THE HOUSE ON H STREET

THE HOUSE ON H STREET

The Conspiracy to Murder Abraham Lincoln

Daniel J. Weingrad

iUniverse, Inc.
New York Bloomington

THE HOUSE ON H. STREET
The Conspiracy to Murder Abraham Lincoln

Copyright © Daniel J. Weingrad

iUniverse books may be ordered through booksellers or by contacting:
iUniverse
1663 Liberty Drive
Bloomington, IN 47403
www.iuniverse.com
1-800-Authors (1-800-288-4677)

Because of the dynamic nature of the Internet, any Web addresses or links contained in this book may have changed since publication and may no longer be valid. This is a work of fiction. All of the characters of the Borin family and the Gotting family are fictitious. The novel uses the historical record meticulously but weaves in fiction when the record is blank. The conspiracy in Lincoln's Cabinet has yet to be proved.

ISBN: 978-1-4401-8275-4 (pbk)
ISBN: 978-1-4401-8276-1 (ebk)

Printed in the United States of America
iUniverse rev. date: 11/17/2009

To my wife, Miriam

My Love, My Buddy, My Inspiration

Jane rolled her eyes back in a quick tilt of her chin. Her eyes snapped back like bars on a slot machine, wide open, bald whites clear and veinless without a trace of iris showing under the lids. Normally there is a slow, heavy reaction, the lids shaking with the struggle. When her upper lids dropped, at my suggestion, it was quick as a wink with eyes still rolled back without strain or effort. It was not the familiar sight of lid muscle working against eye muscle in opposite directions. Even after her fifth visit, looking at the blind eyes that never wavered, it evoked a shudder.

As I went through the induction routine of counting down, the absolute stillness of her body and regular breathing was an indication of a trance state that must have reached its depth just after the eye roll. I was droning along when she spoke but stopped at once. Unlike the slurring monotone of the trance state, her voice was clear and distinct. It was not the voice of Jane Gotting:

"Doctor, I am Mary Surratt."

The interruption was not uncommon. In the trance state many patients feel the need to talk and if the conversation is kept in a soothing monotone it is quite helpful as input. Usually it is a conversation with the other recalcitrant self who does not want to give up smoking or chocolate brownies and will resist all the way. The name she had used intrigued me. It was a name I knew well, a name most Civil War junkies knew well.

"Jane, that name Mary Surratt...."

She interrupted with a quick burst of impatience:

"I am not Jane, Doctor Borin, I am Mary Surratt. Jane is my granddaughter in a direct bloodline four generations removed. She now lies dormant deep within, and there she will lie until summoned."

I sighed in resignation. After the positive results of the previous four visits, was this another mystic looking for a dupe? I had been on a predictable path toward our goal and felt cheated and annoyed. Perhaps it was her manner, quite unlike the polite and hesitant young woman I had been treating. The language was formal and pretentious and she had added the soft overtones of the genteel South. "I" sounded like "Ahhi".

"When were you born, Mary Surratt?"

"In the year of our Lord, 1820."

When Jane (now "Mary") first spoke, her lids had popped open. The eyes, no longer rolled back, stared straight ahead without blinking. In the trance state with eyes open, blinking slows to once or twice a minute and even then it is slow rather than quick-quick. She was no exception and the corneas got their needed bath in an occasional languid drop of the lids.

"It was fate, indeed, that brought Jane to the right mesmerist. When I pushed my great-great granddaughter to go to a mesmerist to cure her barrenness and saw the shelves of your office lined with books about our failed struggle, I knew my search was finished at last".

She said that in slow and measured tones without emotion. I answered in kind, choosing the words carefully:

"I think it would be helpful if you understood my feelings regarding the supernatural. I am ready to help you and if this is an indication of other problems, we will work together to try to set things in order. It would be better for both of us if I discuss this with you out of the trance state. I will awaken you by counting upwards from one to three. When you open your eyes at the count of three you will feel..."

"Stop"!

This time there was emotion. Sitting in my battered old recliner she jerked forward and the foot rest snapped down into place with a loud pop. I stopped and listened. Not looking at me, but staring straight ahead at the Indian wall hanging Naomi had brought back from Costa Rica, the words came steadily, flatly and it seemed to me, without end.

"It has been 143 years since I was hung. No woman had ever been hung in the United States before and my stupid lawyer kept saying they would not do it because of public outcry. Huh, the outcry was for the hanging! Only afterward did the guilt swell from the pulpits of the North. The scum wanted their pound of flesh for the killing of the great baboon and they succeeded. Gentlemen they were, my executioners, they put an umbrella over my head and protected my modesty by belting my skirt around my legs. How good of them. In spite of my shade, the July heat was like the flames of Hell reaching ever closer. Herold was screaming like a pig and Atzerdrodt was mumbling in German. We stood on double traps, my sweet Lewis and I, and dropped together. I heard the word "Mary" through the white linen hanging caps over his head and my own. My daughter Anna was screaming "Mamma! Mamma!" and I gathered every ounce of strength to scream back but the good gentlemen had gagged my mouth with a filthy rag and I could not. Perhaps it was that desperate surge of will to contact Anna one last time, or the Devil was doing his work, but I left my body swinging on the gibbet alongside of my sweet Lewis and entered the mind and body of my seventeen year old daughter who fainted in the process."

At that moment, I had no idea I was hooked but looking back I surely was. Perhaps from the first mention of her name. Riveted by now to every word, I shivered in a flood of memory. The image was clear in my mind of a shocking photograph in one of my old issues of American Heritage. It was taken in a prison courtyard just after the hanging. Soldiers, officers and a sparse crowd stood about, a few on the prison wall above the scene. The rough scaffold looked sturdy, designed for four on double traps. The four bodies, in a terrible, limp stillness, hung below.

Every source that refers to Lewis Paine always mentions his giant physique. Bearing this out in the photograph, swinging alongside of the full-figured, hooded and skirted Mary Surratt, was a huge man whose boots were half a leg below his three fellow conspirators.

It was Mary Surratt who ran the boarding house on H Street where the noted actor, John Wilkes Booth, plotted the assassination of Abraham Lincoln. The small band of conspirators included John Surratt, Mary's devoted young son. The killing plan, evolved after a kidnapping of the President went wrong, included the murder of the Vice-President and the entire Cabinet. Lewis Paine, a hardened Confederate deserter and accomplished killer, was the only follower of Booth to follow through on his assigned mission, a botched and bloody attempt to murder William Seward, Secretary of State. He ran from the scene thinking Seward was dead. "My sweet Lewis" was some sweetheart.

I stopped Jane's flow of words with questions of my own:

"What do you want of me? What purpose is there in telling me this nonsense?"

"Nonsense is it? Before we are finished your mind, your eyes and your soul will recognize the truth. Open your mind, if you have one, and listen! I was a god-fearing woman who fought for my country's cause far better than the poltroons that John Wilkes had so much faith in. I fought the same way to survive for five generations and I won't give up now! I can only do so if my bloodline continues and I can transfer my spirit into flesh of my flesh when Jane Gotting dies. After living in one generation in the body of a great grandson, a lusty one at that, it makes no mind to me whether boy or girl but it would matter to Lewis. Once started, Jane will brood like a sow to have two or three in her lifetime, as many as it takes for us to be assured of boy and girl to continue our immortal union!"

I am a confirmed Civil War buff. To those of us so afflicted, no drug could be more addictive. I could not bring myself to stop this woman's story. I should pull out all the research I could uncover and prove her story false. Armed with facts, I could convince Jane that her possession by Mary Surratt was a product of her own subconscious.

Even as I protested, I knew I was hooked. How educated was this imposter in a time period I was steeped in? I was smug in my concrete box of disbelief but I wanted to hear more. Much more.

"Doctor, it has been 188 years since my birth. I have lived three lifetimes and have soaked in a sea of forbidden knowledge. When my son John escaped to Canada, after the kidnapping of Lincoln failed, an old college classmate sheltered him.

From Anna's mind I came to him in dreams and pushed him to go to Rome and the Vatican where he would be safe. With help from his Canadian contacts he became a Papal guard, dressed in the costumes of bygone ages. Space and time were meaningless to my ghostly spirit and I came to him in dreams again and again, urging him to find and read the tomes of witchcraft and necromancy confiscated and hidden by the Mother Church. In dark catacombs and secret rooms he found those ancient volumes. Not only under the Vatican but many as well in the old monasteries scattered about the Tuscan hills. My power grew with each forbidden word, each month, each year and still grows as I reach out of a world you know not."

What an unbelievable crock. I knew John Surratt had gone to Canada when he took flight before the assassination but it sounded like the wildest fantasy that he wound up with a pike and striped pants as a Vatican guard. That was 1865, there was no Kennedy airport. That "ghostly spirit" crap was one thing, the facts quite another. What a jolt it was to discover in later research that the basic story was true. Almost two years after the murder of President Lincoln, John Surratt (using the name of Watson), escaped the American agents sent to

Rome and fled to Egypt. In the back alleys of Alexandria he was captured, still dressed in the uniform of a Pontifical Guard Zouave.

Shipped back to Baltimore to stand trial, the end of the story raised more questions than it settled. Maryland was a border state. The jury was sure to have several former Confederates on the roster. Admittedly up to his neck in Booth's earlier plot to kidnap Lincoln, after a mistrial the government dropped the case. John H. Surratt Jr., who had equal billing on a wanted poster with John Wilkes Booth, (how that would have upset the actor), walked away scot-free..

He was frail and slight but had inherited his mother's nerves of steel.

Mary (I have begun to call her Mary rather quickly) continued, her deadpan delivery growing more animated as her cheeks grew hot with inner visions:

"My daughter was a naive virgin when she married a milksop chemist, two years after my hanging. My oldest child Isaac, who had fought so bravely at Gettysburg in Lee's army, gave Anna away. John, free as a bird and prosperous in an auditor's job with the Baltimore Shipping Company, sat proudly in the first pew, as Anna became Mrs. William Toney. I shared that pride."

"That night, the sweet taste grew bitter. My spirit writhed in anguish as Toney, grunting with the effort, pumped and pushed six or seven times and rolled over to snore as Anna cried in pain and disappointment. I was but fifteen when I married John Surratt and the old bastard was just the same."

"But ah, my sweet Lewis, with the smooth muscled body of a Greek God he made love to me with unbridled lust and I matched his passionate embrace. I would take his great phallus in any entrance he wished and climax in ecstasy again and again until the final soaring eruption that left us gasping for breath. I want Lewis through eternity and with your help, I shall have him! I shall have him!"

With this last outburst she turned to look me squarely in the eye. I was stunned as Jane vanished and I looked with horror into the contorted face of Mary Surratt.

I knew that face. In the same article showing the gallows photograph was her oval daguerreotype portrait. As was the fashion her hair was severely parted in the center, pulled tight and straight back. Eyes cold and widely spaced, her features were not unattractive but the look was hard as granite. Mary's face was barely wrinkled and her eyes were gray, now wild with fury and lust. The lips were thin, a straight slash with the lined corners turned down in a sneer of hatred.

Goose bumps rippled over my body and my heart palpitated with a rush of pure terror. I fought to breathe but aside from gasping attempts, I could not speak. Beginning to regain my composure, there was an attempt to calm Mary with words of assurance. In hindsight, it was another mistake. She spit words out like foul tasting bile:

"Don't patronize me, Doctor! Don't talk to me as if I was insane. I have shown you my face and still you do not believe? Do you want cheap tricks that would destroy your office?"

"Mary, give me time to think. It's not easy to turn a lifetime of conviction upside down. I must research my facts, catch my breath, and try to reason this out. Jane's inability to conceive is not an easily solved problem. I told her early on that not every case could be successful. The odds are good but you expect a guarantee even as to gender."

Jane of the staring blank eyes, instant and effortless eye roll, Jane of the impossible biofeedback is gone. I now had to deal with her metamorphous as Mary Surratt, the snarling woman who was born almost two centuries ago and now sat scowling at me.

Was this astonishing phenomena real? My thoughts were chaotic as she continued:

"Enough Doctor, let me be fully forthcoming. I can give you what you dream of, leafing through your books. I can bring you to the Executive Mansion in 1865. You will be an invisible traveler in time that can be an eyewitness to all you dream of. I can put you in the box at Ford's Theatre and you as an invisible observer can see the incredible scenes as they actually occurred. See Seward's bloody comeuppance in his bedroom and be an eyewitness to the bravery of sweet Lewis. See anything you damn please, just as long as I get what I want, sweet Lewis in my arms, fathering the child that will be the fruit of our union."

What bait she had offered! My mind reeled with the possibilities. To speak to Lincoln! To see his face! To be an eyewitness to American History's most famous event! There was no Zapruder film for the public to see over and over since Kennedy was shot. For every ten observers that night in Ford's theatre there were ten varying descriptions that have driven historians bonkers.

Was I so seduced by this scenario that I was going bonkers? I was in my office and the year was 2008, that was real. I was talking to a nut that had somehow created special effects in my mind. That was real. Everything else was pure fiction in the hands of an accomplished magician and amateur historian. God, let me end this crap and go back to my orderly world. I would humor her, keep her calm and ease her out of my office with a minimum of stress.

"Mary, I will ask the question once more. Why do you need me? I can understand the desire to see Jane have a baby and your belief in the method that I use to gain that end. Why don't you let the process take its due course? Then you could do what you want with your ghostly lover and enter the child when Jane dies."

"I told you (in tones reserved for children) I must enter flesh of my flesh. Lewis can only enter a body and

11

mind in the deep throes of a mesmerist trance. Your ability to create that trance coupled with your desire to know and see first-hand the stirring events of the rebellion, makes you the perfect candidate. If only you were not so stupid!"

When I get angry, my ears turn red. It is the frostbite legacy of a bitter cold February night's sledding without ear muffs in the upstate Catskill hamlet that was my home. I was twelve, my only thoughts the girl sitting jammed between my legs in front of me, not my ears. A rise in blood pressure still does the trick. My family knows exactly when the choler rises along with the color and I was beginning to warm up.

"If my therapy with Jane is successful and she and her husband have a child, where the hell does Lewis come in? Am I to be a party to placing the ghost of Lewis Paine into the body and soul of her unwitting husband!"

"You spineless dolt! You have been offered the opportunity that a real historian, a real man, would give his life for. Do you think there would be no price for you to pay? I have had enough of your stupid questions!"

The anger within me exploded. It was like a tonic, washing away the sour taste of fear. I lashed out, red faced and trembling:

"I have no fear of you, bitch, and your command of the underworld. Get the hell out of my office and find someone else to haunt!"

Another voice came from the corner of the dark, windowless room.

My heart literally skipped a beat as I turned to see. During therapy the only light is from a pushed down, shaded goose neck lamp. My ears roared with pressure as I tried to penetrate the deep shadows. The voice was guttural but the message was clear.

"You have good reason to fear, Doc."

The light's circle just touched the tip of dusty boots and the skirt of what must have been a khaki riding duster that looked straight out of a Clint Eastwood western. I held my breath as he moved toward me out of the corner. The floorboards creaked with his weight as his huge hands became visible, knobby wrists dangling out of short sleeves. My pulse rate soared as it became difficult to suck in air. In his left hand he held a king size Bowie knife, the top honed back in a serrated razor-like curve designed for the gut-pull after entry. As my chest threatened to burst and my mind silently screamed "Oh God, Oh God", I knew who my visitor was.

Mary's voice was soft and almost inaudible, quite a contrast to her angry last outburst:

"That's enough, Lewis."

Lewis Paine stopped in his tracks and sheathed the knife on a belt holster under the riding duster. Mary's words did not cause Lewis to fade into the woodwork and he stood there looking as solid as a brick wall. Mary spoke again in that same gentle tone:

"Step into the light, Lewis and let the Doctor see what a man really looks like."

I got the crazy memory of Clive, what-ever-his-name, controlling Boris Karloff as the monster in the old Frankenstein movie. This was no movie. This monster stood in my office and stared at me, without expression. He was tall and handsome with the same chilling, emotionless eyes of the "preppie murderer" who killed that young girl in Central Park. His shoulders sloped from a bull neck into long and powerful arms. I knew who my visitor was. I knew him from Sandburg's "The War Years" and the transcripts of the conspirator trials that pronounced his death sentence. I knew him from the photographs and descriptions in American Heritage. All that I knew scared the hell out of me.

His father, a farmer and itinerant Baptist preacher, beat Lewis regularly with a leather razor strop. Lewis, already over six feet, ran away at 16 to join Lee's Army of Northern Virginia. He fought bravely at Gettysburg and was transferred to Mosby's guerrillas on the strength of his reputation as a nerveless slitter of throats when slipping through Yankee pickets. The loose discipline of a Guerilla forager, allowing him to rape, pillage and kill without restraint, suited Lewis and his exploits became camp-fire legends. When Mosby (who conceived of himself as a chivalrous Southern gentleman) finally came across

Paine's handi-work, the mutilated bodies of women and children, Lewis Paine escaped hanging by deserting the Confederacy and melted into the waterfront slums of Baltimore. He was barely twenty when Booth found him, bought him clothes, food and lodging and made him a cornerstone of his plans to destroy the executive branch of the Union. That also suited "sweet Lewis", killing was the thing he did best.

These thoughts raced through my head as I stared back at him with fear and loathing. At the same time I was fascinated, like a spectator looking at a hooded cobra rising out of a fakir's basket. The excitement of looking at and speaking to actual players in the melodrama of Lincoln's assassination drove out every rational thought.

Mary read these emotions quickly and moved in for her victory with soft-spoken, consummate skill:

"Doctor, you were right to take exception to my choice of words. In the emotions released by being so close to my goals, I had forgotten my manners. Please forgive me. If you have read our trial transcripts, you know that Lewis tried with eloquent appeals to clear my name and save me from the noose. He is still trying to protect me."

Trying to calm down and quiet a racing heart, I just nodded as Mary continued:

"Doctor, reach out and grab this opportunity. I can put you in Lincoln's box at Ford's Theatre at the hour of his death. You can be in this time period for days and it will be only be a few moments of elapsed time in this era. Put yourself into a trance state and I will do the rest. When you return to this office, simply awake Jane as you normally would. Do it, Do it now!"

God forgive me, I could not refuse. As I caved in, I knew that I was no longer in command of my own destiny. Mary Surratt had control of Lewis and now controlled me.

Lewis picked up one of the heavy chairs in my office as if it was weightless and seated himself opposite Mary. Ghosts that could make a chair's cushion's flatten seemed astonishing. It went directly against the image of the movie ghosts I grew up with and seemed far more frightening. As he talked to Mary, I studied him intently. I watched his chest and neck muscles. There was no sign of breathing. That frightened me even more. Mary had told Lewis to leave until summoned and he was protesting:

"Mary, if I ain't called up, I ain't here to protect you. It's like goin' back to the coffin and I'm not about to do that." He spoke in throaty, guttural tones softened by a Southern drawl and was far less cultured in speech patterns than Mary, who answered quickly:

"Lewis, sweet Lewis, I brought you here to help us get what we want. It is the beginning of eternal life in living bodies. Bodies whose hearts will pound with the red blood of passion. You must trust me more than ever.

Borin, Jane is deep in trance and we await your return. Our time will move only slightly. One more thing, this basement room has two doors. Fire is unlikely but both exits must be unlocked. Being careful is the essence of survival."

Lewis was erased in the blink of an eye. There was no ectoplasmic image taking a slow exit. Sitting back in my chair, I closed my eyes. Taking a deep breath, I rolled up my eyes and began a deep self hypnotic induction, using the visualization device of standing in an elevator, watching the lights above the door change numbers in a downward sequence from ten to one, instructing my mind to go deeper into trance.

I did so, feeling the familiar sense of total relaxation the trance state requires.

The first request to Mary had been to return to the afternoon of April 5th, 1865, nine days before the assassination of Lincoln and the attempt on Seward. On that day, William Seward, the Secretary of State, was almost killed in a accident. Nine days later on the night Lincoln was murdered, Seward was attacked by Lewis Paine in his own bedroom and left for dead in a pool of blood. I had read an account of the accident and the attempted murder in a diary of his young daughter Fanny.

The story was gory but fascinating. Her vivid description of this terrible night would have, in our day and age, aroused both publishers and moviemakers. Was I really to be there as it happened? I was frightened and at the same time aching to find out.

Chapter 2
Washington D.C. 1865

My first journey through time began with the background sounds of horses. Hooves clattering on the cobblestones and the sharp smell of manure. My office filled with sunlight and I was there! I could think and feel and listen, disembodied somehow, but able to project my presence at will. I could move like a zoom lens on a video camera.

I drank in the picture of the city around me. I was so excited it was difficult to concentrate on any one scene too long. The finished dome of the Capital was etched against a deep blue sky. It was the same huge and majestic sight I was familiar with but the total building looked much smaller. I quickly realized that both houses of Congress were missing. The construction of Congressional wings was in the future. The White House, across the square, also looked smaller and I guessed for the same reason, the renovations that were done closer to our own era. Was Lincoln in the oval office? Was there an oval office? Excited and little disoriented, my thoughts raced unchecked

Dirt, squalor and ripe odors were my immediate impression. On the Congressional Mall the beautiful reflection pool we know so well was gone, replaced by lines of Army tents girded by open, turgid streams of raw sewage. The stump of the unfinished Washington Monument seemed abandoned about a quarter of the way up. Soldiers were everywhere on the streets in Civil War attire. What struck me was the diversity of the uniforms. Every regiment seemed to have designed a different one. Another oddity was the generally small stature of most people, men and women. The rock-solid reality around me was so persuasive, I moved to one side as a bearded officer strode directly at me. Women seemed plain and a bit drab with hair severely pulled back and no make-up. Their clothes seemed comfortable enough, skirts to the ankles and flared out over padded hips. Black and gray were the predominate colors.

This was not a set left over from "Gone With The Wind". I had traveled in time and the only words that came to mind were banal expressions of astonishment. The enormity of what I was seeing was so mind-boggling that profound thinking would have to come later, if at all. I resolved to make as complete notes as I could as soon as possible on return. Would I return? The incredible scene before me blotted out the uncertainty.

The small park of Lafayette Square was lovely as were the stately homes around the park. It seemed like an oasis of affluence, lawns neatly cut with tall elms shading the wrought iron benches. The old black & white photographs I had studied turned into the rich tones of red brick and white shutters, the frontage covered thickly and at random with ivy vines that gave the exteriors color and warmth.

There was an instant recognition in my mind of Seward's house, a three story brick colonial facing the square and as I watched, two young women dressed in crinolines and lace stepped from a large open carriage. They bustled in and out of the house, chattering all the time in happy excitement. It was surely Fanny Seward and her friend, Mary Titus. Fanny, Seward's youngest child, was just twenty and was in the heady swim of young Washington society. Her friend Mary was a girl Fanny had known in her hometown of Auburn, New York and they were inseparable.

I knew with absolute certainty of the terrifying trip they were about to make as I studied Seward and his son Frederick sitting in the carriage waiting for the girls to enter. Seward, slight and pale, reminded me of a Disney turtle with a beak-like nose and long, wrinkled neck. He rarely smiled, except at Fanny.

Fanny was comely but rather pale, her friend chubby and vivacious. They had picked up her father and brother at the State Department. The girls had implored the two men to take a ride in the cool spring sunshine. After the stop for her father's coat they hopped back in the carriage. I was an unseen presence. A hidden observer who could not in any way change the tragic course of events I knew would happen.

The carriage was an open tonneau, graceful in a curved arc and fitted with upholstered seats that faced one another. On the driver's seat was an elderly black man they called Henry, dressed in a bright red coachman's jacket and black, wide brimmed hat. The Secretary of State and his son were dressed in somber working suits for the State Department, white linen shirts and finely striped cravats. The happy girls sparkled in the bright sunshine and wore colorful dresses unlike the less wealthy.

A team of four matched Bay's high stepped at a slow trot up a brick paved Vermont Avenue. There were no bodyguards, no effort at security such as top up and closed curtains. Seeing the Seward family taking an outing did not seem to turn many heads. A family friend, Ben Tayloe, one of the pillars of Washington society, waved a greeting. Vermont Avenue at this spot was a beautiful residential area of Georgian mansions, dappled by the late afternoon sunshine.

The door on the men's side (Seward and his son faced each other) became unlocked and swung open as the carriage hit a rough spot. Frederick made several efforts to lock it and giving up, called to Henry to stop and fix it from the outside. Henry pulled the slow moving team to a stop and dismounted from his high perch. A testy conversation between Secretary Seward and the coachman was going on about keeping the locks well oiled and Henry's surprisingly strong defense made the girls laugh and even Seward smiled. Henry, instead of tightly cinching the reins on the coachman's seat was holding them in his right hand as he protested the Secretary's comments and secured the door with his left hand.

Invisible to all and engrossed in this charming scene, I glanced up to see Lewis Paine on the sidewalk, staring at the carriage with those expressionless, frightening eyes. Just then, something happened to spook the team. The lead horses rose on their hind legs, wheeling sharply and jerking forward as the reins were ripped from Henry's grasp.

Frederick jumped from the carriage in an attempt to grab the lead bridle but the horses, snorting and eyes bulging with fright, were not about to stop. Frederick was thrown roughly to the pavement and as I looked back, he lay quite still where he had fallen. People were running to help as the horses bolted, the girls screaming in fear as the carriage was twisted from side to side. Secretary Seward tried to grab the reins streaming overhead but they were too high. He then decided, despite Fanny's screaming entreaties, to open the door and climb higher on the coachman's seat. As he stepped out of the wheeling carriage, he was immediately pitched headlong to the brick pavement. I looked back to see a limp bundle twisted in his greatcoat, lying still as death.

What happened next might have seemed endless but it was over in just a few moments. Brushing trees and heading directly for a brick wall as the girls desperately hung on, the careening horses came to an abrupt halt as the off horse on the right fell heavily. The lead horses, mad with fear, pulled the team upright before the girls could leap to safety. The momentum however, was slowed; allowing a passing soldier to leap to the bridle and calm the trembling, sweat frothed team. Mary, shaken but unhurt, was helped to a bench but Fanny raised her skirts and ran back to find her father. An act, under the circumstances, that endeared her to me.

Fred, dazed but not badly hurt, had rushed to his father whom he surely believed dead. He found Seward bloody and unconscious as he pulled the greatcoat from over his head. A group of men came from all directions to carry the Secretary of State into his home. One of those men, head and shoulders above the rest, was Lewis Paine. Fanny, frightened and distraught over her father's condition, stayed by his side as the men climbed the stairs to Seward's second floor bedroom off the hall. A large four-poster bed on the left side dominated a high ceiling room with large windows on the right wall. The bed was canopied by heavy brocade colored a deep plum. The heavy curtains matched the canopy. Flowered wallpaper, potted plants and small fireplace reflected the over laden look of the Victorian era. A small dry sink held a porcelain pitcher and large bowl. The white porcelain chamber pot peeked out under the bed.

Lewis, his face in a grimace of exertion, told Frederick: "I'll do better lifting him myself, Mr. Seward" and in an easy motion lifted the slight man and laid him on the bed where Fanny had pulled back the covers.

Turning to Fanny, who looked devastated, Lewis spoke again:

"It's all right missy, just a nose bleed."

She flinched and ran down to the kitchen to get a basin of water and towels to staunch the spurting blood from her father's nose. Seward was insensible, his eyes blackened and swollen and his right arm sticking out at an odd angle. Frederick rushed a manservant to fetch Dr. Verdi, the family physician and to notify the Secretary of War, Edwin Stanton, who lived nearby.

Lewis and the others moved down and out of the house. Lewis did not rush, his eyes alert and active. With the advantage of hindsight, I knew that Seward's ordeal was just beginning.

As Doctor Verdi arrived, an old gentleman whose hands were shaking as he opened his black bag, he began his examination. Other Doctors began to crowd the room. Stanton had notified the Surgeon General, Dr. Barnes, and an experienced Army surgeon, Dr. Norris. He had sent his carriage rushing for both.

I eavesdropped with great interest seeing two competent physicians give a very thorough examination without benefit of high-tech diagnostic tools. The right arm was snapped cleanly between the shoulder and elbow and he was suffering from a fractured jaw and severe concussion (hindsight again, the jaw fracture was not discovered until the swelling went down the next day). The right arm was set without anesthesia (not yet in use) but Seward, in and out of coma, only occasionally moaned in pain. His jaw was so swollen, little could be done and the decision was to wait, using compresses to reduce swelling. Fanny, with grit and determination, stayed with her father constantly, nursing him and praying for his life.

This day, April 5th, 1865, was nine days away from the day Lincoln was assassinated. On that same day of infamy, Good Friday, April 14th, Lewis Paine made a near-fatal attempt on Seward's life as Fanny Seward looked on, helpless and screaming in fear.

At this moment my decision had been made on where I wanted to be. I wanted to be here, in this bedroom as Paine did his bloody work. I wanted to follow John Wilkes Booth as he climbed the stairs to Lincoln's box at Ford's Theatre and lastly to be with Lincoln on the last day of his life.

Interrupting my thoughts, the voice of Mary Suratt was startlingly distinct.

"So, Doctor Borin, you want many things now that the appetite is whetted. What I want is to be reunited in the living flesh with my sweet Lewis! Will you do so?

God forgive me, I needed no more time to think. Yes, and again yes, if my objectives could be realized.

"So be it, Doctor but you must heed my warning. If you attempt to weasel out of our bargain, your hell will start long before you die."

Again, like a junkie that knew his fate, I could not refuse.

"We will start by twisting and compressing time and space to our own liking. In this in-between world, Newton's laws of do not apply. Observe as you wish and move forward or backward as you wish. You can relive the assassination of Lincoln again and again from Wilkes Booth's experience or Lincoln's. Focus strongly on where you want to be and I will see that it will happen. You must return to your office when the moment is right and re-visit 1865 but all in good order. Do you understand?"

I assented and rejoined Fanny in her vigil.

For the next few days Edwin Stanton the Secretary of War, an old political foe of Seward, treated the Secretary of State with tender compassion. A short, plump and pugnacious man with a long spiked beard, he bathed Seward's forehead and wiped the clots of blood forming in Seward's nose. Fanny remarked to her family that Stanton, a man whose temper was feared throughout the War Department, was more adept at nursing than she was. When Seward, days later and conscious, tried to thank Stanton, both strong men broke down in tears.

In these medically less sophisticated times, much of the fight for survival was up to the courage of the patient. Seward did not give up and slowly moved out of crisis.

Nine days later on that fateful Good Friday, April 14th., Seward, with wired jaw, steel neck brace and right arm in a cast, was still suffering from his injuries but well enough to be read to by Fanny and others in the household.

About 10 o'clock that evening, the Doctor had left and Fanny was sitting by Seward's bed as he seemed to be drifting into sleep. Also present was a soldier, George Robinson, who had some experience as a medical orderly during the War and had been at the Soldier's Home, convalescing from war wounds. He was picked to help bathe and tender to Seward, another of Stanton's characteristically practical suggestions. Fred, his wife and his brother Augustus were in the house as well as members of the household staff. Fanny's mother, Mrs. Anna Wharton Seward, was asleep in an upper bedroom.

I knew full well that I could not change the outcome of what I was about to witness. My only contact with this world was as an invisible observer of events. I could not resist the urge to make contact with my mind but was unable to arouse a response even from a stray cat when my mind screamed "SCAT" in the animal's ear.

I was fully aware of the time traveler's paradox. Change one incident in the fabric of lives or pivotal events and the future would change. Change major events and the future might be erased, to be replaced by an alternative probability. In the process, my life and my family's lives might be erased as well. In the time of a waning Civil War, If Seward had been killed by the attempt on his life, would Alaska be part of the Soviet Union? If Booth had been barred from the Presidential box at Ford Theatre and Lincoln had served a second term, would the civil rights issue still be a divisive factor in our country? The speculation is fascinating but the logic is unassailable. We cannot change the past even if time travel were possible. Looking back, such a positive opinion about an unknown possibility seems pretty dense.

It was just before 10 o'clock in the evening, this night of April 14th, 1865. Fanny was quietly knitting in an upholstered rocking chair, glancing up from time to time at her father, just getting to sleep. George Robinson was reading in the corner chair after making sure that Seward was as comfortable as possible before retiring. Seward's wired jaw made it difficult for him to take food but George had infinite patience with the cantankerous Seward and managed to get him enough nourishment for steady improvement in his strength.

I moved (my unseen presence moved) to the windows that overlooked the street below. Graceful wrought iron street lamps, lit by the city's network of natural gas lines, gave adequate light. A few pedestrians moved about, some with the ubiquitous uniforms of war-time Washington. A movement caught my eye about a half block up La Fayette Square. Two horsemen, one very tall and dressed in a light colored duster. The tall man dismounted and tethered his horse with a quick slip knot at one of the many convenient iron posts that were provided for the purpose. As he approached on foot, I saw it was Lewis Paine and if I had a breath it was sucked in sharply.

In an instant I was with Lewis as he strode toward the Seward's front door without the slightest emotion. He did not hurry. The only sign of his inner feelings, if he had any, was the purposeful way he banged on the heavy brass door knocker. A young black man, dressed in a house servant's livery, answered the door in irritation:

"Hush you, hush! Peoples in this house is sleepin."

The young man, William Welles, (his name came from trial testimony) looked at Lewis with unfeigned suspicion. Lewis was cool and confident. He had talked his way out of trouble with Yankee patrols and this harmless youngster would pose no problems.

"I come from Dr. Verdi and I was told to give this medicine (he pulled a small wrapped package from the deep pockets of his duster) to Secretary Seward himself. Take me to him." The last request was made a little more firmly.

"No sir! I'll take the medicine right up to Miss Fanny and she'll know what to do. The Secretary needs to rest, he cain't be bothered by you. Gives it to me."

The argument went back and forth but Lewis never lost his cool:

"Dr. Verdi made it clear that I must give this right to Mr. Seward and nobody else. If I can't do that I'm going to take it back to Dr. Verdi and your gonna get in a heap of trouble."

William hesitated, confused and upset by this turn of events:

"Well..well, we'll takes it up to Mr. Frederick and sees what he wants to do wid it."

Lewis stepped into the front door and followed William up the stairway. The giant did not take delicate strides and the young man turned repeatedly to admonish him.

"Hush, dammit! Cain't you puts your feet a little softer?!"

Lewis said nothing as he followed, slipping open the buttons of his duster and never varying his heavy tread. The hunter was getting close to his quarry and adrenaline began to flow, the killer's breath quickening in short gasps.

Frederick Seward, not yet ready for bed, had heard this commotion and came out of his room, still fully dressed, to stand at the head of the second floor landing.

"You there! My father is very ill and needs his rest. What do you want?"

Lewis, closing in and becoming impatient did not mince words:

"I must see the Secretary, is he asleep?" This was said roughly, his masquerade discarded as he simply pushed past Frederick and turned right to Secretary Seward's bedroom door. Fanny, roused by the noise, anxiously peeked out.

Frederick was just behind Lewis, frantically motioning Fanny to close and lock the door. Lewis, with a singular lack of imagination and almost shouting, asked again and again: "Is the Secretary asleep?"

Fanny answered timidly: "Almost." Frederick took the immediate opportunity to grasp the doorknob and pulled the door closed. Lewis was through asking questions. In a blur of speed he pulled a large pistol from his belt with his right hand and a big Bowie knife from a holster with his left hand. His first choice was the knife and Frederick took a deep gash on his shoulder and arm as he raised it in an attempt to protect himself. The silver barrel of the pistol flashed in the flickering gaslight as it crunched into Frederick's skull with the sound of a dropped watermelon. Fanny's brother had no quit in him and instead of going down he grabbed the giant and hung on.

Fanny, as well as the male nurse Robinson, heard the scuffling and blows, Fanny moving backwards in fright and Robinson moving forward to secure the lock as the men burst through the broad doorway, side by side. Her brother Fred, staggering from a fractured skull and bleeding from stab wounds, incredibly tried to stop Lewis Paine's charge to the bed, failed and crumpled to the floor unconscious.

Fanny screamed for the intruder not to kill her father who had started awake in confusion. The brave Robinson leaped upon Paine's back, jarring loose the pistol in his right hand that Lewis had now pointed at the helpless invalid. Stabbing Robinson and throwing him aside, Paine moved like a panther to the left side of the bed and with the bloody Bowie knife in his left hand, methodically continued his horrible work. The giant stabbed Robinson once more as the veteran, despite his wounds, grabbed Lewis around the neck. Lewis threw him off as he would an annoying child as he struck at Seward repeatedly, spattering the walls with blood.

Seward rolled off the bed by the force of the blows. Robinson, bleeding and faint could only manage to make a feeble attempt at Paine's legs as the killer leaned over to strike Seward again who had raised his heavy cast to instinctively protect himself. The floor, the carpets, the walls and the pulled off bed sheets were awash in bright, slippery blood. My body, sitting in my office chair, must have been breathing in gasps.

With Fanny screaming and Frederick and Robinson lying on the floor comatose from their wounds, Paine walked calmly out the door thinking Seward was surely dead. His slouch hat and Army pistol were left behind but he still gripped the dripping knife. Fanny slipped and almost fell in the blood as she rushed around the bed still screaming for help.

Seward's oldest son Augustus, an Army officer on leave had rushed unarmed from his upstairs bedroom hearing Fanny's screams. He was sure his father had died from his previous injuries. He confronted instead a blood-spattered giant striding out of his father's bedroom.

The struggle was quick this time Augustus was no match for Paine's strength and incredible determination. Augustus too, went down in a pool of blood as Paine, quickening his pace, rushed down the stairs. A young man, a State Department messenger named Emerick Hansell, who had been coming and going the past few days, had let himself in the unlocked front door and was coming up the stairs. Confronted by the grotesque apparition of Lewis, eyes wild and clothes covered with the blood of his victims, Hansell turned to run, frightened out of his wits. Hansell was the last victim of Paine's dripping knife, crumpling on the steps with a slash across his back. William, the young house servant, who had hidden from sight under the stairwell, ran into the street shouting: "murder, murder!"

As Paine went out the door there were several people who were drawn by the shouts and screaming. Lewis went through them like a bull in flight, waving the knife and shouting: "I am mad.. I am mad!" in an attempt to frighten and intimidate. He escaped by running the short distance to his tethered horse and with a quick pull on the slip knot and a expert leap into the saddle, raced away into the shadowed streets of the city. The other horseman had vanished..

My consciousness had watched something so horrendous, I was stunned. Fanny, using a Shakespearean phrase in her dairy, wrote a fitting ending to this awful scene: "I have supped full on horrors."

Incredibly, all of Paine's victims survived. Seward had the left side of his face slashed open so badly, the surgeon who sewed him up could see his teeth and tongue but the leather covered steel neck brace had protected his throat from the bloody knife.

With incredible grit, Seward survived copious blood loss from his wounds. A fractured jaw, fractured arm and what must have been overwhelming psychological trauma. The wounds of the others ranged from critical, as in Frederick's case, to superficial but all the victims recovered.

Booth was much more efficient. At about the same time that evening, a mile or two away at Ford's Theatre, the President, a bullet in his brain, lay dying.

Chapter 3
Ghost Stories

The window in Dr.Parker's office had a sweeping view of Washington Square. The park, looked at from above, had the clean fresh look of springtime. From the sixth floor window the landscaped cobble walks and majestic marble arch looked serene in the dappled sunlight. When I was a graduate student, years before, the graffiti, spent needles and strewn garbage did not offend or surprise the viewer. The hardened New Yorker, like the diving bird-of-prey, develops a transparent necessitating membrane that slides down over the eye and blocks out the filth.

From my birds-eye perch it could have been Lafayette Park as seen from the window of Seward's bedroom. God, it had been so real. I'm not sure how other people dream but I am certainly familiar with my own. Sometimes they can be so intense that I awaken startled and disoriented but no matter how vividly the image, my dreams never waste too much time on background. My trip back to 1865, on the other hand, was rock solid in reality. Smells, colors and sounds were genuine. Lewis Paine's ghost was as tangible as the back of my hand. What the hell was happening! There had to be some rational explanation. Confused and without a clue, I had reached out to my old mentor at the University.

Twenty years before, taking my doctorate in psychology at New York University, my professor of clinical psychology was a man named Edward Parker. He was tall and thin, with intense eyes that were in contrast to his bland and unruffled manner.

Dr. Parker had been a dedicated disciple of Milton Erickson, the foremost of American physicians who used hypnosis as a therapeutic modality. Those early laboratory sessions with Dr. Parker had a profound effect on my career. Those who believed as I did, that hypnosis could be a force of great impact in healing, lived beyond the pale of the medical community. That made most of us cowards and we shoved "hypnotherapy" out of sight, using the euphemisms of "visualization" or "deep relaxation techniques."

As a result of the AMA's animus, Parker could only publish his work outside the medically correct Journals that would have made him famous. He was devoted to Erickson and that meant calling hypnotism by its name. Dr. Erickson was more of a poet than a pragmatic scientist but Parker, almost alone among the Master's disciples, was a maverick realist. Using the broad canvas of Eriksonian methodology, he had lifted medical and psychiatric hypnosis to a new level of precise scientific data collected by laboratory experimentation.

It was not at all easy sitting on the other side of the therapist's desk. I had a preposterous story to tell and if he had suggested that I came regularly for help after a diagnosis of a delusion psychosis, it would not have been a surprise. He made it easy. Those intense eyes never wavered and his expression never changed. Apologetic bumbling marked my efforts but as the experience was relived, goose bumps rippled up my arms and Paine and his knife became real once more. When finished, exhausted, I waited for Ed to break the silence.

"David, if a patient had told me this story my reaction would be as typical as any other therapist. It would have been the same reaction you had when your patient confronted you in the voice and mannerisms of Mary Surratt. What makes this case so unusual is your own involvement. We both are committed to the pragmatic wing of our small niche in hypnotherapeutic healing. The work you sent me on fertility was right on the money and backed by careful research. You haven't lost your scientific detachment. That's why this whole thing so god-damned interesting."

"Ed, this may be interesting to you but I'm scared shitless!"

"Actually, I envy you. We find it easy to lose the cutting edge in the overall sameness in the cases that sit across from us. Sometimes you begin to fit all neurosis into the same three or four bins that are recycled in each day's office hours. Here is a problem that you could die for, pardon the expression. You know, of course, that I studied with Erickson in Phoenix in '78 when I was a grad student. He said something during one of our seminars that has stuck with me. It was a comment during a discussion of professional behavior: He answered a question by stating: ` It would be a good thing to remember there is a fine line between who is the hypnotist and who is being hypnotized. You're liable to find yourself on the wrong end.' We laughed at the time but he was dead serious. "

"The professional healer, whether it is an internist or a psychologist, gets wrapped in their own ego. The knowledge that you have worked so hard to obtain is rewarded the title of Doctor. That makes it hard to admit that a patient or a layman can possibly be as clever as you are. We are sadly aware that therapists can manipulate patients. Manipulation of therapists by patients, however, is not only possible but is a rather common occurrence. Teachers seduced by students, lawyers convinced of a client's innocence; the list covers us all. The psychologist, in a one on one therapeutic modality, is particularly vulnerable. Very often your own psychological needs seek satisfaction."

"Jane Gotting might be a master hypnotist who has an agenda to control you in a really innovative way. If instead she suffers from a multiple personality syndrome and is unaware of her evil twin she must be treated accordingly. Check her background more thoroughly. Find out about her prior knowledge of hypnosis. Do more work with the lady who lives in the present. The rest does not exist. I am sure these incredible adventures are as real to you as breathing but we both know the rational explanation will eventually be revealed."

A window had opened and the sunlight streamed in. The sense of relief was intense.

I was very grateful to my old friend and left his office with the determination to end this charade with Jane. The conception of a child was the goal Jane and I had set in our therapeutic relationship but this serious neurosis had to be cleared before any headway could be made.

Was Jane, the stolid unimaginative woman I was treating, a hypnotist that had used my love of history to implant post-hypnotic suggestions in me? Was she a dual personality? I was moving past LaGuardia Airport on the Grand Central, heading east just before the rush hour and my mind had switched to automatic pilot. My thoughts were interrupted by my occasional mumble of; "bastard!", as someone cut in front of me but by and large the session with Ed Parker had an exhilarating effect. I was a professional and good at what I do. It was about time to put my talents as a therapist to work.

Our home had been cut into a hillside well back from the main road that ran down hill and alongside the finger of Long Island Sound that cuts into the North Shore. The driveway was wide and extra long and as I pulled in and parked well back from the house, my teenage son snapped the net with a arching three-pointer and turned to smile in triumph. Donnie was 15 and though I am a tall man, he was already on eye level.

"Hey Dad, how about a 10 point game of one on one?"

"Is that fair, you bum, you have been warming up for an hour. However, since I can always whip your ass, just give me enough time to put on my sneakers."

Forty-five minutes later, winded and ego bruised, I climbed the stairs as Naomi bustled about the kitchen making dinner. She never saw a pot that could be moved quietly.

Cooking was a one-gal-band. Jennifer, just back from Junior High cheerleader practice, brushed by me with a mumbled: "s'cuse me Dad", on a dash to her room. By the time I reached my bedroom, Jen was halfway down the hall in her red terrycloth robe, stooped over to hide Mom's legacy, an abundant bosom for a 12 year old.

I had an automatic reaction: "stand up straight!" Jen's reaction was also automatic, a rueful smile and nary an effort to comply as she locked the door in the hall bathroom.

I made a mental note to talk to Naomi about it one more time and went in to take a shower of my own. I had to check if Jen's shower had stopped running as we would both get cool water and stuck my head back into the hall. It was then that Lewis Paine, still in that dirty khaki duster, stepped right through the locked bathroom door and turned to look at me, grinning and licking his lips in delight.

"Doc, she's as tasty as hot apple pie."

In an explosive rush of adrenaline I traded roles with the beastly thing laughing at me. The shout in my mind screamed: "KILL! KILL!" The last thing I remember as I leaped for his throat was his eyes and expression. He looked surprised. I hit the floor, grabbing nothing but air and sat there gasping for breath, shaking as the tide of anger ebbed. The hallway was empty.

Naomi, involved in her symphony of pots and pans, had heard nothing. I had to steady myself against the wall and moved back to my room. Rest and trying to think was the immediate goal. In a few moments my breathing returned to normal and my chaotic thoughts became a bit more focused. Was an implanted hallucination created by hypnosis? At the same time the entire Lewis incident had Freudian implications I could not ignore. Was Lewis a reflection of the beast that is buried within? Was this the acting out of stray fantasies that are tucked deeply into the subconscious? It was surely possible that a skilled layman could use hypnosis to implant post-hypnotic suggestions that would mirror deeply hidden sexual repressions. Was my reaction of bloody rage and attempt to kill, a rage that was directed at myself?

My mind began to race, quickly finding plausible and rational explanations for the awful experience of the last few minutes when there was a tap on the door:

"Dad, can I speak to you for a moment?"

Jen was still in her red robe, thick black hair still damp from her shower. Looking at my beautiful child, I had that same pure rush of love I have had since the first time I saw her cradled in her mother's arms. Quite suddenly, my theories were not quite as plausible as they had seemed. Jen looked pale and frightened.

"Daddy, I locked the door of the bathroom and pulled the shade way down as I always do but as I got ready for my shower I had the funniest feeling. The running hot water always makes the bathroom steamy and warm but somehow I felt cold and do you know how you get in a room when someone is staring at you?" "Yes I do , Jen"

"Well that's how I felt. only 10 times as much. It was sooo creepy. I closed the handle on the shower door and when I was finished and stepped out to dry, the feeling wasn't there any more. When I think about it, I still feel the goose bumps. There is something else."

With a steadily sinking feeling in the pit of my stomach, Jennifer led me back to the hall bathroom. She silently pointed to the fluffy throw rug on the tiled floor. Outlined quite clearly on the damp rug were the tracing of two footprints. The soles and heels of a heavy shoe or boot in a very large size.

I got that bad, bad feeling in the pit of my bowels, the sliding out of control feeling. It was like opening an final exam in grad school and looking at a question you had not studied. Mixed with that helpless nausea was a rising tide of anger at this violation of my home and family. At the same time my daughter turned to me, Mr. Fix-It, for an explanation and I forced an attempt to remain calm and impassive.

My mind raced to find a plausible answer. Naomi and I never raised our children by the book but we do have a few unwritten commandments. One of them is never to lie when asked a question. Evade, if absolutely necessary, but no lies. I lied.

"Jen, you remember about the top hinge on this shower door being a little loose? I was in here before you came home and was just checking to see what sheet metal screws I needed to do the job right. I had gone down to the tool room and didn't have the right size and went back upstairs when you rushed past me. When you steamed the room up with the shower, the foot prints became clear."

"OK, what about those spooky feelings?

"Baby, you know that old saying about the mind playing tricks on you. It happens to adults as well. It happens to me all the time. Maybe when you started your shower your mind way down deep noticed the faint outlines of the footprints but didn't tell your awake mind about it. Remember when we talked about the conscious and subconscious mind? Ghost stories were always a favorite of yours and this was a great time to invent one deep inside and not let your aware mind know about it except for the chills and the spooky feelings."

"Maybe you're right, Dad. What you say may be so but I get the feeling that you're all bent out of shape as well." She looked at me with those big eyes. I had to dance as fast as I could.

"Jen, when you are troubled, I am troubled. We both enjoy that TV baloney but this is the real world and you must not mix reality with some scriptwriter's effort to scare the pants off you. There is a not always a defined boundary between what's real and what is not. You are tough enough and smart enough to tell the difference."

Jen smiled and this small crisis was over. Getting back to the privacy of my room, I knew with absolute certainty that there was much more to come. I was no longer afraid, no longer uncertain. I must rid my home of these evil apparitions. My thoughts were clear, focused and, I must admit, murderous. Jane Gotting was an unwitting pawn. The thing inside of her must be stopped at the beginning, 143 years before, hanging by the neck in a prison courtyard. Lewis would disappear with Mary.

That same night, propped up in bed reading without focus, I knew that Naomi needed to be brought up to date. Even at the considerable risk my image would be severely tarnished, I needed her strength and support.

When I finished, right down to the conversation with Jennifer, Naomi said nothing.

She had listened with quiet patience without a hint of her feelings. When she did speak it was in her usual direct manner, without a hint of mockery or disbelief:

"David, when we met in school and fell so deeply in love, I knew then as I know now that the things that made you special, the honesty and integrity of your character, would never change. For me and your children when the sun is shining and Dad say's it 's raining we all grab umbrellas. I'm not saying that I won't question, probe and find all the answers I can. Many times we have changed our course because we trusted each other's input. I won't follow blindly and agree to every action but my basic reaction is quite simple. If you believe all this to be true then I believe it too. My first suggestion is to go downstairs and bring up that bottle of Merlot in the pantry, a box of crackers, two stemmed glasses and a hunk of cheddar and we'll sit in bed and get wasted. While we do, let's cover all the bases and work out a way to hit back." I get emotional whether it's "Hail to the Chief" or an embrace of father and child in the movies. This was no exception. We talked to the wee hours and slept late. Jane's appointment was that afternoon.

I started Jane's next session with taking detailed notes on her reactions in sex with her husband since erotic post hypnotic suggestions had been implanted as part of her therapy. By and large there had been a good deal of success. Erotic fantasy had helped her in becoming aroused. Orgasms, which had been infrequent, were becoming a steady and welcome reaction. During orgasm and ejaculation she was instructed to visualize the sperm traveling to the womb, meeting the egg with strong feelings of loving contact. Her results were fuzzy and not sharply focused. However, it was a great start. I suggested a few texts in the library with realistic illustrations of the sperm's inner journey, to help her visualizations.

The small success I have had in working with couples who have gotten nowhere in the traditional medical approach to fertility can be traced to a short research paper published a few years ago. I read it in a Dentist's office waiting for a root canal. The research had found a statistical basis to what had been considered an old wives tale. Couples who had no medical reason why they could not conceive a child very often had a natural conception after adopting. This careful research, using a study group of 680 couples over a period of five years, seemed to conclusively arrive at the same opinion my Aunt Sarah always had. Sarah's only other claim to fame was her cheesecake.

It seemed to me that the "must succeed" stress these people have in sexual union was inhibiting the natural flow of the many physiological responses needed to make the female egg fertile. Knowing full well that hypnosis can achieve bio-feedback responses such as a sharp rise in body temperature or brain waves that could be recorded on an EEG test, I began to explore the possibilities. The book by Desmond Morris, "The Naked Ape", had a marked effect on my thinking. His thesis, boiled to the bones, was that every physiological response of both partners in heterosexual sex was designed by nature to propagate the species. If, in foreplay, both partners would achieve passionate arousal, at penetration the firm, thrusting penis of the aroused male would ejaculate explosively up the vaginal canal. Rapid breathing, heart rate and body temperature would increase in both partners giving the sperm a proper environment to start a successful journey. As the female orgasm took place, muscles in the vaginal tract would alternately constrict and expand, literally sucking in the sperm as the dramatic increase in body fluids would protect and nurture the wriggling cells as they moved upward and in, ever closer to that fateful encounter with the egg.

After 20 years of hypno-therapeutic practice, I am acutely aware of the minds ability to produce a auto-immune response to cure a sty, wart or a boil overnight. In my own particular use of the mind's ability to produce a healing serum, I ask the patient to visualize this serum moving directly to the site of the skin eruption and destroying the problem as an army would destroy an enemy. The percentage of success is remarkable, particularly with problems of the skin. Destroy could become create.

The therapy in helping a woman conceive would use the same logic in reverse. There would be enhancement at the site of conception, not destruction. At the moment after orgasm, a post hypnotic suggestion would be triggered. The woman's thoughts at this fateful moment could help the brain's production of hormones and bio-chemicals needed for successful fertilization. A visualization of warm and loving acceptance as the sperm meets the egg would enhance the brain's ability to produce the hormones and bio-chemicals to make fertilization a success.

The key was uninhibited passion not hampered by the stress of failure to conceive.

The basic problem was the lack of good sex in many of the couples I treated. That was an important focus of the hypnotherapy. Using the Master's and Johnson approach of individual erotic fantasy, coupled with the inclusion of post hypnotic response, was appropriate in both partners. Success, in the first patient and in many others, led to a succession of invitations to Baptisms and Bris. I wasn't too fussy in what turned them on. I found out that there is no better marriage counselor than good sex. In couples deeply in love, perhaps reaching back to a teen age eroticism would prove helpful. In a hostile relationship, sadly the more prevalent possibility, there were no holds barred. Anyway, whatever the motivation to arouse, breakfast sure becomes a lot more friendly. In some ethical studies, a white lie for a greater good is permissible. To use an erotic fantasy of a different partner is a lot more common than generally believed. Not being foolish, I'm inclined to read the ethics I agree with.

Jane Gotting was a "perfect". A subject that could get into an hypnotic trance with an eye roll and could achieve startling success in biofeedback. Until the chilling voice of Mary Surratt scared the hell out of me, we were almost done with our sessions. I was determined that they would not end until Mary and Lewis were exorcized.

Mary did not wait long to make her contact. Jane became very still and her breathing deep and regular as she went deeply into the trance state. It was only a moment when she turned to look at me, her eyes now gray, the face lined and the mouth thin and straight:

"Well, Dr. Borin, do you still have any doubt of my occult powers?"

"You haven't contacted me for bullshit and you need no affirmation from me to feed your ego. Letting Lewis free to roam in my home and his despicable actions in leering at my child has made up my mind. I will not cooperate with you further unless I set the ground rules."

"Ah, the mouse speaks harshly to the cat. The only thing the mouse can accomplish is to be eaten."

"And I'm gonna do the eating." Another voice entered the room and Lewis moved out of the shadows.

"Is this real enough for you Doc? The huge knife flashed in the light of the desk lamp and slammed into my desk, vibrating with the force of the blow."

"You slimy bastard, you couldn't even kill an old man lying sick in his bed when you were alive. All you're good for now is Halloween."

Even his eyes seemed red as he lunged toward me and then was gone, as was the Bowie knife, just as if someone had turned off a television set. My finger reached out and there was no scar on my desk. So far, Naomi and I had guessed right.

"Your gamble was right Doctor but I'm still here." Mary indeed was still staring at me but seemingly unperturbed about the incident. "Lewis needs a living body but unfortunately for you, I have one. A healthy young woman that I can control and used to destroy both you and your family with impunity. Will you tell your tale to the local constable?"

"I'll take my chances. Whatever happens, you and sweet Lewis have not been able to fornicate in 143 years. I'm your meal ticket, damn you."

Mary was not one to spend much time on decisions:

"Very well, Doctor, what are your ground rules?"

"If myself or my family are ever confronted by Lewis again, you may remember your host is in my office. I can direct my therapy in any way I choose. You will never see her pregnant. I will work with negatives instead of positives to make sure she will stay infertile. You and your murdering boyfriend will never fuck again! "

"Damn, you're a pistol!"

Mary actually cackled in glee in a heaving fit of laughter.

"So you think this is funny, you bitch.." I rose and began to move around the desk.

"Sit down Doctor Borin. That comment was said in admiration, not jest. I was beginning to think that except for my sweet Lewis, real men didn't exist in this damned generation. I will agree to your terms. When Jane conceives, you will never see me or hear from me again and as an amateur historian you will be famous in using your experiences to write the truth of what happened to the great baboon in the Executive Mansion."

Wary of that evil woman sitting across from me, I was not about to be thankful.

The concept of her soul entering into Jane's child and letting those two zombies loose in our world was unthinkable. Our plan had a lot of gaps that would have to be filled in but the goal would always be the same. Remove the evil in our house. For now I must get back to the Civil War time era. Only there could Mary be stopped but at this moment my mind churned and found no definitive answer.

"OK, here's the next step. I want to follow Lincoln from the time he awakens the morning of April 15, to the moment of his death in the Petersen house across the street from Ford's Theater." There is a lot more I want to see, but more of that later." I tilted back the armchair and rolled my eyes up to initiate the trance state.

The trip to the Capitol in 1865 was not the Hollywood concept of time travel. There was no portal of crackling electricity making colorful wavy lines. One moment I was in my office and in the next heartbeat my invisible presence was at the door to the White House on a perfect Spring morning in April, 1865. Will we ever see such mornings again along the present megapolis from Richmond to Boston? The sky was a breathtaking blue swept clean by unpolluted air. The morning was crisp and dry. The odors of the open sewers a few hundred yards down the hill were dormant in the low humidity and no match for the blooming lilacs of the White House gardens. For a moment the beauty of the scene blotted out the reasons I was here. This was the day the first assassination of an American President was to occur. Not just a President, but also a man so revered by his people that the shock waves of this deed still reverberate a century and a half later. I was to bear witness to a brutal murder, a crime that will never be erased from the nation's collective memories. I moved past the pair of armed soldiers at the door and stepped into the large foyer just beyond. The executive mansion was decorated in the overblown manner of a Mississippi river boat. Thick hangings tucked back by velvet ropes, flowered wallpaper, and heavy furniture and potted palms in abundance. Stuart's superb portrait of Washington dominated the room. As I moved up the grand staircase to the President's family quarters above, the grandfather clock on the first landing showed seventeen minutes before seven.

My first sight of Abraham Lincoln was his back turned to me as he sat in a large rocking chair in the center of what looked to me as a family library. Head tilted forward, he wore a knitted shawl over a white nightgown and spectacles that rested low on his nose. My emotions were chaotic. I was awestruck in the presence of this American icon. I knew that I must observe and remember but for a few moments could only stare without a coherent thought. I moved slowly around the chair.

He was as homely a man can get.. A shock of unkempt black hair went in all directions and his ears were long with hanging lobes. He had an unhealthy pallor and his sunken cheeks emphasized his sharp cheekbones. I got the sense of a man exhausted and underweight. His shoulders were broad and with knees drawn up, his long body seemed too big for the chair he was in. His hands were huge and his arms stuck out of the sleeves of his gown. For all of this, there was a look of majesty in his bearing, an aura of extraordinary power.

The giant was reading the Bible, balanced on his lap. His lips moved slightly as he read but he made no sound. After a while, Lincoln glanced at the clock on top of the ornate fireplace, put the velvet bookmark in place, sighed and unfolded from the chair. He put the large Bible on a handsome reading desk with a leather top and unhurriedly walked back to his bedroom to start the day. It was to be a day that will be remembered as long as there is a United States. April 14th., 1865.

Unseen or not, I was not about to intrude on the President's privacy as he dressed and got ready for the day. I used the time to move around the empty halls as one would in a museum, in this case a little seedy and in need of some repair. There were cracks over the door jambs and on the hallway walls the paper was beginning to peel. The inevitable potted plants seemed healthy and in a few moments I saw why. A teenage young black man dressed in valet livery came up the stairs with a watering can and went about seriously doing his thing. The great house was beginning to stir and a young man in his 30's walked by and pulled a watch from his vest pocket, mumbled something and sat down in a chair opposite the bedroom putting a large briefcase on the floor beside him. I assumed it was either Hay or Nicolay, one of the President's secretaries. As I later found out, it was John Nicolay.

When Lincoln strode from the room he greeted the young man with warmth and affection, I got a jolt listening to his voice. I had assumed it was like Henry Fonda's but instead it was higher pitched. Not unpleasantly so but not the deep, booming tones of an orator. The accent was dignified, with country roots like the old men who sit on the bench in front of the town barbershop swapping stories.

"John, my son Robert was at Appomattox with Grant at the surrender and I can't wait for him to tell me all about it." Lincoln and Nicolay strode down the hall to his upstairs office. With his arm on the young man's shoulders, he towered above him. Dressed all in black, the President's clothes seemed a bit baggy but still gave him a distinguished look with white starched collar and pearl gray cravat. His hair had been brushed and parted but still looked as if he really did not care much about the strands that were still untamed. "Well, you mule driver, what have you got for me today?" He had sat down at a shiny mahogany upright desk, somewhat like a secretary with a large foldout writing shelf and many cubbyholes stuffed with papers. The large windows behind him were bright with sun and the Potomac sparkled in changing accents. John Hay walked in with an assortment of letters and newspapers but both he and Nicolay, according to a comment by Hay, had been up since dawn culling only the few things they thought the President should see. His staff was efficient and attentive and an observer like myself could sense the great admiration and respect in the way they interacted with the President.

The agenda for the day was a series of appointments with political cronies and a very important Cabinet meeting that was pushed up to 11:00 o'clock to accommodate the press of business. It was the first Cabinet meeting after the Appomattox surrender of Lee's Army to Grant and much machinery had to be put in place for the days ahead.

When I heard that Grant was to attend the meeting, my pulse rate (if I had a pulse in this disembodied state) speeded up again.

About an hour had passed and Lincoln excused himself to have breakfast in the family dining room on the floor below. His son Tad and the First Lady would be waiting.

My first impression of Mary Lincoln was that of a dumpy woman with a pudgy face who never seemed to smile very much. She did fuss over the President and seemed concerned when he ate very little. Breakfast for him was one egg, a cup of coffee and a strip of bacon. Tad was irrepressible, leaping into his father's arms, ignoring his mother's pleas and chattering away with questions throughout the meal. Lincoln was calm, loving and patient and it seemed that if Tad had turned the table over, it would not have upset him. Mary, on the other hand, remonstrated non-stop. This particular breakfast was not a very relaxing one for the President but he adored his little boy and Tad could do no wrong.

The President brightened when his son Robert walked in and joined the family. The Lincoln's oldest son was just twenty-two and had graduated from Harvard college the previous Spring. His face was apple-cheeked with a pale hint of a beard, a face that favored his mother. Proper and trim in what looked like a custom made Captain's uniform, Robert was intelligent and articulate, making his story of the Appomattox surrender come alive in a colorful description. He called Lincoln: "Father." as did Mrs. Lincoln and Tad.

Mary was able to bribe Tad away from the table and Lincoln relished the details of Lee's surrender. Robert had brought in a print of a portrait of Lee, a man whom Lincoln had never seen in person. He was taken with, as he put it:

"..the face of a noble, noble brave man." For Lincoln, who had suffered the great casualty lists of the war that flowed in to the War Department by telegraph, battle after bloody battle, to look upon Lee with such strong and positive emotions was a remarkable picture of his soul.

The President seemed particularly pleased by Robert's description of the contrast between Lee, the patrician Virginian in a spotless, bemedaled uniform and the simple Grant, wearing a private's tunic with muddy trousers and dirty boots. Lincoln asked about Grant's terms to Lee's beaten Army of Northern Virginia. When Robert read from his notes about the humane and simple instructions for Lee's men to return home, keeping their horses for the Spring ploughing, the President nodded in vigorous assent. The time flew and John Hay came in to remind the President of his schedule.

Lincoln's last words to his son was a fatherly but still firm suggestion that he should leave the military and return to Harvard, as he put it, "to read for the law." With a reluctant sigh, the President rose to leave and meet his first appointment of the day with Schuyler Colfax, the Speaker of the House.

Colfax walked in with a Congressional colleague who, as it turned out was also a trusted friend of the President, formally announced as Cornelius Cole of California. The atmosphere was not a formal one but rather a happy reunion of old friends. It was obvious to me as an observer that chums or not, the line of authority was clearly drawn. It was not a matter of first among equals. The Presidency had the same mantle of respect then as it does now. "Mr. President" never gave way to "Abe". All three were jubilant about the end of the War but some serious business was discussed.

Colfax, newly arrived from Indiana, was leaving in a week or two for a long trip to the West to test political waters. He was making sure that the President would not order a special session of Congress that would require his presence. Cole was to start his trip to the family home in California and was the first to leave.

Lincoln began to talk about the West in an uncanny glimpse into the future. My notes were made after my time travel and I cannot be exact in my quotes but things were said that were so striking I won't ever forget. Making the point he would give "his eye teeth" to make the trip West with Colfax, Lincoln started to talk about the mineral resources of the nation and commented on the almost inexhaustible supply of our natural resources. Now that the nation was not engaged in the tremendous expense of running the War, we could encourage migration to the West for the thousands of returning soldiers both North and South who must seek employment and, as well, the rapidly expanding influx of immigrants from the poor European continent. There was enough room for them all. The expenses of supporting an all out war effort had stopped all Government support to Western expansion and the now united nation needed growth and prosperity.

The following is a remembered quote and the words still ring in my mind:

"Tell the miners for me that I shall promote their interests to the utmost of my ability because their prosperity is the prosperity of the nation. We shall prove in a very few years that we are indeed the treasury of the world." The words were said in the poetic cadences of the Gettysburg Address and I was stunned at this prescient look into the 20th Century. That trip of the Speaker was not postponed but it turned out to be a sad duty for an old friend. He was to mix Lincoln's advice with eulogies for a fallen leader as his audiences wept.

A string of politicians moved in and out as morning quickly moved toward mid-day.

The Postmaster of Detroit, a Senator or two, all to effusively congratulate the President on the end of the War. The President seemed to enjoy every handshake and sometime overblown praise. His replies were always depreciating and modest. My admiration, no. it was more than that, try "adoration", grew with each interview.

Prudes seemed not to be welcomed in Lincoln's inner circle. The room rang with ribald jokes about lusty old maids and gun toting fathers, all with a country flavor. It reminded me of the old films I had seen of Will Rogers entertaining on stage. Lincoln could really have been a stand-up success. He reared back and laughed with his mouth wide open and told three stories for every one he heard. His were better, as was his instinctive timing as an experienced raconteur. The stories were not told as jokes, per se, but always to illustrate a particular point of view. Most were at the expense of some of his political opponents in the Congress. They would start out; "Talking about old Thaddeus, that reminds me of...." A good deal of serious work was done as well. He was very firm as to the principles the War was all about. Slavery was over and that would be enforced. The national authority would rest in Washington and nowhere else and any and all Southern armed forces were to be disbanded immediately.

Many of the visitors rubbed their hands in glee about getting even and hanging all who led the Confederacy. Lincoln's replies were firm and consistent. No more bloodshed except for criminal acts. The South was to be treated with respect and humane treatment. Not every visitor, even the powerful ones in his party, took that advice graciously. Lincoln tried humor first and if that did not work he made it perfectly clear who was responsible for this policy. He seemed to have an utmost faith that the American people would agree with him and put his policy right on the line. As long as he was President he would not change his stance. "With malice toward none, with charity for all" was a theme of his second inaugural and to one visitor or another he reminded them of his commitment to that pledge.

Hay and Nicolay seemed like men on a dedicated mission, making notes in remarkably swift shorthand of every spoken word (I wondered if that included the racy jokes) and making sure the President would keep his appointments on time. I kept the two of them apart because Nicolay had a little less hair and a small beard and Hay was the one with a curled, full mustache and shaved chin. They were both slight men, black haired and dressed like undertakers. As for the 11:00 Cabinet meeting as far as I could see, the President had studied no position papers. From my own reading of his habits, staying up late and absorbing the important details was probably done the night before.

I suppose I was so awestruck that leaning over Lincoln's mail and reading his written replies for the sake of historians never occurred to me. I was content to soak in the scene and my own previous reading assured me that every letter, every note, was already in the record. I was seeing Lincoln in the flesh, alive and in full command of his office. I did not want to get buried in minutiae on this day. The last day this great man would live.

As the morning moved along Lincoln seemed to get in a better and better frame of mind. A man moved into his office announced as Senator John Creswell of Maryland.

Lincoln evidently liked the man as he rose from his desk, shook his hand and exclaimed with joy:

"The god-awful war is over, Creswell and you're up early. Must be important!" I gathered from the gist of the conversation that Creswell, a firm Unionist from a border state, had done much to keep Maryland in the Union. He was there to get the President's signature on a letter that would pardon a Confederate family friend in a military prison. Lincoln was no stranger to the Presidential pardon. His political opponents made much of his "disloyalty" to the memory of fallen Union troops. A man with rock solid belief in his instincts, the President never wavered in his humanity. This incident stands out because of a funny story Lincoln told the Senator.

It was a story of a hayride that took a scow across a river and the men and ladies picnicked on the other side. The scow broke loose during the afternoon and drifted downstream requiring the men to choose a lady and carry her back across (with a wink or two during the telling). The last ones left were a very thin, short man and a tall, rather large, lady. The man almost went under but he and the lady made it. "Now don't you see Creswell, you petitioners will get everyone across the river except me and old Jeff Davis!"

Creswell roared along with the President. That was one time I did lean over to see as he took the Senator's letter requesting the pardon and wrote on the back of it: "Let it be done. A. Lincoln. April 14th, 1865"

I do not have a photographic memory. The story was longer and funnier than it sounds and any conversation quotes are as close as memory allows. I became emotional looking at that pardon as one of his last official acts and I shall never forget it.

Not every caller got what he wanted as easily as Senator Creswell. Several of his visitors, particularly those with personal axes to grind about money they felt was due them, were given polite, but short shrift. I got the feeling that Lincoln, carrying the awful responsibility of the thousands upon thousands of Americans who sacrificed livesin the war, had no patience for those with a monetary loss.

The process of getting an appointment with the President was not very difficult. During the War there were two armed soldiers at the door of the mansion but people were not asked for identification going in and out. As such the White House was host to many others than political or military dignitaries. A petitioner would walk up to the desk in front of Lincoln's office and ask one of his staff to be put on the appointments list. They would wait to be called, seated on sofas that lined the long corridor. Time restraints and Lincoln's needs would determine how many daily visitors would move through. Members of Congress and friends of the President would, of course, get preferred treatment. Very often a note would be passed into the office and the President would cut short an interview and quickly see an important visitor.

Today, the President told Hay to leave him enough time to go to the War Department, a quick walk, in that era, out the East wing of the mansion. He wanted to check the telegrams from General Sherman who had not yet received the surrender of Joe Johnston's Army of Tennessee.

In the hallway just outside his office were two attractive ladies. Lincoln smiled and asked their names. His eyes were alight with pleasure as he asked them to come and look at his favorite lemon tree in the garden, alive with fresh fruit and blossoms. Hay never left his side. One of the ladies had introduced herself as Mrs. C.D. Hess, the wife of the manager of Grover's Theatre. The lady with her was Mrs. Moss, her sister in law. The President, an avid theatre buff, knew Mr. Hess and had received an invitation from him to attend that evening's performance of "Aladdin". Lincoln had decided instead to go to Ford's Theatre to see a ribald comedy called: "My American Cousin". Rather than have Mr. Hay send a courier and a note, he asked Mrs. Hess to make his apologies to her husband. All smiles and quips, he picked a lemon for each of them and called over the gardener to pick a bouquet for both. The scene was extraordinary, the President obviously enjoying the encounter as did the two thoroughly charmed women.

When the President walked, he did not seem to rush but his long legs made Hay take two for one and the young man looked harried. Lincoln, very formally, was wearing the familiar stovepipe hat which made him seem even taller. Around his shoulders was a gray shawl which Mary had insisted at breakfast that he wear if he left the White House. Entering the old brick building of the War Department, Lincoln waved everyone "at ease" as they jumped to attention, saluting his presence as Commander in Chief. It must have happened every day but he still seemed embarrassed. After checking the morning dispatches from Sherman, it seemed the Confederate troops under General Johnston were still holding out. Lincoln expressed the hope to the young Lieutenant in charge of the telegraph office that the surrender would take place soon. As a matter of hindsight, I knew that it would take about two weeks for Johnston to finally lay down the arms of his men. Lincoln would never read that dispatch.

Across the hall the door way was open to the office of the Secretary of War. Like all the office doors in the building, the door frames were hung with screen doors inside the entrance doors. The only air circulation in this era was the open windows and doorways. Sanitation was primitive at best and with troops encamped in every unused land area, open sewers were common. Flies were a constant irritant.

Lincoln moved across the hall and with a rare show of irritation, swept the shawl off his shoulders and draped it over the top of the screen door. Hay looked like he made a mental note to retrieve the shawl on the way back. He protected his President in many ways, not the least of which could have been a scolding from Mary Lincoln.

Lincoln greeted Stanton with warmth but the Secretary seemed to be annoyed by the interruption. It was my first look at Edwin M. Stanton in his seat of power and what I saw certainly contradicted the warmth and compassion he had showed in taking care of Seward after his near fatal accident. There were many unanswered questions in the written history of the Civil War and Stanton was one of the enigmas. I was to pay very close attention.

Lincoln was not unaware of the threats on his life. From all sides he was constantly cautioned to be careful. Most of the time he made light of the subject, but today he seemed to be preoccupied with his trip to Ford's Theatre and who to have along to double as body guard and escort. The Secret Service was an intelligence unit at that time, not a guard for the President. Lincoln had requested that Grant and his wife Julia should accompany the Presidential party but the General gave the excuse that if he could finish his duties that day early enough to make the evening train to Burlington, New Jersey, his three children were at home and he missed them dearly.

It was the kind of excuse the President could not turn down.

The conversation with Stanton was not about the many details of winding down the War. It was instead a testy clash of wills between two powerful men over a rather simple duty. Stanton scolded Lincoln about courting trouble by visiting public places like Ford's Theatre, citing intelligence reports that threats were being heard in every saloon in Washington. When Lincoln answered:

"Stanton, I had no idea you had the time to visit saloons," even the crusty Stanton chuckled. "Really Mr. President, if you are determined to go you should have a personal guard at the Theatre." The Secretary knew full well what the President's response would be. Lincoln hated any show of ceremony and considered it a display of cowardice to go about with armed guards. He felt that a sturdy companion that would be part of his party would be more suitable. It is on the record that the President did not know that Stanton had spoken to Grant that morning and insisted that the General did not join the theatre party for reasons of safety. It would seem to me that a warning like that would beg a question from Grant about the President's safety. I would try to eavesdrop on that conversation if I could, but now, back to business.

"Stanton, do you know that Eckert can bend a steel poker over his arm?"

"I did not know, Mr. President, why do you ask?"

Major Thomas J. Eckert was Superintendent of the Military Telegraph and answered directly to the Secretary of War. His great strength had left a strong impression on Lincoln who was proud of his own physical prowess and admired it in others.

"A while back, I saw Eckert bend 5 pokers over his arm when he was upset about some contractor selling the Government shoddy steel. I'm thinking that he'd be just the right man to come with us tonight."

"Mr. President, the Major has a important assignment that will keep him very busy tonight and cannot be excused."

This exchange between these men has been known to most avid readers of Civil War history. Being there was quite something else. Stanton's face was flushed and he seemed more nervous and upset than the situation warranted. The President was relaxed about it at first but when flatly turned down he stiffened.

"Well, by heck, I will ask Eckert himself and he can do that important work of yours tomorrow."

As Stanton blustered, the President turned his back and strode out. Hay, ever vigilant, swiftly retrieved the shawl from the door and scurried along. A conversation with Eckert then ensued. Eckert's chest stretched his uniform buttons and it looked as if he could bend pokers even if the steel was first rate. Lincoln immediately saw the man's predicament in not following a direct request from the Secretary of War and ending the Major's stammered and halting answers, got him quickly off the hook. Eckert sighed with relief as the President, with a quip or two, left to attend the important first Cabinet meeting after War's end.

Perhaps my feelings were colored by my foreknowledge of the appalling events of that evening but my assessment of Stanton's behavior certainly jolted my thinking. I guess I'm one of the few holdouts that believes the Warren report's conclusion of a single assassin in the death of President Kennedy. A hidden conspiracy theory was not on my agenda. My quest was to see at first hand the events of that awful day in 1865 and if I could, rid my world of the wandering, evil spirits of Mary Suratt and Lewis Paine. As much as I needed to stay focused on my goals, as I observed these events my mind wandered. I was the perfect spy. Was it my responsibility to uncover a plot against the President? If I did, nothing could be changed and how could I make it known in 2008? My thoughts chaotic, I followed Lincoln and Hay back to the White House to begin that specially called Cabinet meeting.

Both Hay and Nicolay escorted the President to the Cabinet room down one of the long corridors as the clock rang 11:00 AM. In front of the twin doors Lincoln greeted several members of the Cabinet as they arrived and moved in together, the President towering over every man in the room. A striking figure among the group, walking with a cane, was a man in his 70's with a full white beard and what looked like a curled light brown wig. It was Gideon Welles, Secretary of the Navy, probably the most loyal of the President's supporters reaching back to his nomination in Chicago. Other than Welles, whose likeness was a staple in History texts, I must confess that I relied, in most cases, on the President to greet them by name. Frederick Seward, whom I had traveled with on the wild carriage ride that seriously injured his father, represented the Department of State as Assistant Secretary of State. He looked overwhelmed and aside from studious note taking, said little.

The President's Cabinet, according to the memoirs of Nicolay and the diary of Welles,were not a very happy group when together. By the end of the War, meetings were infrequent and sparsely attended. The President was always firmly in control and there was no question where the primary authority lay. Welles of the Navy and Seward of State were the only members that had been on board from the beginning of his term.

That day the mood was upbeat and jocular with back slapping all around about the surrender of Lee's forces , the President smiling and making small jokes at everyone's expense. In 1865 there were only seven members of the Cabinet and the meeting was small enough for all to express their views. Stanton was late and arrived in a bustle of briefcases and rolled up maps. The last to enter was someone I did not recognize who I later found out was John Usher, Secretary of the Interior. When all were seated the President said:

"Gideon, if you will" and the man who looked like an Old Testament prophet thanked the Almighty for the Union's victory and asked his blessings on their deliberations and on The United States of America, once more indivisible.

After four years of bloodshed to reach that goal, this was an emotional moment. I did not know these silent men but as I looked around the massive mahogany table I was choked by pride and patriotism. Lincoln, his hands on the table sticking out of starched cuffs, looked like the awe inspiring statue in his Memorial. For a moment I remembered my first sight of the Daniel French masterpiece. It was on a High School bus trip to the Capitol and all of us stopped the horseplay and looked up in reverence. I looked upon this remarkable scene with the same strong feelings.

The meeting started with a discussion as to the treatment of the members of the Rebel government. Would they be captured and tried for treason? Would the good of the country be served if there was harsh treatment? My notes, that were written when I returned home, say it was James Speed, the Attorney General, who asked the President:

"I suppose, Mr. President, that you would not be sorry to have them escape out of the country?" Lincoln answered with his usual droll comment: "Well, Speed, I should not be sorry to see them leave the country; but I sure would be for staying on their tails to make sure of it!"

Ulysses S. Grant entered the room after a staff member knocked and announced him. All present, including Lincoln, stood up and applauded. Grant looked embarrassed and took a seat near the President. Today he was resplendent in a trim uniform tunic with the 3 stars of Lieutenant General on shoulder bars of blue and white. True to form with this self depreciating man, he wore no decorations. He was much younger than his portrait on the fifty dollar bill. Black hair and beard neatly trimmed, he looked all Army and no nonsense. His voice was a bit hoarse and the events of the last few days showed in his tired eyes as he graciously answered the many tributes. Answering the President's question he recounted the humane terms of the surrender to Lincoln's obvious approval. As to the current military situation regarding the Army of Tennessee, Grant said he was expecting favorable news very shortly from General Sherman.

The President shifted in his chair and said he was sure the news would be favorable.

He then told the group about dreaming, last night, a recurrent dream about a strange ship carrying him to a distant shore and that he had this dream before some of our great victories such as Vicksburg and Gettysburg. Knowing what awaited him, the comment gave me a chill. I can only presume that every man in the room must have had the same thoughts 24 hours later.

Stanton then took center stage. A strong nose, spectacles and full gray sprinkled beard, Stanton was like a pudgy pouter pigeon happy to strut but within a few minutes I listened with admiration at his command of the details that poured out. With each heading on his list there were maps and explicit details of how to proceed. It was an outline of a master plan for immediate Government action at the end of all hostilities. The Treasury Dept was to take possession of the Rebel custom houses, the War Department should move quickly to garrison or destroy Rebel forts, The Navy was to occupy harbors, take possession of Rebel shipping and Naval ordnance, The Interior Dept should send out surveyors, Indian agents and set them to work, The Postmaster General should reopen Southern post offices and establish national mail routes. As he went on and on Stanton never hesitated and his suggestions seemed more like orders to subordinates. He sure got their attention but there was much shifting of chairs and clearing of throats.

The President sat with a bemused expression admiring Stanton's overview but gently made sure that each head of Department had his say, pro or con. I think he felt a need to placate those whom Stanton, one among equals, might have offended by his detailed "suggestions."

Lincoln, after praising Stanton for his well organized and meticulous efforts, again spoke at length about establishing the ground rules for humane treatment of the South. There were many men at that meeting who made accurate notes of what the President said. Welles, Frederick Seward and John Nicolay to name a few. I shall put in quotes this reading from my delayed notes but I'm sure the existing record is more accurate. Where I can be of service is his emotions and delivery of what he had to say: "There will be no persecution, no bloody work, after the War is over."

He looked around the table and pronounced each word out carefully and slowly: "No one, No one should expect me to take part in hanging or killing these men, even the worst of them!"

There was dead silence. The President had each of them, in agreement or possibly opposed, focused on every word. "Frighten them off, open the gates and scare them away." He waved an arm in emphasis and then began to speak more softly:

"Too many lives have been sacrificed. We have to temper our resentments if we are to expect harmony and union. Too many in Congress want to be masters and dictate to the defeated states. We must treat them as fellow citizens. Many show little respect for their rights." Again the President pronounced each word slowly for emphasis:

"I do not sympathize in these feelings!"

Several times during the meeting, couriers would slide silently in and out leaving notes with Lincoln's trusted secretary, John Nicolay. John would read them silently and put them, I presume, in order of importance to be addressed with the President at a later date. One such note was brought in sealed with wax and Nicolay rose to Lincoln's side and whispered something I could not hear. Lincoln looked at the envelope and, ever curious, I had glided over to read it as well. In flowing script was the sender's name: "Colonel Lafayette Baker, for the President only." The President, without expression, read the short note, tucked the envelope in the inner pocket of his dress coat and said to Nicolay: "Please send a note to Mrs. Lincoln that we will be taking our drive to the Soldier's Home". Baker, I knew, was the man who started our present Secret Service that guards the President. In 1865, the colonel was the head of army intelligence.

The rest of the meeting discussed questions that needed to be addressed regarding the political makeup of the Rebel legislatures most of which were hotbeds of hostility :against the Union. There were many opinions as to procedure and all recognized that a mountain of work was left to be done in the coming year. The President, with a chuckle, was grateful Congress was not in session and if he and they moved swiftly a good deal could be accomplished.

As the meeting broke up with two or three men making their views felt at either end of the table, Lincoln's words reflected his concern for the common soldier as he spoke to the Treasury Secretary, McCulloch: "We must look to you, Mr. Secretary, for the money to pay off our men as they muster out." With the Secretary's assurance to the President, McCulloch expressing faith in the generosity of the American people, the meeting disbanded.

General Grant hung back to talk privately to the President: "Mr. President, It seems I shall be able to make the afternoon train to Burlington after all. I have just received word from my wife that she has expressed her regrets in a note to Mrs. Lincoln about not being able to attend the theatre with you both. Please accept my own regrets."

Lincoln expressed his disappointment and reminded Grant that the people would like to see the General and his lady. Grant wavered a bit but, like most husbands, probably feared his wife's wrath more than that of his Commander in Chief. The President, as was reported, had to deal with a neurotic wife who saw designing women everywhere around her husband. At a recent social gathering, Mary Lincoln's remarks about Julia Grant paying too close attention to the President, upset Mrs. Grant to the point of intense dislike. How much of Grant's refusal was about his desire to see his children or instead to placate his wife, the written record was speculative.

Our young Mr. Seward, representing the State Department, was the last to speak to Lincoln as he left the room. Seward asked the President to give him an appointment the following day to present the newly arrived British ambassador, Sir Frederick Bruce. Lincoln was always uncomfortable with ceremony, in marked contrast to the pomp and circumstance the British held so dearly. The President sighed but knew it was a necessary duty. They agreed to meeting the ambassador at 2:00 PM in the Blue Room the following day. Lincoln, in his half joking way, said something to the effect that Seward should be sure to send to his office the required welcome speech in time for him to read it beforehand. No one seemed downcast by the responsibilities thrust upon them. Least of all, the President. The Cabinet meeting ended at 2:10 PM.

Secretary Stanton turned to leave with John Usher, Secretary of the Interior and moved to the left to descend the great staircase. Lincoln and his staff walked to the right down the long corridor to his office. I paused for a moment and followed Stanton down the stairs and out the East Wing. As I moved through the tree shaded walkway, I was no longer there. I looked up and stared into the unforgiving face of Mary Surratt. She was seated in my recliner with the bustling folds of a gray, Civil War era dress, sweeping to the floor around her.

"Doctor, you are not playing by the rules that we had agreed to."

I needed a moment to take a deep breath and adjust to the jolt of being yanked like a puppet from past to present. I glanced at the desk clock I use to time my patients visits. A day in the past had taken only a few minutes in our own era. I had witnessed things that could not fit into our orderly world and this suspension of the natural laws of time and space did not seem unusual. My only concern was dealing with the harridan in front of me.

"Mary, the whole purpose of my acceptance of your demands was to satisfy the need to know the truth about the assassination. You bragged about your participation in the plot. What difference does it make to you that I follow that need to know?"

"Your sympathies are with Lincoln and the Union. If the truth becomes known you will portray our loyal band as villains and cowards, not as the brave patriots we were."

"Who do you expect me to portray that to? Shall I start by saying that I overheard the facts in a conversation I listened to? The only ones I'd be left to tell would be the other inmates at an asylum!"

"Once again, Doctor, you underestimate my ability to see through you. This is too juicy a tale to leave unspoken. I'm sure you are already working out the means to publish your findings."

"What findings? Is Stanton involved in the assassination? Was Booth backed by members of Lincoln's cabinet?"

"Enough, Borin! Lewis and I were questioned by far better inquisitors than you, under threat of death! We did not speak then, do you think I will speak now!

Mary was just warming up: "In one respect you are right, I really don't give a damn what you find out but I am getting very impatient for my end of the bargain to be met. You will tell Jane at the end of this visit to bring Alfred, the idiot she married, to the next visit for therapy needed to accomplish your fertility goals. That is If Alfred can achieve an erection! Ha!

The derisive laugh was barked at me. It is hard to describe the ferocity of her words and manner. It was fascinating, revolting and more than a little frightening.

"When Alfred is here and in a trance state of sufficient depth, sweet Lewis will enter the fool and command his body and soul. We will conceive the children that will be the start of eternal life together!"

God forgive me, at that moment getting back to 1865 was the only thing that mattered. I rationalized my moral predicament by the inner promise to make good on our final goal; to cut the bond between Mary and her daughter at the moment she dropped through the hangman's trap. That would not only free my family but Alfred and Jane as well. I did not want to dwell on the overriding fear of never getting back. There was much to be thought out. For now, I wanted only to return to that short garden walkway between the White House and the War Department in 1865. I agreed to her conditions, sat back in my office chair, closed my eyes and my senses were again assailed by the smell of clean crisp air and the sweet odor of a lilac tree.

Chapter 4
The Navy Yard

There was a clattering of hooves off to my right as an open carriage drew up in front of the White House portico. The President and his wife came out of the entranceway between saluting guards and moved slowly to the carriage to the applause of the many onlookers who had gathered for just such a glimpse. Lincoln and Mary Todd entered the carriage, the President helping the short-legged lady up the step, and closed the half door. I moved invisibly to the opposing seat, making the quick decision to stick to my original plan to stay with Lincoln to the end.

The morning had been balmy and beautiful but the weather had turned a bit colder, a few gray clouds moving in quickly erased the sunlight.. The Presidential couple sat close, Lincoln, dressed in coat and shawl and black stovepipe hat firmly in place.

The only witness to what was said during that ride, and for that matter where they went, was Mary Todd Lincoln. Knowing her past history of jealous rages, hysteria and depressive behavior, historians have never been sure that her memoirs were self-serving or accurate. My observations turned out to be a good measure of both. On the crowded streets around the White House were banners and bunting hanging from every house. It did not matter that there were still pockets of Confederate resistance that still had to be mopped up by the Union. Lee had surrendered and that meant the War was over! The excitement and celebrations were non-stop. Many times the horses reacted in fear as firecrackers went off but the firm hand of Burke, the coachman, a grizzled Union veteran, kept things calm. Mary reacted with jumps and cries but Lincoln remained impassive. He smiled at the many waves and shouts from the sidewalks but to me he seemed lost in thought. Mary, on the other hand was cheerful and generous with her waving back, enjoying each moment.

When they left the White House area, Lincoln asked the driver to take them to the Navy Yard. Mary remonstrated sharply, reminding the President he had sent her a note that they were driving to the Soldier's Home. He was gentle and humorous in reply reminding Mary that as President he had the right to veto.

Mary was not amused. She was annoyed because the route was not a scenic one and had to take them to the less desirable area of the city. Lincoln, citing his daily involvement in Army affairs wanted to acknowledge the debt the country owed to the Navy, stating that the warships had fought gallantly and a Presidential visit of appreciation were due. He was firm and the matter passed although Mrs. Lincoln went into a silent pout. The carriage turned to the southeast and we traveled in a steady trot through the city. Carriages, open and closed of all sizes, moved in opposite directions. Individual horsemen, mostly in military dress, moved in and out of traffic with occasional bursts of speed. The city was decked out in celebration and many times we saw that celebration spill onto slatted wood sidewalks from saloons that seemed to be on every corner. Groups of men, some of them in uniform, would stagger down the walks, some carrying beer steins, shouting in the joy of Union Victory. I saw one instance of a beating broken up by a policeman. Washington was a border city with a large representation of Confederate sympathizers. This was a good day for adherents of Jefferson Davis to stay indoors.

The Lincoln carriage, open and unguarded, was a focal point of interest. Several came close enough for comfort. One man running along side was shouting words of praise and encouragement. Lincoln was now smiling and animated, giving small waves and nodding his head in acknowledgment. Mary too was caught up in the adulation of the crowd and seemed in good spirits at last. The President called to Ned, the coachman, to move to more residential streets even if the way was longer. The scene changed from cobblestones to dirt roads and the green canopies of the trees on either side added calm contrast to the boisterous scene we had just left.

Arriving at the docks without notice, The President and First Lady were immediately surrounded by cheering officers and men who surrounded the party. Lincoln and his wife were clearly invigorated by the reception and Mary's mood brightened considerably. She spotted a young officer in the crowd from Springfield and drew him over to remind the President of who it was. Lincoln was pleased to see William C. Flood, the grandson of an Illinois political crony. The young officer was acting ensign and executive officer of a small Union steamer, the Primrose, docked nearby. Lincoln asked which of the warships was the Montauk since he had been told of her bloody engagements with the enemy. When the ship was pointed out Lincoln pressed the young man into service as the escort for himself and Mary to tour the battle scarred cruiser.

The Commander in Chief was piped aboard with all due ceremony to the obvious discomfort of the President. Mary beamed and took the arm of young ensign Flood as he moved to describe the first set of gun turrets on the main deck. A Warrant officer named Foley, stepped up to the President and whispered something I could not hear. Lincoln turned to Flood and said he was going to tour the decks below, too crowded and stuffy for Mrs. Lincoln. Mary, basking in the attention of all these officers and men hardly knew he was gone. I followed Lincoln, with young Mr. Foley leading the way, down a tight gangway in which he had to remove his tall hat and stoop to avoid hitting his head. Always jocular, he asked his guide if all Navy men were required to be as short as General Sherman. The President was ushered into the Captain's quarters, a rough-hewn timbered room about eight foot square and barely six feet high. The portholes were open, the air making the room comfortable. At a bare oaken chart table sat an imposing and handsome Union officer. It was Col. Lafayette Baker, head of Army intelligence. He moved quickly to his feet and saluted smartly. Lincoln waved him at ease and was pleased to sit down and not keep crooking his neck to avoid the ceiling. He took off his coat, white gloves, shawl and with the earlier removed stovepipe hat, entrusted the considerable package to the awestruck Foley who left the two men together and stood guard outside the thick oak door. The President's long legs were also a problem he solved by sitting sideways.

"Well Baker, I got your message this morning and was quite surprised. I heard you were in New York on intelligence business."

"Mr. President, that was a ruse. My train pulled into a siding just outside of the city and my aide met me there with horse in tow. After you have heard what I have to say, the meaning for such a deception will become clear."

For the next twenty minutes Baker outlined a plot on the President's life. Not simply a warning of saloon gossip around the city but a plot that seemed to involve members of Congress and possibly a member of the Cabinet. The Colonel was meticulous in his details and absolutely sure of his sources. I sucked in my emotions and listened as intently as the President. When the President asked the obvious questions of naming names, Baker said he did not yet possess the incontrovertible truth and would have such proof within the week. His adversaries were brilliant men who burn notes and leave no solid evidence but Baker had managed to infiltrate the offices of one of his suspects by planting an agent of his own as a recorder of shorthand. He could not move without such evidence and would not destroy reputations on hearsay no matter how reputable the informer.

I looked for signs of fear or emotion in the President but his breathing was steady and his body and hands motionless. Lincoln's next question was soft spoken without a hint of anxiety: "Do you have any information about when or where the attempt will be made?"

Baker was blunt and direct: "The assassin and a small group of followers have no idea of who is footing the bills and backing the undertaking. The backers are setting the killers up to die for their foul deed. They would then have a clear path for their ambitions, which is to destroy your plans for reconstruction and wreck havoc on a defeated South. The plotters have created a collective monster that could break its shackles at any time. Your going to Ford's Theatre tonight, as is advertised on broadsides tacked up all over the city, is simply an invitation to disaster."

Lincoln did not speak for a few moments and when he did it was in soft and measured tones: "Baker, Almost five years ago when my administration began, I listened to my close advisors, including Army intelligence, and against my better judgment I agreed to sneak into the Capitol in the dead of night because of the threat of assassination. New at the game, I figured I had to trust in men more experienced than I. I have regretted that action ever since and my political enemies have rejoiced in my discomfort. Can I be less resolute than the multitude of brave men who have given their lives in this conflict? I know full well that this heinous crime can be committed at any time by a man willing to risk his own life. It is the price I have to pay for accepting my oath of office. If the Almighty wishes it to be, then so be it. Our nation will survive and many good men will follow who can and will do a better job than I."

This humble man could not foresee the hundred years of racial strife his untimely death would cause. He was, at that moment of history, irreplaceable. Col. Baker, all Army to the tips of his polished boots, was now the one to be silent. My own emotions were chaotic but the great man's words remain indelible in my memory. Baker spoke again:

"Mr. President, let me at the very least put a troop of seasoned veterans around Ford's Theatre?"

"Absolutely not, Colonel, the last thing I want is for the public to be aware that the President needs an honor guard like some foreign potentate."

Lincoln said this with a lot more emphasis than his previous remarks but the brave and dedicated Colonel did not back down. The next few minutes were a haggling session about security. The President finally agreed to a group of Baker's best men, in plain clothes, mixing with the audience. In a way, at Ford's Theatre that horrific night, the present Secret Service was born. Col. Baker was to be its first chief of staff.

Before the President took his leave he asked Baker to come to the White House early the next morning and be prepared, regardless of the Colonel's reservations, to lay all the notes and interviews with agents before him. He put it firmly to Baker to be prepared to name names and would not heed any objections to this order. Baker's only reply was: "Yes, Sir." A meeting, I knew, that would never take place.

As the President prepared to take his leave he said: "Come now young man, don't look so glum." Then proceeded to tell Baker about an old turkey on a farm that always managed to escape the axe each Christmas dinner. The punch line was said with a chuckle: "They haven't got this old turkey trussed up yet."

When the President came up on deck, word of his arrival had spread, the officers and crews of all the ships in the Yard gathered about on the dock and on the Montauk. Men were hanging from the lines above and cheered with enthusiasm. I was at his side as he leaned down to his wife and said: "This will do more for my health than all the doctors in America." An impromptu speech in all the noise was not possible and the President looked as if he wanted to beat a strategic retreat. He and his wife shook hands with the Captain and his officers and asked Flood to escort them back to his waiting carriage. When seated he invited the young Ensign to the White House for dinner, saying that Robert, who had known Flood in Springfield, had some great tales to tell of the surrender at Appomattox.

Finally in the carriage together Mary said: "How wonderful the reception we have received. Father, it must make you very proud indeed. I burst with pride for my husband."

"Mother, the other side of the coin of love is hate. There are editorials each day in powerful radical newspapers calling for my head. There are members of my own party who would cheer at my demise. My concept of 'Malice toward none' is like waving a red flag in font of a bull. The Radicals thirst for blood and vengeance and I must somehow overcome those deeply felt beliefs for the sake of an undivided Union."

Listening to the President and still churning with emotion from the information that Baker had given the President, I knew that I had to somehow squeeze in time to follow Stanton like a fly on the wall. With my ability to move time frames back and forth it could be done without giving up my plan to experience this day all over again with the infamous Booth. Lincoln's day had been recorded by many sources hour by hour. Booth's day had gaping holes in the record, which I intended to clear up.

The time away from my home and family, whose security was a constant worry, would still be measured in minutes rather than days. My office clock had confirmed that on my last trip. In my own time era, Mary Surratt would have given up only a few minutes of Jane's appointment.

Mary Todd was warm and affectionate and the President moved into a better frame of mind. They talked about the things they wanted to do when his work was over. Visiting Jerusalem and touring Palestine was discussed at length. He felt there might also be the possibility of a move to California, a State that Lincoln felt would be a leader in industry and commerce as the Nation grew. He became animated as he talked about the old days in Springfield and the practice of Law. Mary refreshed his memory on many instances of those days. As it always is in retrospect, life was better then.

In contrast to the somber beginning of the journey they were both in a fine mood as the carriage pulled back into the White House driveway. When they stopped under the portico entrance, Lincoln helped Mary down. As he turned to go into the executive mansion he spotted two old friends walking away from the grounds. I was a little startled when he shouted: "Come back boys !" The two "boys" turned out to be the Governor of Illinois and a General from the same State.

The President took them up to his office and without waiting to find out the purpose of their visit, said: "Boys, you have to hear this.." and started to read a recently published book by a humorist he admired who used the pen name of Petroleum V. Masby. Lincoln was an accomplished reader and acted out the homespun satirical dialogue to the delight of his guests who obviously put whatever their mission was aside. I found out through the visitors log the Governor was Oglesby and the General was Haynie. He was Mr. President to both men but Lincoln, as was his custom with young and old, called them by their last names.

Getting the President to stop his reading was not easy. The doorkeeper, who Lincoln called Tom, came at least twice to remind him of the dinner hour. The third time Tom evoked the name of Mrs. Lincoln who said to remind the President of the theatre after dinner. Tom, to the merriment of the three men said: "You'd best come, Mr. President" The grandfather clock in the reception room chimed six.

Dinner with Mary Todd, Robert and Tad was a happy meal. The glow of Lee's surrender had not worn off. As they left the table Lincoln walked to his office for some more unfinished appointments, promising to keep them short. His son Robert remarked that he had never seen father thinner or more tired and that a good night's sleep might be better for him than going out. Mary remarked that he would not disappoint the people who came to see him and that a good laugh at a play he enjoyed would be beneficial.

Thomas Crook, I knew from my own studies, was Lincoln's armed bodyguard and accompanied the President on his after dinner visit to the War department. He turned out to be a trim man in his mid twenties devoted to his charge. Both men left the White House portico and began the walk to the War Department. Crook was a battle hardened Army veteran, now a D.C. policeman assigned to the White House.

The President and Crook were passed by a small group of rough looking men, which made Crook uneasy enough to unbuckle his pistol holster. Lincoln seemed unperturbed but somber: "Crook, do you know I believe there are men in this city plotting to take my life?. and they might just do it." Crook was shaken and wanted to known why the President thought so. Lincoln did not answer directly and Crook said in an unsteady voice: "Sir, I pray you are mistaken. I would give my life to stop it."

The President was moved and told Crook of the confidence he had in all his guards (just four on single shifts) and then replied in much the same words he had used with Col. Baker: "I know they will pay for it with their lives but preventing it might be impossible." Cook's relief that night, was John Parker, late as usual. Cook had known Parker from the Police Dept.and felt poorly of him.

When The President came out of the War Department, Crook beseeched him to let him extend his shift and accompany the theatre party. The President said for Crook to go home and rest, that one good man would be enough. Listening to this exchange and knowing John Parker was going to betray his trust, was agonizing. In that entire day everything that could have saved this noble man seemed to ride a wave of predetermined destiny that would end in his death. Crook, in his memoirs has said that the President said "Goodbye, Crook", which I had just heard clearly at the White House entrance. Crook said he was struck by the fact that he did not say: "Good night, Crook " as he always did. The loyal guard became convinced, in later years, that the President had a premonition of his death.

It was incredible to me how many times Lincoln's evening was interrupted. Speaker Colfax, two or three Senators, a Judge and a member of the Cabinet, all tried to get a piece of him before he left with Mary. As the President passed his son's room he called out: "Come see the play with us, son." Robert, already preparing for sleep, said his preference was to get a night's sleep in a real bed rather than an Army cot. Lincoln gently agreed. Robert Lincoln suffered over that brief exchange all his life.

About 7:30pm, with just a footman and coachman along, President Lincoln and his wife Mary Todd Lincoln drove away from the White House. I moved quickly and invisibly slipped once more into the opposing seat. As the carriage jolted over the cobblestones, I looked at the great man, sad and withdrawn, and writhed in frustration.

The President and Mrs. Lincoln were on their way to pick up young friends of Mary Todd, Miss Clara Harris and her fiancé, Major Henry Rathbone. Clara's father, Senator Ira Harris, was a staunch supporter of Lincoln and his daughter had on several occasions been a guest of Mrs. Lincoln at the White House. With all the turned down invitations that the President had proffered, the First Lady, had made the arrangement. Rathbone had served with distinction in several bloody engagements under Grant's command and Lincoln was pleased when Mary mentioned her choice of guests.

When they pulled away from the grounds of the White House, Mary seemed troubled by a change in her husband's behavior. He had lapsed into an almost melancholy silence. Given his wife's history of what would be diagnosed today as borderline paranoia, he had not apprised her of the secret meeting with Colonel Baker that afternoon. He chose instead to answer her queries with a discussion of a dream he had on Wednesday night, saying it still disturbed him:

"Mother, do you remember that after dinner a few days ago I had described a dream to you and Ward Lamon."

Lamon was Lincoln's crony from the old circuit riding law practice in Illinois. He had been invited to live at the

White House and became a self-appointed bodyguard. Big and powerful, he was obsessed by the President's safety and at least once, sat all night armed to the teeth, at the Lincolns' bedroom door. Lincoln entrusted Lamon as a personal courier. In another instance of fated destiny he was on a mission for Lincoln in Richmond and would not be back for a few days.

"Mother, you were preoccupied with Tad at the time and probably were not listening."

"Then please tell me again Father, and I shall listen intently." (Father and Mother would seem to be the way they addressed each other, at least in private. In public Mary would address him as Mr. Lincoln)

"About ten days ago, I had retired very late. I was weary reading dispatches from the front. I fell quickly into a fitful sleep and began to dream. I heard sobs and wailing and seemed to rise from my bed, barefoot in my nightclothes. I moved through the halls. The mourners were invisible but the rooms were well lit and familiar to me. The sounds became louder as I moved down the stairs toward the East room. I entered to a shocking sight. Before me was a catafalque which bore the long body of a corpse whose face and figure were covered by white vestments. Soldiers were standing guard and a line of mourners, sobbing and wailing , moved slowly past. I asked a guard:

'Who is dead in the White House?' 'The President,' he said, 'killed by an assassin'.

A loud burst of grief awaked me and sleep was no longer possible. Look, Mother, as I repeat this story my skin ripples on my arm." With that, he pushed up his sleeve.

I had read this story previously in Carl Sandburg's; "The War Years". When Ward Lamon heard that dream the first time he was shocked and that very night had committed the words to his private journal. Sandburg had used Lamon's journal as a source. The story had affected me when reading about it but hearing Lincoln repeat the tale on the way to Ford's Theatre, my very soul shuddered.

Mary Todd, to her credit did not wail or get upset and said: "Father you have always been a believer in dreams. I myself think it is the natural fears that anyone who has had to bear with death and dying might feel. Your burden in this War could have driven lesser men mad. Crook and Lamon are always talking to you about the need to be vigilant. You laugh it off with some story but I think it must affect a deep place within you."

"Mother, you may be right. We will look forward to the evening and talk of it no more."

He said this as the carriage stopped on H street (another coincidence) to pick up the young couple. The footman escorted them into the carriage, my unseen presence had plenty of room, and we drove the seven blocks to Ford's Theatre on 10th street. During that ride the vivacious Clara and the handsome Rathbone, both in there twenties, brightened the President and his lady and there was no more talk of gloom. On the street corners near the theatre were torches, brightly lit, stuck into the top of barrels. Street barkers were shouting the way to Ford's Theatre and this festive mood seemed to lighten the heavy air and fog that had moved into the city after sundown.

The theatre, which could hold more than 1500 people, had a good crowd but it was not jammed. Of the eight boxes that could hold six patrons each, only the Lincoln party occupied these most expensive seats. The other boxes were empty. It could possibly have been the prices that were raised this night or the fact that it was Good Friday. The play had already started and I noticed several empty seats throughout the house. Ford's Theatre was the newest and best theatre in town and was decorated, considering the period, in relatively good taste. Burgundy velvet hangings predominated. The Presidential box was, in fact, two boxes with the partition removed They were colorfully draped with red, white and blue bunting with an engraved portrait of President Washington framed by two bright Navy banners.

Not arriving till just before nine o'clock, the Presidential arrival stopped the production and the house erupted with loud cheers. The actors on stage doing as much clapping and shouting as everyone else. The

Lincoln party turned left to the stairs leading to the dress circle and the Orchestra broke into "Hail to the Chief." A program boy, about 12 years old, seemed awestruck but Lincoln smiled and took a program from his tightly clenched hand as did the others. The party, led by the Chief Usher, crossed behind the dress circle to the passage that led into their box. I wanted time to stop, my head spinning with emotions. It did not, and as the minutes passed and the really awful play moved on, I knew that very soon I would witness an act that would shock the nation and burn itself into American History with the searing permanence of a branding iron.

The President, visibly embarrassed by the pomp and ceremony, pulled the large rocker supplied for him almost to the wall and back into the shadows of the velvet curtain. He seemed to feel a chill and put his coat back on before he sat down. Mary and the two guests were well forward and could be seen clearly by the audience.

The play 'Our American Cousin' was described by a critic of that era as '...being of little substance..' It had however, decent audience turnouts for the many cities it had visited. It was just the type of backwoods humor that Lincoln needed to mindlessly relax. The President was a great admirer of classical playwrights and would regale his family and guests with readings from Hamlet or Macbeth but for escape it was backwoods and barnyard humor that he would turn to. It was reminiscent of President Kennedy's penchant for Ian Fleming's 007.

'Our American Cousin' was about a country boy who was trying his luck in snaring the daughter of an English titled family. A family that were distant relatives. The humor was as corny as it gets, even for 1865. Booth knew the play well and some of his good friends had leading roles. I did not look for Booth, I would be with him step by step on <u>his</u> Good Friday and would again visit the assassination looking over his shoulder at every step he took. I steeled myself to stay where I was and mentally record my impressions of this senseless murder of our greatest President.

Mary, nearest to the President , was pleased to hear Lincoln chuckle at the lines and put her hand over his in affection. Clara, so attractive in a small cocked hat and silk blue dress, clapped and laughed along with her fiancé. Mary at one point remarked that Clara and the Major might think she was very forward hanging on to her husband. Lincoln smiled and said something about the two only having eyes for each other, making Mary laugh as well. At that moment The President leaned forward and moved the drapery to observe the audience. The Box was about nine feet above the stage.

On stage a haughty Duchess had made an insulting remark about a lack of good manners, addressed to the American country bumpkin, a character called Asa Trenchard, played by the actor Henry Hawk. He turned to the wings and gave the Ladyship a shouted scolding as she walked off:

"Don't know the manners of good society, eh? Well I knows enough to turn <u>you</u> inside out, old gal...you sockdologizing old man trap!"

The audience roared and Booth, who knew the play well, used the cover of that laugh and applause to open the door of the Presidential box and walked in unheard. That line of dialogue on the stage were the last words President Lincoln would ever hear.

I was only a few feet away, staring into Booth's eyes. Dressed in a tightly cut black suit with a light black coat, bareheaded and gloveless, he held a tiny Derringer pistol in his right hand and carefully sighted down the barrel, moving forward with arm extended. In his left hand was a large Bowie knife. He seemed perfectly calm and moved deliberately, his eyes narrowed in intense concentration. Black hair was cut long over a pale face, set off by jet black eyes and a curling mustache. Of medium height, dressed impeccably, Booth's eyes looked as murderous as a raven with a unwary field mouse.

In a reflexive jump, I thrust myself between Booth and the President. The little pistol exploded in a cloud of white smoke and a tongue of flame. My invisible being was no match for the .44 caliber ball of iron that ploughed into Lincoln's brain, jamming bone and tissue along with it. The smoke and sharp report of the shot seemed too much for such a small weapon. The President slumped forward and to the left, hitting the wall. His left hand jerked in a spasmodic reflex action but he did not make a sound.

The brave Rathbone was the first to react. Booth was moving towards the balcony rail and had dropped the one shot pistol, artfully shifting the Bowie knife to his right hand. Rathbone leaped to grapple with him and Booth thrust the knife at the Major's chest.

Rathbone parried with his left arm and received a wound that cut to the bone. He staggered and fell back but had no quit in him. Booth turned and attempted to vault the rail as Rathbone grabbed at him again. The Major's arm gushing blood, he was no match for the assassin who shook him off and vaulted over the balustrade.

Rathbone had upset Booth's timing and he banged his right leg into the heavy portrait of Washington, spinning it around. Going down, his spur caught one of the Navy flags and he fell awkwardly to the stage in a heap, grabbing at his left leg above the ankle. He had made these vaulting leaps to the stage in Macbeth and Hamlet with a dancer's grace and an actor's flourish. How disappointed he must have been to look like a clumsy oaf, spoiling what was planned to be his supreme moment.

Despite his injured leg, he managed to stand erect. Brandishing the bloody knife, he shouted oratorically: "Sic semper tyrannis !" The Latin phrase is also the motto of the state flag of Virginia taken from the words of Brutus as he murdered Caesar. "Thus always to tyrants." In the wild pandemonium, few were listening. Oblivious to his pain and waving the knife, Booth ran, in an grotesque hippity-hop gait, straight at the only actor on the stage, Henry Hawk. The poor man's eyes popped in fright and he bolted into a gap in the scenery.

The audience was in a screeching panic, shouts of "stop that man!" from many parts of the house. In the Box the wounded Rathbone had been the first to yell the warning. The audience was slow to understand the enormity of what had happened. None screamed louder than Mary Lincoln but she did not bolt in flight, trying in heart rending pleas to rouse her husband. He never cried out or spoke a word. A small trickle of blood ran over the back of his collar, his powerful body deathly still. I looked down on the stage as Booth, waving the knife, knocked one man flat after stabbing him and escaped in the wings. Two men gave chase as the audience finally erupted in chaos.

Clara had tried to comfort Rathbone, pale from the copious bleeding that soaked his shirtsleeve down to the cuffs. He kept mumbling: "see to the President, see to the President." Clara stood over the railing and shouted for a Doctor. The cry was taken up by people who had climbed upon the stage. People nearest the Box helped up and over the railing a young man not in uniform. He identified himself to Mrs. Lincoln as Dr. Charles Leale, an Army surgeon. Mary, attended to by a distraught Clara, was almost in hysteria as she pleaded with Leale to save her husband. Assuring her, Leale turned quickly to the President and with the help of others who had climbed in lay Lincoln gently to the floor. In another twist of fate, I recognized a grim faced Ensign Flood, the Lincoln's Naval guide that afternoon, who had climbed in as well.

The Doctor cut away the President's jacket and shirt in an attempt to find the wound. Only when attempting to help Lincoln breathe by mouth-to-mouth resuscitation did he grasp the back of his head and found a matted blood clot in his hair. He removed the clot and realized the wound was from a large caliber ball now in the President's brain. Lincoln, the intense pressure in his brain momentarily relieved, began to breathe. Dr. Leale had treated far too many bullet wounds and sadly declared the wound a mortal one. By now near collapse, Mary's reaction to Leale were repeated piteous pleas to God to spare her husband's life.

One of the others in the box was Dr. Charles Taft who was entreated by Clara to stop Rathbone's bleeding. The Doctor, with the help of an Army scarf from a soldier in the Box, applied a tourniquet under the Major's armpit, gave Clara instructions and turned back to aid Leale with the dying President. The weakened Rathbone, holding the bloody scarf in place, had enough strength and presence of mind to stagger to the door of the Box where people had been pounding to get in from the time of the shot. They were stopped by a 2" by 4" wooden brace that Booth had jammed against the door to foil pursuit. The Major kicked it loose. The brave man was not to get proper medical attention for hours.

Running to the box were soldiers, doctors and even Laura Keene, the star of the play in make up and costume, trying mightily to share top billing. The Doctors conferred over the next course of action and it was agreed that Lincoln could not survive a ride back to the White House. Giving instructions to four soldiers, Dr. Leale had them gently lift the President and carry him out of the theatre to find the nearest house. The Doctor was at Lincoln's head keeping the wound from clotting again. I moved with them, suffering my own private agony.

Outside, in the cool mist and flickering lights, two more men joined in to keep Lincoln's great frame from sagging. An officer had to draw his sword to make a path through the surging crowd. A young man was standing on the porch of a three-story brick building across the street, the tears streaming down his face but shouting strongly for the men to bring in the President. This was the Petersen boarding house. On this night, it was the President's final destination.

The procession moved up the stairway to the first floor of the house following the young man who had brought them in. He was a boarder in the house, waiting to cheer the President's departure from the play like so many in the crowd outside. I heard later that his name was Henry Safford. He stopped at first at the larger rooms but they were locked and then led the Lincoln bearers to a small bedroom at the end of the hall. The room was narrow and fairly long. Neat as a pin with a small four-poster bed and simple walnut furniture. My thoughts were of this great man, born in the only bedroom of a small log cabin, now to lay mortally wounded in a spare and plain room on a bed so short for his frame that his bearers had to lay him out with his knees sticking up.

Despite the efforts of strong men to break off the footrest, the sturdy furniture held fast and the only way to have him fully straight was to place his body corner to corner.

The third and largest room on that floor was to become the War Secretary's command post. Troops had broken the locks of both rooms on orders of the officer present. A inconsolable Mary Todd Lincoln, attended by Clara Harris and later on a few friends, Clergy and relatives, used the smaller room next to the comatose President. Robert Lincoln arrived and would come in and out of Lincoln's room to check on his mother. Several times she asked Robert to take her to see her husband. Those few visits were heart breaking, marked by the intensity of her grief. Stanton arrived in a little while and after standing at the bedside with tears falling, he took command.

Dr. Leale was never to leave the President's side. There were other doctors far more famous and experienced than Leale present in the room but medical ethics decreed that the young Army surgeon who was first on the scene was the doctor of record and Lincoln was his patient. Leale was humble and grateful for any advice, allowing any procedure to be carried out by the physician most qualified. He held the President's hand, constantly monitored his pulse and kept the wound from clotting.

With churning emotions, I watched as the doctors had an officer clear the room in order to strip the President from head to toe for a complete examination. I was surprised at the President's muscular development and skin tone. He had not the sags or flabby skin that would be usual in a man of 56. Doctor Taft remarked that his body was that of a young athlete. The pale face was worn and lined without expression, his eyes closed. Under the left eye a purple swelling began to get worse. Dr. Leale announced a steady heartbeat but the President's breathing had become labored. Later there was an effort made to remove the bullet with thin probes but all that came forth were bloody bits of bone. He was given mustard plasters to raise a falling temperature and his icy feet, sticking out over the corner of the bed, were wrapped with an Army blanket over a hot water bottle. When all that could be done, an operation was discussed but deemed useless. The door was finally opened.

The room filled quickly with dignitaries, family and friends. The air became stuffy and many times people had to walk out to the cool night outside. I recognized the Cabinet members and some other people I had seen that day. My memories of that night are chaotic and how many came and who they were has been recorded by in minute detail.

I am aware of the conflicting memoirs of people there and like any momentous event in history more people claim to have been present than humanly possible. My memories of that night concern certain unique individuals. People who deserve remembering.

There was a young girl who lived through this horror and never faltered in her duty to Mrs. Lincoln. With her betrothed's blood spattered over her dress, Clara Harris stayed at the First Lady's side when Mary had almost slipped into madness, trying to calm her and take care of her. History seems to have passed her by. As for the brave Rathbone, fainting from loss of blood, he was taken to the Harris home and attended to there. During the evening Senator Harris advised Clara that their family doctor had said that the Major's stab wound was only a quarter inch from a major artery and that had it been severed, would have taken his life before he left the theatre.

There was the heartbroken Robert Lincoln who berated himself for not going with his parents and would not believe the doctors who said there was no hope. Except for the time he was comforting his mother in the adjoining sitting room, he too, never left his father's side.

Lincoln's faithful secretaries, Nicolay and Hay who loved the man like a father stayed with him throughout the night. Their memoirs provided most of the reliable memories of that agonizing ordeal.

I admired the elderly Gideon Welles, Secretary of the Navy, whose devotion to his President was moving and eloquent. He stayed out of the way and in deference to his age they found a chair for him but his welling eyes never left his dying leader. His poignant memoirs of the deathwatch were a prime source for historians to come.

Another indelible memory was that of Robert Tanner, a boarder in the house and government clerk who had lost both legs by shellfire in the second battle of Bull Run. Only just 21, he was on artificial legs and crutches. When Stanton, interviewing witnesses to the murder, bellowed a request for someone who could take shorthand, he volunteered immediately. He was remarkably accurate, reading testimony back word for word when required. Only once or twice, when the piercing cries of Mary Todd's despair reached a peak in the next room, did he ever ask a witness to repeat a line of testimony. He was seated at Stanton's side, his crutches in the corner nearby.

Finally, the most enduring memory is that of Edward Stanton, Secretary of War.

That night the United States Government came close to being a Dictatorship. "Dictator" sounds negative and I don't entirely mean it in that sense, but it is the only word that can describe his actions that night. The Secretary did an end run around the Constitution. With the Generals and their troops at his beck and call he was able to bypass legal niceties and set about calling in witnesses to pin down who was responsible for this most despicable of crimes. During this time, he moved men, Generals, Judges and investigators, issuing orders in a non-stop display of intellect and energy.

Stanton by his own decree proclaimed the investigation of the President's murder to be a military matter without consulting Chief Justice Chase or anyone else. From that moment on he was able to take absolute power. The faint voices that objected were drowned out the by the almost universal cry for vengeance. The later questions of a few in Congress that opposed a military Court Martial, rather than a civil trial, were not heeded. Those questions were based on the fact that all the accused were civilians, as was the President. The public was not concerned and any opposition was swept away by the power of momentum that Stanton had set in motion.

The War Secretary, as he had shown that morning at the Cabinet meeting, was a master administrator, in his glory, snapping orders to every one in sight. Telegrams were dictated and taken by fast horses to the War Department. The room was like a tempest with Stanton as its forceful and efficient storm center. General Grant was summoned to Washington from Philadelphia. There was some concern the Confederates would strike quickly in some prearranged, last gasp attack. The talk of the crowd outside the Petersen house was rife that the Confederate Army was behind the assassination. The Army and Navy were to close every exit from the Capitol, roads to the North and bridges to the South. Stanton and his cherished maps and charts was on top of every detail. Chief Justice Chase was alerted to come with a Bible to swear in Andrew Johnson, the Vice President, when the President finally died.

One of the telegrams was to Col. Baker in New York to take charge of the manhunt. It was sent to a hotel where he was supposed to be a guest. I knew from Baker's meeting with the President today that he was in Washington incognito. I wondered how he would handle the emergency. Thinking of Baker's top secret information about a traitorous plot, my concerns were about some strange inconsistencies I had observed in this crowded command post.

One of the first witnesses to testify was Harry Hawk, the actor on stage who ran from Booth's waving knife after he jumped from the Presidential Box. Hawk, now frightened of retribution from Booth, was a little hazy about a positive identification. He was asked directly if he was still frightened and was promised protection. Hawk knew Booth well and so did the other actors the assassin ran past in the wings. He finally swore on his life it was Booth as did the others. That testimony was elicited at about 11:00 PM. I expected a flurry of action in pursuit but Stanton did not mention Booth's name in dispatches to the newspapers or requested his name and picture posted until 3:20 AM.

James Tanner, the shorthand whiz , wrote a letter to a good friend on April 17th. He confided: …"In fifteen minutes I had testimony enough to hang Wilkes Booth, the assassin, higher than ever Haman hung." Stanton heard every word Tanner did.

By 3:20AM Booth was long gone in northern Virginia. As if leading a charmed life, he galloped south over the Old Navy Bridge and joined a fellow conspirator, David Herold. Despite Stanton's careful study of maps and charts to order the Capitol's bridges to the South shut down, that bridge was not guarded. My mind reeled with questions.

As the sky began to lighten in the pre dawn hours of April 15th, the President grew steadily worse. By 6:00 o'clock, the loyal Dr. Leale could hardly find a pulse. The breathing had turned into a high-pitched whistle and even those were fewer and fewer.

The Surgeon General, Dr. Barnes, went in to summon Mary Todd Lincoln to the bedside. At about 6:45 pm Mary sat by the bed and wailed uncontrollably. Robert Lincoln had to be supported in his grief. Tad was deemed too young to be present. Lincoln again expelled one of his breaths with that high-pitched whistle. It caused Mary to scream loudly and fall to the floor in a faint. At that awful moment I was shocked to see the Secretary of War at the doorstep, waving his arms and shouting:

"Take that woman out of this room and do not let her in again!" Whether it was fear of Stanton's wrath or concern for the mental and physical health of Mrs. Lincoln, she was gently lifted and taken to the sofa in the sitting room. She never again was to see her husband alive.

The 10x18 foot room began to fill with dignitaries. Robert, his oldest son, by his bedside, sobbing. Many other men wept as well. Lincoln simply stopped breathing and a moment later Surgeon Barnes pronounced him dead. It was 7:22 am.

For what must have been five minutes the people in that room, including my unseen presence, were frozen in common mourning and the shock of the President's death. Stanton gave another order, this time gently, but firmly. It was for the Reverend Gurley: "Doctor, if you are to say anything, do it now." After a short and moving prayer, Stanton uttered a phrase that has become an immortal part of American history:

"Now he belongs to the ages."

I stood on the street outside the Petersen House on a cool but cloudy April morning, watching a simple Army wagon bear Lincoln's body back to the White House. Wrapped in white linen, the President was borne back to his mansion surrounded by troops and followed by weeping crowds of white and black mourners that had never left the wet and chilly streets during the long, sad night.

I do not know what prompted me to join this procession. Grief in the men and women that surrounded me was deep and genuine. Marching in center of this heartbroken group, the men and women around me sobbed the words: 'Father Abraham.' The words seemed particularly apt. A great leader who had been cut down was also a beloved and universal parent who felt deeply for every one of his children. He had mourned for all that had fallen in battle and shared in the grief of their families. The lyric poetry of the Gettysburg address affirmed that his children included the legions of brave Confederate dead that joined the fallen Union troops. To the President it was a brotherhood, linked in grotesque postures of death across the forest and farmlands of a nation that had been torn apart and drenched in blood.

Chapter 5
A Family in Danger

My thoughts turned to my own family as the entourage came closer to the White House.

Even though the elapsed time in my own era was less than a half hour, to me in 1865 it seemed like a very long time. I had much unfinished business. My plan to follow Booth in his escape was still ahead. Baker had talked to Lincoln of a conspiracy and the possible complicity of Stanton in Lincoln's murder had to be addressed. Finally, and most importantly, I had to stop the transfer of Mary Surratt's soul to that of her daughter Anna at the scene of the hanging. With so many historic events taking place in front of me and the inability to think clearly about my family's final security, I must take the time to work out a feasible plan with the realistic and valued input of my wife. Moving away from the procession as it moved past Lafayette Park, I moved to a bench underneath the stately trees and focused on home.

There are always a few unsteady moments coming out of a deep trance state and the empty room did not register at once. When it did, I felt a chilling sense of unease. Where was Mary Surratt? Was my family safe!? I bounded up the stairs of the basement office and quickly checked the living room, den, library and kitchen. No one was there. My unease had progressed to a full-grown panic. I moved up the stairway at a faster pace, my heart racing in fear. There were sounds coming from Donnie's room down the hall to the left. The sounds of sobbing.

I walked into Donnie's room and found my wife daughter and son sitting on the bed.

Naomi was tightly clutching the both of them, sucking in her sobs as loudly as the rest.

To see them safe was pure joy. To see them in this state was a whipsaw of emotion. Seeing me was not followed by joyous acclaim. Sobbing turned to near hysteria and it took quite a while to calm things down. I begged my family for forgiveness. Flooded by guilt, I knew without getting any coherent details that Paine, Mary or both had terrorized them. It was I who moved into this Hell, blinded by the possibility of time travel to the Civil War. If I refused at the very beginning to cooperate in Mary's schemes, my family would not have suffered. It is hard for me to convey to the reader my despair at that moment. It is to the credit of our unshakeable faith in each other that no recriminations or blame were tossed about in that room filled with the posters, sports equipment and high-tech speakers of a teenagers domain. Donnie was the most reluctant to talk and Jennifer was still too frightened.

It took hours to calm things down helped by a family favorite, egg plant parmesan, served in the kitchen. It was not until Naomi and I were in bed together that I was able to get a sense of what had happened in the hour of therapy allotted to Jane Gotting that afternoon.

As best as they can be recalled, Naomi's words are what follows: "What I'm going to tell you David, will require patience on you part. I've got to get a grip on reality and face this problem with you. I'm going to give you each small detail as an attempt to strengthen that grip, so don't hurry me or interrupt: It was about four o'clock and the kids were home from school and upstairs. I was in the kitchen, making dinner. I took two eggplants out of the refrigerator and put them on a vegetable board near the sink. (I groaned, but just a little) It took me about ten minutes to peel the plants with a peeler and then rinsed them in the sink. They were then sliced into thin rounds. The breadcrumbs were spread on a paper plate. Three eggs were beaten in my colander, whisking in a little water. I dipped the eggplant rounds into the egg wash and dredged each one into the bread crumbs. A small amount of olive oil had been simmering in my cast iron frying pan and I flicked water from my fingers into the oil. When the oil is the right temperature the sound is a little zizzt or pop."

I nodded vigorously to humor her, hoping she would hurry up. She didn't:

"Then I slowly fried the discs of breaded eggplant into a golden brown on both sides.

I ripped up two brown grocery bags into four flat pieces and lay each fried disk out to drain. Turning each of them once and then covering the bottom of a large baking pan with a layer of tomato sauce, laced with fresh garlic and herbs. Then I laid the eggplant rounds on top of the tomato sauce. Tomato sauce was spooned in on the top of each disk. That was followed by a sprinkle of parmesan cheese on each disk as well as a teaspoon of ricotta cheese. After that I sprinkled a generous amount of shredded mozzarella all over the layer. I repeated the whole procedure two more times. The final layer was topped by a thick helping of tomato sauce with a topping of plenty of parmesan and mozzarella cheese. My oven was then set at 350 and I adjusted the baking time for 45 minutes. I was washing up and turned to my left when I saw him through the glass patio doors. He was standing in the middle of the side lawn, looking directly at me.

It was a bright, sunny afternoon. Cars were moving by on Ridge Avenue, Cindy's collie next door was barking at a squirrel and all was right with the world until that horrifying moment. He was dressed in a crew necked light blue cotton shirt tucked into khaki pants. On a wide brown belt was a holster for a large knife that had a horn hilt.

The pants were tucked into riding boots. He was very tall, with a bull neck and the sloping shoulders of an athlete. He must have been staring at me for quite a while as I concentrated on the eggplant. He looked as handsome as a model for Ralph Lauren casual wear except for that wicked knife and eyes that would make anyone shudder in fear. I knew exactly who he was, you had described him right down to the long arms and huge hands.

I got mad as hell and opened the doors, screaming at him to get the hell out of here.

I locked the glass doors, looked up and he was gone. I debated the need to knock on your office door and started for the stairway down as I heard a sound from upstairs. I ran back to the kitchen and grabbed the frying pan drying on the rack at the sink. Yelling God knows what, I ran up the stairs.

Paine's back was to me, his pants had been dropped and his big hairy ass was staring back at me. His knife was at the back of our son's neck. Donnie was sitting on the bed, his eyes popping in fear and making the strangled sounds I had heard downstairs.

Paine's voice was soft but deadly:

'Go ahead sissy, wrap your big mouth around Mr. Johnson. You won't never see another like it. Iffen you don't, I'm gonna slit your scrawny neck.'

David, I think I went crazy then. I only remember Donnie taking the frying pan out of my hands. He told me later that after screaming 'you fucking bastard!' I had smashed Paine on the head. Even though the pan hit nothing but the dresser, I had kept swinging and shouting after the giant dissolved in front of our eyes. Jennifer had heard me come up the stairs and had watched the scene from the doorway, screaming in shock and fear. I do not remember her screaming, only sitting on the bed afterward hanging on to one another. We all will never forget what happened next.

In the doorway to the bedroom stood a woman who stared at us with a face set in stone. Her black hair was parted in the middle and pulled back tight at the sides.

She was dressed like 'Melanie' in 'Gone With the Wind' complete to the drab gray of the dress that fell to the floor over bustled hips. Her ample waist was drawn in tightly under an equally ample bosom covered in lace. I was frightened to nausea as were the children. Mary Surratt spoke directly to me:

'Mrs. Borin, I must admit you are a spunky bitch but you are not dealing with a ghost in me. I inhabit a live and healthy young woman who is my granddaughter thrice removed. I can harm you, the Doctor or your children if I so choose. I made a bargain with your husband and will not break it if he lives up to his obligations. I did not send Lewis to harass you today, he is a man who makes up his own mind and has spent a century and a half in limbo. I will not apologize for his actions but if things go as I wish, I will try to curb his excesses. If there is the slightest deviation from my goals, you will not sleep another night in peace.

The threat to your lives will be from me and there is always sweet Lewis who is quite capable of driving your children mad with fear.'

With that said she turned abruptly and was gone. That was about fifteen minutes before you came through that door."

When Naomi and I finished talking about three hours later, we had a final plan. Donnie and Jennifer, having come this far, would play significant roles in a joint effort . The children's help to expunge these evil creatures from our lives would be a positive way for them to come to grips with any trauma they might have suffered. Failure was unthinkable. Without having the luxury of alternate possibilities our plan had no fall back position. We had to succeed.

The next day, Jennifer chose to stay home in an attempt, with our help, to come to grips with reality. Donnie, while a bit morose, decided to go to school. When he returned, Naomi and I prepped the children on the plan we had to rid our lives of the loathsome pair that had bedeviled us. Their anger, along with ours, overcame the fear. We got some positive suggestions that in one instance, was incorporated into our design. Dinner was upbeat as we turned to the many other things that made up our daily lives, such as eggplant parmesan.

I had left a message on Jane's answering machine and she called back the next afternoon during a break I had between other patients. Jane told me her memory of that last session was fuzzy. She did not remember the usual discussion we had after hypnosis and became fully aware of her surroundings when entering her car, parked in our driveway.

I made light of the memory loss and said it was often a side effect of a deep trance state. Jane's safety when driving was of real importance and I assured her I would make certain she was fully aware and responsive when leaving my office. Somehow I felt Mary must have been sniggering in contempt, deep within her host. We confirmed another appointment for the following week that would include her husband. At this news, Jane's parasitic host, Mary Surratt, must have gotten her confirmation for the exchange of the ghost Lewis Paine into the soul of Alfred Gotting. My family would probably be safe from any ghostly activity before that appointment.

Some of my time, aside from the normal flow of patients, was spent at my computer putting down the experiences I had witnessed in 1865. The plan became the focal point of our family's concentration. We required some equipment that Donnie helped me to bring back to the garage from Home Depot. Naomi, the children and I rehearsed our roles over and over to make sure of success. We were as ready as we could have been when the day quickly came. All of us were jumpy and tense and each one of us beset with private misgivings. Only my wife and I discussed the dreaded possibility of failure. Perhaps the children also realized that my ability to come back to our world when making a time trip rested on Mary Surratt. Would I be trapped forever in a different dimension of time if her soul died with her on the gibbet? Logic, if that is the right word for this surreal happening, told us that if we succeeded in blocking the transfer of Surratt to her daughter than all of what had occurred would cease to exist and I would awaken from the trance state naturally, safely back home. My memories might be erased but my computer had an outside chance to retain my journal.

Alfred and Jane were right on time and after a brief discussion, moved to hypnotic therapy. In a few minutes they were both deeply in a trance state. The therapy was a dual exercise in the enjoyment of sex helped by the visualization of erotic imagery.

When Mary abruptly appeared in the place of Jane her cheeks were flushed with the anticipation of having her favorite stud in her bed once more. My therapy in erotica had only enhanced her excitement. The small office was getting crowded. Lewis Paine, dressed in his long tan duster and slouch hat, stood in the corner.

I looked at him with anger and disgust. In spite of Naomi's wise advice to cool it, I vented just some of my feelings: "May you rot in hell for the anguish you caused my family!"

Mary jumped in quickly before Lewis could react: "Doctor Borin, get on with it now!"

"Hold it Mary, we have some unfinished business. Our bargain was for me to return once more to follow John Wilkes Booth to his death and uncover the truth about a possible conspiracy to kill Lincoln."

Mary erupted in impatient fury but I held fast. She was close enough to taste her victory but knew that I held the final trump card. Mary could not accomplish the transfer without my help and sputtering in frustration agreed to give me twelve days with Booth and two days with Stanton. This time period in 1865 translated to a little over forty minutes of time in my own era. She was unaware (I think) that I had developed the ability to move as I wished across time segments once I was in the Civil War era. I had to end my odyssey at the moment of her execution. One day with Stanton would suffice.

The math was consistent and based on the slight movement of the clock in my office as it applied to time travel. Our plan would have the time needed and my family was ready to put the design in motion. Before I went into a self induced trance state there was one more comment I had to make:

"Mary, if I return to find my family terrorized again by your mad dog, there is nothing you can do, in this world or yours, to make me help in the transfer between Lewis and Mr. Gotting."

Mary, almost unable to contain her impatience, said: "Doctor, you have never seen what my anger can bring forth. Don't push me any further. Your family will be safe. Start, damn you!"

Mary was then directed to place me on the sidewalk in front of the National Hotel in Washington, D.C. The day was the same, now to be seen from the proximity to our nation's most infamous assassin, John Wilkes Booth.

It was Good Friday, April the 14th, 1865, just about sunrise.

Chapter 6
John Wilkes Booth

I knew that so much was still to come. I had to follow Booth the same way I had followed Lincoln, every moment of Good Friday, April 14th, 1865. I had to uncover the truth of the assassination plot that Lafayette Baker had outlined to Lincoln. If I have to visit Ford's Theatre three times, from every perspective, I will. Most importantly I had to save two people's souls, Jane and Alfred Gotting, and to rid my home of the ghostly spirits of Mary Surratt and Lewis Paine.

Almost 144 years ago John Wilkes Booth, by profession an actor, shot and killed Abraham Lincoln. Consider our present day and one of our Hollywood leading men was to assassinate the President. In 1865 the same shock wave swept the nation when the news became known about the identity of the murderer. Who was this man?

Booth came from a family of renowned actors. His father Junius was the leading actor of his day, the earlier part of the 19th Century. Three of his sons, John Wilkes being the youngest, were acclaimed as the finest actors in America, particularly in their interpretation of the classics. Most famous, his oldest brother Edwin. Wilkes made his acting debut at seventeen, pummeled for years by the critics for hamming it up. Noted was his scene stealing by inventing leaps and bounds at every entrance and shouting his lines without dramatic phrasing. Jealous of his brother Edwin's "greatest actor" fame, he worked hard to refine his talent. Nine years later, only twenty-six, his fame had exceeded Edwin. Perhaps not with better reviews but certainly at the box office.

At every theatre, adoring women besieged the strikingly handsome Booth. From city to city he did his best to accommodate as many as possible, leaving a trail of broken hearts from Boston to Richmond. Fan mail was held for him at every theatre he played and some of the contents could make today's reader blush. He was one of those rare handsome matinee idols who also had a strong male following. His feats of daring on the stage, leaping from ten-foot walls and skill in swordplay, earned him a fearless reputation. The teen-age shouter had matured into a talented actor.

There was a darker side. His father, the famed actor Junius Booth, had spells of madness that included sudden violence. He was jailed once for attempted murder. The record also includes several attempts at suicide. Most of the children were stable but his actor brothers, Edwin and Junius Jr., had bouts of "melancholy" and missed performances. Wilkes was no exception to the deep, dark moods but only he inherited the violent outbursts. On record were several instances in dueling scenes when John lost control and wounded other actors, even in rehearsal. A friend he knew since childhood once shared Booth's train compartment. This friend, later to marry his sister Asia, disparaged Jefferson Davis, President of the Confederacy. Booth leaped at his throat and tried to strangle him. He was pulled off by other traveling actors as the victim turned purple.

Booth was a bigot who considered slavery the just condition for the inferior Negro in a superior white world. He considered Lincoln to be an uncrowned Emperor that he, in the role of Brutus, would kill to save the Confederacy. On April 11th, Lincoln gave an impromptu speech to a crowd in the White House garden. Booth was there with Paine at his side. When the President outlined a plan to give free Negroes the vote, Booth was livid and grabbed Paine by the arm, making this theatrical but ominous vow:

"By God, I'll run him through! That's the last speech he will ever make."

A key factor in this strange mind were the signs of megalomania. In his early teens, he confided to his sister Asia that he had a recurring fantasy. He saw himself as destroying an imaginary world famous statue that stood astride the Straights of Gibraltar like the ancient Colossus of Rhodes once stood in Crete. In crashing the gargantuan monument to the ground, he would gain immortality even if he was killed in the attempt. In President Lincoln, Booth finally found his Colossus.

In trying to reconstruct Booth's entire day of the assassination, there are many gaps in a record that historians have pieced together. I was determined to follow Booth from the time he got out of bed the morning of April 14th, 1865 to when he took refuge that night in the house of Dr. Samuel Mudd, where he had stopped to treat his broken leg.

My weightless, formless self glided through the closed door of room 228 in the National Hotel where John Wilkes Booth had spent the night of April 13th. It was 5:45 AM.

He was sitting on the edge of a rumpled bed, yawning, stretching, and quite naked.

Under the bedclothes to his right was a woman whose blond hair cascaded over the pillow. She was still sound asleep.

Booth rose and moved to a large standing full-length mirror. He spent the next few moments admiring himself with muscle displays. He then took a key from the dresser, tossed on a robe and went to a bathroom in the hall. His body was lithe and hard with very little body fat. I noticed a scar on his neck that looked like the healing of an old wound. Crudely drawn by indelible ink on his left wrist was three letters, JWB. He had style to his movements, quick and decisive, flipping on the robe with a flourish and walking erect with shoulders back. His demeanor was calm and relaxed.

I stayed in the room. Watching Booth pee was not on my list of priorities. He returned to find the girl stirring.

"Ah, fair Ophelia, you rise at last."

All day, Booth usually talked to the people he came in contact with as if they were an audience watching one of Shakespeare's plays. He rarely let this affectation slip.

"Come back to bed, Johnny." As she raised her arms in supplication.." I'm damned good in the morning."

"I'm sure you are my dear, and as I have mentioned before, I am not 'Johnny' to anyone. My friends call me 'Wilkes'." He said this with a hard edge and the girl pouted.

She also had some spunk: "Well I'm not 'Ophelia', my name's Marie and you are not being very nice."

Booth was smooth and to the point: "Then sweet 'Marie', you must arise quickly. The hotel will soon be astir and your supervisor will expect you soon. Please make the bed and tidy up, I must start my day."

The girl, a little mollified, moved without modesty, not making an attempt to clutch at any cover. The young lady got dressed when Booth moved to a small dressing room. As it behooves a good historian, I paid sharp attention.

Marie, dressed in a maid's white uniform, black apron and black high laced shoes, moved to a hall linen closet and came back with fresh sheets. Soon the small room was tidy. Booth was still seated at another mirror working on his appearance as if he about to answer a prompter's call. The girl brightened considerably as he gave her a few bills, but there was no further display of affection before she left. After this curt dismissal, Wilkes Booth went back to his true love and with the help of some jars and bottles of various colors whose contents were used on his skin and hair, he finally began to get dressed.

And what a finished product it was! Ruffled shirt with high collar and silk gray cravat.

Gold cuff links and gray gloves. A tailored black suit and vest. Polished black leather boots shone from the night valet efforts. When he stood again by the tall mirror, he leaned on a curious gold-topped cane to strike a debonair pose. The gold handle was shaped in the form of a calf's foot. He took no weapon with him and did not prepare any tools for the evening's work ahead.

Booth left his room and moved down the ornate stairway into the hotel lobby. It was still quite early and the large lobby, replete with overstuffed couches and comfortable chairs, was in the same overblown, potted plant look that was so popular at the time.

The room was deserted this early and the night clerk was not at his post, probably napping in the Manager's office. He moved directly into the hotel dining room now serving early risers for breakfast.

The breakfast was laid out in a buffet, formally attended to by waiters in black trousers with crimson vests and the inevitable white gloves. Booth had excellent manners and moved down the buffet in an unhurried fashion. I was impressed with his appetite and I was even more impressed by the thick slabs of bacon, shirred eggs, fresh rolls and many pots of different jams. The meat platters and spiced fish all looked delicious. A disembodied wraith, like myself, was not supposed to be hungry.

I wondered how this man who was to murder the President that night would not be a little queasy about eating breakfast. He was moving through this day without an outward worry. My original goal was not to study Booth's pathology but his behavior did not fit into normal patterns. For now, I put these thoughts aside and focused on his next movement.

Making his exit with the usual flair, he went through the lobby door and moved to the desk. The Assistant Manager was now on duty and gave Booth the message that some men were waiting outside to see him. Booth dropped off his key and pulled a letter out of his coat for mailing. I caught only the last name, "Booth", on the envelope. The clerk gave Booth four or five letters and the actor sniffed them, rolling his eyes with a knowing smile and getting the desired chuckle.

Booth stepped into the street through the Hotel's main entrance and was greeted by three roughly dressed men. I looked at the tall one and shuddered. Lewis Paine was in a slouch hat and wore the same duster he had on when he made his appearance in my office. The same duster that I saw splattered with the blood of the Secretary of State. The beautiful Spring morning turned cold. I searched my mind in panic for the logic that could calm me down. Mary Surratt and Lewis Paine had not yet dropped through the scaffold so I should be safe and unseen. Logical, but not very helpful.

David Herold, as well as the third man, George Atzerodt, looked dirty and unkempt. I found out that my sense of smell in a disembodied state was not only attuned to lilacs. Paine, on the other hand, was freshly shaved and seemed clean even to the fingernails on his huge hands. As tall as Lincoln, with perfect teeth, handsome features and an awesome physique, his accomplishments as a rapist and killer could be betrayed only by his eyes. The dead eyes of a shark.

Booth's first comments were acid: "I paid for your hotel rooms that certainly have fine bathing facilities. Paine seems to be the only one who has done his libations.

When I meet with you at Surratt's on H street, I expect you both to be clean. While you are bathing the hotel laundress will wash and iron your clothes. George, how did you even get lodgings in the Kirkwood House?"

Atzerdrot was a small man in a battered leather cap who spoke with a thick German accent. He mumbled an abject reply. Herold, who lived only to please his master, reacted like a scolded devoted pet.

Booth led the three men into a small park across the avenue and they sat on a park bench. Paine, towering over the lot, stood and said little. He called Booth: "Capt'n".

Booth was intense about the maps of his escape route. Herold had spent the week studying the towns and villages of northern Virginia and Maryland and surprised me with good detailed notes and hand drawn maps that pleased Booth. Atzerdrodt was a problem. He whined about joining only to kidnap Lincoln, not to kill him or anybody else. Booth's face reddened and he threatened George with death if he did not carry out his assignment to murder Vice President Johnson in his suite at the Kirkland Hotel. Lewis spoke, and it was cold and deliberate: "I'll take care of it Cap'n."

With that he moved toward the smaller man and with little effort lifted George by his collar until his feet swung freely. "George, the Yank's can only hang you. Has you ever seed a man choked and kill't by his own bloody balls?"

When George, white faced and trembling, was put on his feet he went to his knees on the curb and vomited. Paine had unbuttoned the duster and his heavy pistol and handle of his Bowie knife stuck out of his belt. He looked like the angel of death.

Booth, pale now and spitting the words out, turned to Atzerdrot: "Get up and stand on your feet! We will all meet at H Street at four o'clock. If you are not there George, Lewis will track you down like the rotten animal you are. If you complete your mission, get your money from Mrs. Surratt, and disappear from the company of brave and honorable men."

"Lewis, yesterday I arranged for that big one eyed bay you liked and Herold will take you to the home of Seward."

"No need Cap'n, I looked over the house when I carried the old man up to his bed after he got busted up. That skinny girl he got might be tastier then she looks.."

If Paine was joking, Booth's mood was all business: "Lewis, Seward has two sons and servants, there will not be time for pleasure. You will need David, if only to find the Navy Bridge. Let him act as lookout. You should be out of Seward's home in ten minutes. Failing that, David must join me and you are on your own. Timing is vital."

"George, have you been down to room 67, the Andrew Johnson suite?"

In a thick and guttural accent, the still shaken Atzerdrodt replied: "Yes, Wilkes, but there is always a man in the chair outside. A fat man or a skinny man."

"You have a 4 shot repeating Calvary pistol. Screw your courage to its sticking place and do your work! Shoot the bastard, shoot the lock and kill Johnson!" Erect as if commanding a troop, Booth continued: "I will see you all at H Street around six o'clock. Our moment of undying glory is at hand."

The weather was beautiful and in the mid 60's as Booth took a six or seven block walk up Pennsylvania Avenue to E street near Grover's Theatre. At a barbershop whose sign identified it as "Booker & Stewart", he removed his jacket and loosened his cravat. By the way he was greeted and fawned over, it was obvious he was a regular patron.

Prepared by hot towels, he was shaved, ending with brisk, lilac scented astringents. His long hair and curling mustache, thick and black as obsidian, was carefully trimmed. The barber, whose name was on a printed card over the mirror, was Charles Wood. Barbers were the same in 1865. A steady monologue ensued about the wonderful news of Lee's surrender, to his client's obvious discomfort. Booth said little but his fingers began a steady drumbeat on the chair. What kept him on an even keel was the attention he received by a few customers who also knew the actor well. The banter directed at the actor could best be described today as sophomoric. Booth, admiring himself with satisfaction, said his goodbyes as if he were making an exit in Hamlet. Prophetic, perhaps, considering the ending of today's tortured events.

Grover's Theatre was only a half block away and as Booth entered the house, he knew and greeted by name, every stage hand, actor or ticket taker on his way up to the office of C. Dwight Hess, the manager and part owner. According to my prior research on the assassination, I knew that on the 13th, Hess had told Booth that the President and First Lady along with General Grant and wife had been invited as a joint party to attend the performance of "Aladdin" on Good Friday evening. Quickly, using a friend who owned a billiard parlor and bar above the theatre, Booth had made arrangements to purchase a box in close proximity to the Presidential Box always used at Grover's. Imagine if you will, the steely resolve of this man. The thought of Grant and Lincoln, two formidable men with a presumed entourage of guards, did not even slow him down.

This morning of April 14th, he wanted to confirm the President's attendance that evening. C.D. Hess was standing and talking to two smartly dressed ladies about to leave for a stroll. Ah, my good friend Booth. John Wilkes, these ladies have the better of you. They know who you are but I must introduce you to them. This is my wife Caroline Hess and my brother's wife Helen Moss."

Removing his hat, Booth was all gallantry and smiles: "Ladies, even the spring blooms with have to take a back row seat to your bright and charming appearance."

The ladies blushed like schoolgirls and after shaking hands with plenty of flattery all around, left in a gay mood. It was later, after the night's events engulfed the nation in grief, that the ladies remembered the coincidence of shaking the hand of the President and his murderer within the space of an hour.

Hess told Booth the President had made other plans to attend Ford's Theatre to see Laura Keene's production of "Our American Cousin". Booth was impassive but left quite abruptly. Hess, in the questioning that came days later, remarked that Wilkes' behavior seemed strained but not so that the theatre manager would find it unusual.

As Booth stepped quickly down the stairs he was not so impassive. I was close enough to hear him mutter: "Damn, I must hurry!" I had no trouble sailing right along with him.

It was only two blocks back on Pennsylvania Avenue to the Kirkland House where Atzerdrot had rented a room on the floor above Vice President Johnson. I was not sure what was on Booth's mind but I knew that the confrontation with Atzerdrot had shaken him. He needed a man with courage and reliability to murder Andrew Johnson.

In the barbershop that day, was the inevitable talk on politics. Someone had made a joke about Johnson being drunk while taking the oath of Vice President. Booth said he hated Johnson but if anything happened to Lincoln, Johnson might be better for the country. He leaned toward pro-slavery and would be more acceptable to the South. That spoken thought and the possible botch of Johnson's assassination by Atzerdrodt might have prompted an unusual change of mind regarding the Vice President.

Striding to the desk he asked if Johnson was in residence. When told he was not, he pulled a blank card from the desk and I watched as he wrote: "Don't wish to disturb you; are you at home? J.Wilkes Booth." Relying on his fame to be admitted to the Vice-President's room, did Booth decide to kill Johnson before Lincoln? The meaning of that note bothers historians to this day. On my next trip to the Capitol, I was to find out as much as I could of a conspiracy that went higher than Booth and his band of misfits. My guess as to Booth's intent was a tip-off to Johnson to betray Atzerdrodt and have his guard eliminate a future possible danger to himself.

John Wilkes went out of the Kirkland and down the alley to the rear of the building. He opened the rear door and moved up the stairs to the room that Atzerdrot had rented.

That too was fruitless. The room was locked and gentle rapping without an answer in reply convinced Booth the room was empty. Wilkes then started his short walk back to his hotel, the National, down Pennsylvania and Sixth. You must remember that compared to today's cities the Capitol of 1865 was like a small town. A man of Booth's celebrity would find it hard to make any kind of excursion in town and not be stopped and spoken to by one of his many friends and acquaintances. Social mores were also quite different. A Vice President could have rooms in a crowded hotel and dine in the restaurant without causing a stir. Lincoln or Seward took open-air carriages without any concern of invaded privacy. So it was that a celebrated actor could take a walk and only people he knew would have the temerity to stop him for a conversation. The autograph era had not yet been born.

Wilkes walked several blocks and bumped into the editor of a local newspaper, Thomas Florence. From the way they spoke, he was more acquaintance than close friend and in a way the conversation sounded like a short interview about Booth's plans for the future. The actor talked about his prospects in Canada and said he had many offers for theatre engagements. He said that he might be on his way to Canada shortly. Listening, I thought of his possible plans to escape capture in the next few days. For some reason his focus then blurred and he whined about losing six thousand dollars on oil speculation in Pennsylvania. As the discussion ended, I felt by the body language of Thomas Florence that he too seemed puzzled by the remarks.

In the lobby of the National, Booth found a childhood friend and school classmate, Michael O'Laughlin. He had been a participant, with Booth, in a prior adventure to kidnap Lincoln that could have come straight out of "The Three Musketeers". Dreamed up by Booth, the plan could have been proposed by a present day screenwriter.

In September, 1864 nearing the bloody end of the Civil War, Booth dreamed up a plan to kidnap President Lincoln and turn him over to the Confederacy to force the Union to sue for peace. The actor and his gallant band would be heroes forever. Booth, using the spell binding oratory of a fanatic leader, recruited a strange band of misfits among whom the most sensible (or sane) members were O'Laughlin, Samuel Arnold and John Surratt. Arnold was a old schoolmate as was O'Laughlin. Surratt was a young Confederate spy who crossed lines carrying secret dispatches. All three had seen service for the Confederacy and were brave and determined men. The other three were Paine, a deserter, rapist and murderer, Herold, a frightened drug clerk and Atzerdrot, a wagon maker who hauled pigs and supplies for the Rebels. You have met them.

During the year that followed it is not certain whether Booth was working with the Confederate leadership and being funded by them on this "enterprise." That was the word Booth used as a code name for the kidnapping. Most of the written evidence and interviews by Army intelligence support some Confederate involvement in the plan.

That was not very unusual, the Confederates supported many wild schemes, even the burning of New York City. That incredible scheme was attempted on a night that the three Booth brothers were on the stage together for the first and only time. It was Friday, November 25th, 1864 at the Winter Garden in New York. The play was

Shakespeare's "Julius Caesar". No, Wilkes did not play Brutus; he was the noble Marc Anthony. Aside the busy fire wagons, the torching of New York City was a failure.

On the afternoon of March 20th, Booth and his band of merry men made the attempt to kidnap the President. An actor friend who was in the cast told Booth that Lincoln would attend a performance of "Still Waters Run Deep". It was a melodrama that the President was fond of, to be staged at the Soldier's Home, about six miles out of the city. Lincoln was not in the habit of having any guards when he used a carriage except for a coachman and footman.

Armed to the teeth, the conspirators sat on spirited horses in a wooded area along the road to the Soldier's Home. Booth, a superb horseman and crack shot, was about to achieve his dream of glory. A closed carriage approached at a good clip and at the expected time. Charging from the cover of the nearby trees they bore down on the moving carriage and overtook it with drawn weapons. They were to quickly find out that the man inside, frightened and trembling, was not Abraham Lincoln.

When the frustrated group got to the house on H Street, Booth had a showdown with the group who felt the failure was due to the plot being uncovered. The three most sensible members of the endeavor, quit on the spot and refused to be part of Lincoln's assassination.

O'Laughlin, Arnold and John Surratt left after futile threats from Booth to keep them together. Surratt, a dependable spy for the Confederacy, bolted to Canada. The other two, home to Maryland.

That brings us back to the lobby of the National Hotel where O'Laughlin waited for John Wilkes, late in the morning of April 14th. The two men were not all smiles at his meeting. Booth, for the first time today, seemed to lose some of that cool and unruffled demeanor. They walked up the stairs to Wilkes' room without speaking. Once inside there was none of the courtly manners I had come to expect from Booth. They got down to business quickly, both taking a seat facing each other.

O'Laughlin spoke first in a grim, no nonsense manner to his old schoolmate: "Wilkes, I took six months of my life to follow you down a rat hole. The blame is mine for being stupid enough to believe your fancy talk. As our leader you were paid well for the "enterprise" and have money to burn. You owe me that money whether we were successful or not. I know all of your plans and you are in no position to turn me down."

Booth, his lips tight and face flushed, answered and kept himself under control:

"Michael, we have known each other for over twenty years and you must be aware that unlike you and Arnold, I am not a man you can frighten or blackmail. You lived like a prince in fine hotels and frequented the better whorehouses, all funded by me. You quit this enterprise of your free will and I owe you nothing. As a matter of fact, I'm sorry now I let you live!"

"<u>You</u> let <u>me</u> live, you fop bastard!" With that O'Laughlin pulled a pistol from his coat jacket and said: "If I shoot you where you stand I'd be a hero and earn my freedom."

Not for the first time, I admired the icy bravado that Booth exhibited. Looking directly at O'Laughlin, without a tremor, he faced him down: "My murder will not go down quite so easily. I would be avenged within days but even if you lived, you would be branded as a traitor. Would you like to live with that Michael? If I complete my mission I will be the hero of the great Confederacy that will rise again after Lincoln's death."

In the high emotions of this confrontation, I sensed that Booth seemed to take control. When Michael answered, still gripping his pistol, I could feel a slight change of resolve even before he spoke: "I came here for you to settle your debt to me and I won't be put off. I did not join your enterprise for an act of murder that once done, would seal the doom of each of us."

"Michael, you are already doomed for your complicity in the kidnap attempt. Your only chance is my success. You better pray that I do not miss whenever that time comes. If you betray me, Paine will hunt you down and you will pay the going price for traitors."

O'Laughlin stood, the pistol steady at a belt high level: "As long as I live, Wilkes, I am a threat to you. A threat that can be solved only by paying what was promised to me or killing me. I will see you again, in hell or on earth, for our business is not finished." He waved the pistol as he said: "Stay seated and don't make a move."

With that he backed to the door and carefully let himself out. Booth let out a deep breath and the blood drained from his face. Pale, but not unsteady, he moved to the ceramic basin and pitcher in the small dressing room, washing with a towel and cold water on wrists, neck and face. That done, he moved back to the mirror and checked his appearance. He left the Hotel after using the hall bathroom, still ashen.

Walking the five blocks to H Street straight up Sixth, the sparkling day seemed to invigorate Wilkes Booth and his jaunty step returned, his skin not as pale. He had told his men the meeting was at four and I wondered why he was headed to the Surratt house. Booth strode through the large entrance door after ringing the bell and was greeted by the owner of this neat and well-tended boarding house. It was a fine two-story brick house with wide porch and iron stairway. I was as startled seeing Mary Surratt as I was seeing Lewis Paine an hour ago. Lewis had not changed, but Mary certainly had. The dress was the same as was the black hair parted in the middle but her features were not that of the snarling woman in my office. She had firm, clear skin and her mouth was not in the hard slit I remembered. I saw a full figured, attractive woman in a chaste high-buttoned top, cinched waist and flaring full-length skirt all in pearl gray. Mary was aflutter with smiles and flirtation, as were all the women that Booth had talked to this day.

Booth was direct and Mary turned serious as he outlined his needs. Mrs. Surratt was being driven by carriage to Surrattsville, some ten miles South of the Capitol, where her late husband had owned a bed and board Tavern. Now a widow, she sold it and used the money to buy her boarding house in the Capitol. The cover story for the trip was that the new owner was late on a mortgage payment. Her real mission was to make note of any Union Army pickets posted on the road to the South and take with her a parcel that Booth had left at her house previously. The supply parcel, containing field glasses, maps and compass, was needed after the deed was done. It was to be picked up by an escaping Booth, Herold and Paine that night at Surratt's Tavern. A boarder named Louis J. Weichmann, who worked as a clerk in the War Department, was suspected by Booth to be a Union spy and Mary was to maintain tight security.

The mother of John Surratt, a Confederate spy, and the widow of a affirmed secessionist whose rebel flag was proudly displayed during the War, has been painted by many historians as a woman wronged by the verdict of guilty. The conversation I heard and the last thing Booth said to her was damning: "Mrs. Surratt, I must be on my way to Ford's to plan the final act of our play. Your children and your grandchildren for generations will be proud of what we will do today. The men should expect me around four o'clock." Mary told Booth of a letter from her son John in Canada who escaped the month before after the aborted kidnapping. The letter was about his renewed Confederate contacts and a mission he was on: "He pledged to you, Wilkes, that he will always be loyal to our cause."

It was only a short walk to Ford's Theatre over on Tenth Street but Booth again seemed uncomfortable and very pale. He stopped first at a small stable behind the theatre to see if it was unoccupied. It was locked, to Wilkes displeasure. As he moved back and closed the small gate, a pretty girl called to him: "Wilkes, stop for a moment."

It was a young actress getting a breath of air from the rehearsals of tonight's play:

"Wilkes, my memories of our night together in Albany are sweet indeed. Tell me of your future engagements so I can get my agent to book me in the same play."

Booth's way with women was astonishing. In a few minutes of flattery and charm, promising nothing, he was able to get on his way and leave a happy girl behind. As he turned the corner on Tenth and moved toward the theatre entrance, a young man was sitting in a cane chair near the ticket booth with some friends. It was one of the Ford family who was in charge of the box office, Clay Ford. He spotted Booth and called out: "There comes the handsomest man in America." According to the lobby clock, it was 12:10 pm.

John Wilkes Booth's success in "The Apostate" in November of 1864 at Ford's Theatre, had given him a working knowledge of the seat locations, exits and entrances into the scenery, wings and the passageway under the stage for quick entrances from stage left or right. The doors leading to the alley and stable and the entrance from the Theatre building to Taltavull's Star Saloon were all familiar territory. What is more important was a long friendship with the owner, John Ford. That and his celebrity status that earned him deference from stagehands to leading actors, gave him unrestricted access to every part of the house without a breath of suspicion.

Booth's first move was up the stairs on the left to the dress circle. "Peanuts" was cleaning the aisles and making sure the cane seats were secure. He was a boy in his early teens who was a jack of all trades and a gofer whose hanging around the Theatre had earned him a place to sleep, tips from actors and crew and a small stipend from John Ford who was working him into a stagehand. His real name was John Burroughs. He was destined to play a small but significant part in tonight's proceedings. He knew Booth well and was generously tipped for running his errands.

That might have accounted for his ear-to-ear smile: "Nice to see 'yall' Mr. Booth, will you be attending the performance? The President and General Grant are 'posed to come."

"Peanuts, I wouldn't miss it for all the Saint's in Christendom. Now I want you to run downstairs and tell Mr. Spangler I want to see him alone for a few minutes."

Peanuts was gone in a flash and in a few minutes Spangler appeared. He was the assistant stage carpenter and had been so since the Theatre had opened two years before. A large stolid man in early middle age, he had the red cheeks and watery eyes of a drunkard. Without a family, he also used the Theatre as a place to bed down.

Spangler spoke first and was quite nervous: "I don't have much time, Mr. Booth. I am working with the stage hands on Act 2 scenery."

Booth answered sharply: "Edward, will two hundred dollars buy me five minutes?"

Spangler became apologetic and mumbled something about his loyalty to the cause. He moved quickly when Booth motioned him toward Box 7 and 8 to the right of the dress circle.

"Edward, when we had that last drink together a week ago, your strong sympathy to the Southern cause was evident. I told you then that you might possibly help me in a mission of grave import to a cause that now seems lost but is still not defeated. As luck would have it, that time is now." Spangler's greed had overcome his reluctance.

The outer door to box seven was tested and the lock, as usual, was broken. There was a small vestibule inside with a door to each Box. Neither door had a working lock.

In Ford's memoirs he wrote that keys were constantly getting lost and he decided not to fix them each time it happened. No President had ever been assassinated up to 1865.

Security was not a high priority except to the small group around the President.

"Listen carefully, Edward, this will be the only time we will speak. At this time they were standing inside the outer door to the Boxes. "Get a sturdy piece of scrap lumber to act as an inner lock. Cut away a niche in the molding for jamming it into place. Do not use a hammer and chisel, I want no noise and be sure to clean every scrap of shavings that would alert someone. The niche can be made with a sharp knife. Use a hand gimlet to make a small hole in this door panel." Booth pointed to the lower left corner of the upper door panel: "It must be small and unobtrusive, but large enough to peep through." The actor grinned: "Most boys have drilled those holes, but this one will perform a more noble duty. The entire job should take under ten minutes. Be sure that any shavings that drop on the carpet after drilling, inside or out, are carefully removed."

Spangler had listened to the simple instructions but was so nervous he stammered:

"I don't know what your doing and I don't want to know but I'll do as you ask iffen you tell me that no other soul knows of this." Booth smiled in a tight grimace and said:

"You have that assurance on my honor as a gentleman. There is one more thing; the rear door leading to the back alley has a habit of sticking. Don't fix it, just make sure it is slightly ajar at the end of the first Act. Here is one hundred, the remainder will be in an your mailbox tomorrow. Get it done soon, I wish to make an inspection about 3:30. Now get back to your duties."

Booth kept his promise regarding secrecy between he and Spangler. As a result the carpenter, while indicted as a conspirator, kept his neck intact. Incidentally, the friend of Booth who was supposed to drop the other hundred, threw the envelope away in fear when he learned that Booth was Lincoln's assassin. Edward Spangler, sent to an American "Devil's Island" as a conspirator, was short changed to the end.

The morning rehearsals for "Our American Cousin" were coming to a close. Booth, now in the back of the Theatre on ground level, watched intently and glanced at the lobby clock as if timing the action on the stage. When the rehearsal ended, William Withers, the orchestra leader stayed with the orchestra to practice a piece he had written especially for the Presidential party; "Honor to our Soldiers". Booth unhurriedly walked down the aisle and climbed the small stairs on the side of the orchestra pit to get up on stage. He greeted Withers, so busy with the music the man could only nod in return. Wilkes Booth then quietly checked the stage out through the wings to the alley door. It still had a sticky latch. Moving back he watched Clay Ford, keeper of the box office, as he decorated the Presidential Box for the evening. The regular decorator was ill. Booth chatted with Clay as Spangler and Peanuts removed the heavy partition between the Boxes to make one large box for the President and guests. Clay Ford and his helpers moved in a sofa, chairs and a large upholstered rocker for the President. It was placed in the President's usual spot, in Box 7, to the far left on the audience side hidden behind the draperies. Booth had played the lead in "The Apostate" on that same stage six months before. The chair was in the same place when Lincoln had attended a performance He knew exactly were his peephole should be drilled.

The two boxes were a huge splash of color with large American flags draping both, a blue Naval banner below the balustrade, showing a fierce golden eagle and to top it off, an engraved portrait of Washington was.fastened on the center pole between. When I previously lived through this nightmare with the President, I was not in position to admire Clay Ford's talents. The box was little overdone for my taste but magnificent just the same.

All this while Booth, on stage, had been talking to several actor friends, never staring at the Box or attracting attention. They were all flattered by Wilkes promise to attend this evening. Laura Keene, a star in her own right, who was the female lead and producer, had billed the performance as her farewell to the stage. Performers in 1865 had as many farewell performances as George Burns had in our own era. Laura Keene, pushing forty, was no exception. She was gracious in her thanks to Booth for his promised attendance. Booth was on stage and the actor played his role to smooth perfection. He was like a visiting Prince showing favor to the common folk.

Wilkes called to Clay: "I'm coming up to see how well you are doing inside the Box"

Ford's answer, a quick: "Come ahead."

I took a shortcut and floated upward as Booth traversed the dress circle. In those few moments I checked Spangler's handiwork for myself. The job was efficient and did not look freshly done. The peep hole, a little below Booth's eye level, was tucked into a corner of the door molding and unnoticeable. The weathered piece of 2x4 was leaning against the wall in the dark corner of the outer door and when the door was opened, blocked from sight. The mortise slot gouged in the molding to hold the wood stake, was unobtrusive. Spangler had earned his money.

Wilkes moved into the box and while keeping the tone light with Clay Ford, did not miss anything. Clay was in a jocular mood and joked with Booth about General Lee and Jefferson Davis being in the next Box to the

President. Booth darkened and hoped Lee, who he called a coward, would not be paraded in chains as the Romans were wont to do with captured leaders. All day, Booth's moods were mercurial and his physical well being shifted hour to hour. At this juncture, his surreptitious checking of Spangler's handiwork served to bring his mood back to a high. With a shout he called from the Box to two friends: "Hey Bill, why don't you and Maddox let me buy you a drink! I'll meet you at the Star down stairs."

"Bill" was a friend, William Ferguson, an actor in tonight's play and James Maddox was the property manager. The Star was Taltavull's Star Saloon that abutted the Theatre on the South and could be reached by a hallway on the ground floor. The two men were more than agreeable. The bar and furnishings of the saloon marked it as one of the better class establishments in town. Women and horses seemed to be male bar conversation. In 143 years just change horses to automobiles. Booth, who drank his whiskey neat, at one point asked Maddox about the key to the stable. He was told Peanuts always left it on a nail by the rear door. After downing two or three glasses, Booth made his goodbyes in a bon vivant spirit and walked to the Theatre entrance.

This complex man, perhaps feeling the whiskey, then stopped to chat with the twelve year old program boy. He patted the boy on the shoulder and advised him to become an actor: "You have the face for it, Joseph. When the boy expressed some doubt, Booth said: "The world will think better of actors, some day." Giving the twelve year old some change for candy, the next comment was indicative of a sense of resignation: "Try to think of me once and awhile." The boy, Joseph Hazelton, became a successful actor on the boards for fifty years and never forgot this brief exchange.

John Wilkes was headed for Pumphrey's stable behind the National Hotel on C Street.

He had rented a spirited bay mare and wanted to be sure the horse would be ready for the evening. Stopping at the National first, he asked Henry Merrick, the day clerk, if he could have paper, pen and envelope and use his office to write a letter. Booth's appearance and manner was that of a wealthy man and Merrick chided him by asking:

"Mr. Booth sir, have you made a thousand dollars this day?"

Booth answered in a low and serious tone: "No, Mr. Merrick, but I have worked hard enough to make ten times that amount."

Looking over his shoulder at a handwriting that was difficulty to read, the letter was a long, rambling apologia for what he was about to do. His mind was so shaken at this point that he asked the clerk whether the year was 1864 or 1865. Merrick, asked if he was joking. He replied: "Merrick, I can assure you that I am perfectly serious". The letter was another confirmation of history's snap diagnosis of megalomania. I would have added as well, the mood swings of a manic depressive. The quotes of the last paragraph of the letter do not imply total recall. It's been a long day.

"I have devoted my time, energy and fortune to achieve an end that failed. I must now change my plans. Many will blame me for what I am going to do but posterity will justify my actions. Men who love their country better than gold or life, J.Wilkes Booth, Paine, Herold and Atzerdrodt."

Was it his country that he loved? This overwhelming need to justify this murder speaks of some doubts as to his place in history. Was he worried that this bloody deed would not create the same hero worship as did Caesar's assassin? Putting his conspirators' names down, men he did not admire, was an act of unfettered ego. If he paid the piper, so would they. As long as the actor got top billing.

The letter was sealed and placed in his pocket. He got up as if sleepwalking and went to saddle his horse. At the stable he bumped into an old friend and unloosed an intemperate tirade about Andrew Johnson. Intemperate, considering he was talking to an Army Colonel, C.F.Cobb. It ended with the comment: "If I was there when he made that speech I would have shot the son of a bitch." Cobb, in later questioning, said he thought Booth was drunk and did not report him. Booth had made an effort to see the Vice-President and also an effort to see Atzerdrot. Whatever he wanted to change, it was too late. The day's events had a momentum all their own.

He made a full gallop run up Pennsylvania toward the Capitol and reined in the horse when he spotted Maddox. He wheeled the bay in front of Ford's on Tenth Street. Chatting with Maddox about the horse, seemingly recovered from his dark mood, he spotted a man on the porch of a restaurant across the street: "James! See what a racer I have: "Now watch; He can run like a cat!" He pulled the horse around and in a full gallop, went back down the broad Avenue. Booth reined in the horse again to greet an old friend, the actor John Matthews, also in the cast of "Our American Cousin". This was the same Matthews who had casually mentioned to Booth that the President was coming to see "Still Waters Run Deep" at the Soldier's Home the month before, precipitating the kidnap attempt. Booth looked wild eyed and flushed after the gallop, so much so that Matthews asked him if he was ill. He brushed the question off and at that moment a ragged group of Confederate prisoners shuffled by escorted by troops on horseback. Booth, still seated on the restless horse, struck his forehead with the back of his hand and emoted: "Great God! I no longer have a country."

From the expression on Matthew's face, I sensed he was worried about his old friend. Wilkes Booth pulled out the letter he had written at the National and said to Matthews:

"John, I'd appreciate a small favor. I'll be leaving town tonight and I have a letter here I wish to be published in the 'National Intelligencer'. Please attend to it for me unless I see you before ten o'clock tomorrow; in that case I will see to myself."

Tonight, John Matthews would see Wilkes rush wildly across the stage after shooting the President. Later in the privacy of his room he would pull out the letter, read it twice and then strike a match and watch as it became ashes. Matthews said he burned the letter, fearful of being implicated in Booth's deed. He later gave what I know was truthful testimony and was never charged with destruction of evidence or anything else.

Reading that letter before the play was not the only way he could have alerted Army intelligence. Several months before, Booth had hounded Matthews to join the kidnapping scheme. Matthews flatly refused and he was one of the few old friends that once spoken to, Wilkes trusted to keep quiet. I have no knowledge of the facts but I did have the thought that Matthews might have been the one who revealed the attempt to Army intelligence. I also wondered why, if tipped off, there was no Calvary troop to capture the adventurers. Was it Stanton's hand in the affair, saving his patsy Booth for the assassination or just a stroke of luck?

Coming at a quick pace down Pennsylvania Avenue, heading away from the White House, a closed carriage clattered by with two occupants. Booth's back was turned but Matthews noticed that it was General Grant and his wife Julia. He mentioned it to Wilkes who looked startled and galloped after the coach without his usual courtly exit.

Booth sat a horse as if joined to the animal. The gallop over the cobblestones seemed effortless as he urged the horse on. Pulling up alongside, he peered into the coach with the wild look that often came over him, convincing himself that it was the General. The master plan was breaking down again. Like the switch from Grover's to Ford's Theatre he would have to improvise. As he followed the famous couple, Julia Grant was becoming nervous about this dark rider with the wild expression. When they turned at First Street toward the Baltimore and Ohio Railroad Station, Booth was visibly upset.

Deep in thought and the horse at quick trot, he moved back up the Avenue to the corner of Fourteenth Street.

The Willard Hotel was the Grant residence when the General was in the Capitol. It surprised me just how many people Booth counted among his acquaintances. It would seem that every hotel clerk in town was on the list. On second thought, I should not be surprised that a man with his amatory conquests would know his way around. The clerk at Willard's was only too happy to tell the celebrated actor that the General and his wife were on the way home to New Jersey and would not attend tonight's play. With a sigh of sympathy the clerk said: "A good many people like yourself will be disappointed." Booth's wry smile was his only reply.

From Willard's, Booth then trotted his horse down Pennsylvania to Twelfth Street and dismounted again at the Kirkwood. This time he did not use the rear entrance and inquired at the desk for Atzerdrot. Again, George was not there. His worry about the reliability of this man must have been gnawing at him all day.

As John Wilkes moved down the stairs of the Hotel he had a brief conversation with a young Union officer he called Devaney who must have been an old friend. The conversation was about Booth's further plans on the stage. Wilkes made a statement to Devaney that he was giving up the stage to manage his oil investments. The Major wished him luck and Booth said his goodbyes and remounted the bay horse, which was not an easy handful. The horse had a mind of her own and needed firm handling on the way to Tenth Street to Ford's Theatre. Booth had that sure handed expertise. I might add that "expertise" might also be a good term to describe his relations with men and women, aside from the occasional loss of self control. I had mentioned that Lewis Paine had the good looks and dead eyes of Chamber's, the preppie strangler. Booth had the same handsome, dark look and sociopathic mannerisms of Ted Bundy, the cool serial murderer.

Booth moved down the alley to the back of Ford's and looked for the key to the stable. It was hanging on the nail in the resting place used by Peanuts. He opened the stable, dismounted and then yelled for Peanuts. The boy seemed to pop up like a jack-in-the-box, eager to help Booth find Ed Spangler and have him get a halter for the mare. Booth took the few minutes gentling the mare and feeding him a sugar cube he had filched in the National's dining room.

When Spangler arrived with the halter, he unloosened the saddle strap. Booth let him know that the bridle, saddle and blanket should remain. Ed Spangler nodded his head wisely and said not a word. "Peanuts", said the actor: "Are you old enough to have a glass of ale?" The boy assured Wilkes that he had not joined a temperance society. "Then go find Mr. Maddox and tell him all of us are meeting at Taltavull's"

After Peanuts scurried off Booth turned to Spangler: "Be sure to leave the rear door very slightly ajar after the first act. And Ed, busy yourself in the back of the scenery drops and mind your own business whatever happens."

Without another word, Spangler and Booth left the stable and went to the saloon. Maddox, joined by Peanuts, was waiting at the bar. John Wilkes Booth, according to his friends at the conspiracy trial two months later, was drinking heavily since early March. John Deery, the bar and billiard parlor owner, described it as occasionally downing a half to a full quart in a four to six hour span. He also said that Booth, aside from darkening his violent mood, showed very little effects of these stunning amounts. He had spoken to Booth in an effort to find the cause of his friend's binges but Wilkes was never forthcoming. Deery also testified that, over many years, Booth could best be described as a moderate drinker.

That fateful night he was not a moderate drinker. Half glasses were the vogue. I don't think a shot glass had then been invented. My count, over the space of an hour, was three. Booth led a loud and ribald ribbing of Peanuts as to his experience with the ladies, or was it non-experience? The bar, as was the custom, laid out a free lunch and the cheese, rolls and spiced meats were replenished time and again. A good old time all around. When the actor left around five, he walked with a steady gait to the house on H Street and seemed unaffected by the drinking. The afternoon sky had become cloudy and a cool breeze ruffled his hair.

When Booth walked in to the white clapboard house on H. Street, he asked Mrs. Surratt's seventeen year old daughter Anna if her Mother had returned. I stared at Anna, who held in her hands the fate of my family and that of Jane Gotting and her husband. This was the young and pretty girl I had to keep from a macabre appointment. The hanging of Mary Surratt, Lewis Paine, David Herold and George Atzerdrot. Anna was the daughter who received the spirit of Mrs. Surratt the moment the rope broke Mary's neck at the end of a six foot drop. A sweet faced teenager in a blue hoop skirt was to launch a series of demonic possessions in a line that led to my office 143 years later.

Anna said yes to Booth. Her mother had returned from Surrattsville and was upstairs with Mr. Paine and did not wish to be disturbed. Booth did not seem at all perturbed and asked the girl for tea to be shared with her in the front parlor. Annie bounded from the chair in a nervous, giggling flutter and made the preparations quickly in the adjacent kitchen. Proud of her home making ability she came in bearing a silver tray with a polished silver service, her mother's best, to serve the actor tea, scones and cookies. I knew Booth would not miss the opportunity to regale an pert audience of one with stories about the world of the stage. I went upstairs.

There were three rooms upstairs but only one had a closed door. I glided through the door and into an empty parlor. I turned right and moved silently into the bed room.

Mary was on the end of the bed, belly down, feet on the floors and almost nude. Almost, because her long white stockings and half girdle cinched about her waist, were in place. Lewis was dressed in a cotton pull over and had dropped his trousers and underwear over his boots, displaying powerful buttocks. His large phallus moved in and out of Mary's ample, firm buttocks with languorous, repeated thrusts. He was silent, his eyes closed, his head moving in dreamy rhythmical arcs. His actions surprisingly gentle. Mary's heavy, deep breasts, bobbed back and forth to the ecstatic beat as she pushed upward from the bed with her forearms. Mary was not silent, urging Lewis to probe further and further into the depths of her body, murmuring with pleasure.

I was drawn into erotic fascination as the passion moved to a noisy climax. Lewis spoke at last, breathing heavily: "Mary, I a'int never wanted to please anyone but myself and never said this no body; I love you." Mary took his face in her hands and they kissed deeply as I moved out of the room, feeling exactly like the voyeur I was. I heard her say, again and again: "Sweet Lewis, I love you too."

I believed it. Perhaps, if she had twenty years to turn this killing machine into a human being, a change might have been accomplished. If Mary's patriotic love of the Confederacy had not drawn her into Booth's deadly scheme, the demon in my office would not exist. She had once said to me that her spirit transfer might have been the Devil's work. I was beginning to believe that as well.

I moved downstairs and laughter came from the front room parlor. I waited with Booth and Annie for the odd couple to come downstairs. In ten minutes Mary and Lewis walked into the parlor. Booth rose and bowed to Mrs. Surratt with practiced gallantry. Ladies in 1865 were known to pinch their cheeks and bite their lips in an era almost free of cosmetics. Mrs.Surratt needed no self abuse to achieve her rosy glow. That and the sheepish expression on Lewis, made John Wilkes flash a knowing smile. Annie was oblivious of anyone but Booth.

"Lewis, I have spent too much time at Ford's but there was much to be done. Please tell Atzerdrot and Herold to meet me at eight o'clock in your room at the Herndon House around the corner from Ford's. We will go over the final arrangements. Mrs. Surratt, were you successful?" At that moment Louis Weichmann, who might have been standing on the porch for a time, walked in with Herold and Atzerdrot. The entrance only had an airy screen door and Booth was upset. After the greetings, Booth said: "Mrs. Surratt, may I see you privately for a moment. I'd like to settle with you for my rooms last month."

There was no hint of panic in Mary: "I keep the accounts ledger in the closet office off the kitchen, Please come with me, Mr. Booth."

They moved without haste to the kitchen.

"Mary, the Judas might have been outside but he cannot know where or when we will strike. No discussions about the enterprise unless it is safe. Keep him here tonight if you have to get him drunk. Get Herold alone and tell him to meet me in my room at the National at 7:00 tonight. Now please go on with what happened on the trip."

"Wilkes, David will get your message. You will be pleased to hear there are no Army pickets on the road South. I asked a Union officer, in the guise of a frightened woman, 'where are the pickets?' He told me the President had canceled the order to require passes to northern Virginia and Richmond and all pickets have been withdrawn."

Wilkes nodded affirmatively as Mary continued:

"Lloyd, the sorrowful man I sold the Tavern to, was so drunk I had to give the parcel to Mrs. Offett, his sister in law but I made sure that I went with her to stash it. I'll tell Herold exactly where it is and if Lloyd is sober enough, he will get you the carbines and pistols Herold gave him to keep for you. If he's drunk, Herold was there when he put them in the rafters. He'll get them."

"By God, Mary, good news for a change! If you were a man you would be riding with me tonight. You have more courage and intelligence than any one of them."

With that, Mary hugged the actor and wished him Godspeed. It was the last time she would ever see him, alive or dead.

Booth walked briskly down the five blocks on Sixth to the National Hotel. He stopped briefly at the tea room to fortify himself for the evening ahead. Tea time at the National, like the huge English breakfast, was not only cakes and cookies. Booth found some hearty food to tide him over and moved through rather quickly. Calm and focused, he went to his room.

I watched intently as he moved through a carefully planned routine. The day's finery, suit, vest and light overcoat were hung in an armoire. His shirt, gloves, even his under- wear were removed and tossed into a basket in the corner. Donning a robe, he moved to the hall bath to remove the grime of the Capitol's streets. On return he changed into long underwear and a black broadcloth suit that would withstand the rigors of the evening. He would still wear a cravat, the shirt not formally ruffled and the sleeves buttoned instead of linked. The finished man was still dressed fashionably but in a more informal style. The polished boots were the same complete to the spurs.

The trousers came over the boots, not tucked in, western fashion. With no time for a valet he used a small boot black kit to restore the shine. The cane was left in the closet. He pulled out two saddle bags and began to pack.

His packing was rather light . I assumed he thought that on the run he was certain to be taken care of by his Confederate compatriots. Some bare clothing essentials. A black slouch hat and sturdy leather riding gloves. A makeup kit that included false whiskers, spirit gum and theatrical cosmetics interested me. A small chipped mirror, brushes and cotton went with it. Another black coat, longer and suitable for riding was draped on the chair. In an inside jacket pocket he put a worn notebook and pencils.

In the other saddlebag went a large repeating pistol and a box of shells. He then moved to the closet and took out a small case and a Bowie knife in a leather sheath. Putting the Bowie knife in the saddlebag, he opened the case and took out a pistol small enough to fit in the palm of his hand, putting it on the table. I looked with some horror at this tiny weapon that would change the fate of a nation. The pistol was labeled "Deringer - Philadelphia". I always thought Derringer was spelled with two "r's." I am not a gun buff and this move-by-move description on how to load the pistol is only as accurate as my overloaded memory. He first cleaned it with a rag and small vial of oil. Gunpowder was not poured in. It was pre-measured in a small cotton bag. And tamped in by a tiny rod. The bullet, an iron ball about a half inch in diameter, was pushed in through the barrel. A small percussion cap was set in place to be struck by the trigger and the spark would light the gunpowder, exploding the lethal pellet from the barrel.

All of Booth's movements were slow, careful and deliberate. He softly whistled a tune throughout the process. When finished, he wiped the pistol again and slipped it into the side pocket of his coat. If there was any thinking about the enormity of what he was about to do, it was not apparent to me. The man was within a trigger pull of the immortality he hoped for and everything else was of secondary importance.

Before he left the room, he again went to the full length mirror to check his appearance.

This time however he stared at his reflected image, sighed and moved to his trunk. From a padded inside pouch he pulled a small packet tied with some string and opened it. He spread out on the table five photographs of very beautiful women. I recognized only one from an 1960's article in "American Heritage" that featured Lucy Hale, the daughter of a U.S. Senator. The article I had read discussed Lucy Hale, a Washington belle that had been courted by some very famous men. Oliver

W.Holmes, Robert Lincoln and most successfully by John Wilkes Booth. The Hale family for generations denied an engagement rumor that was rife in 1865. This night, in the actor's hotel room, she was on a short list of five, tucked in his wallet as a final sentimental flourish. There was a knock on the door.

Booth said: "Just a moment" and without undue nervousness, went to saddle bag and loaded the repeating pistol. At the ready, he asked who it was and was answered by David Herold. The actor let him in without greeting or handshake, a foolish grin on Herold's face. Booth gave him the saddle bags with an order to bring them to the stable behind Ford's and without attracting attention, retrieve the stable key from the nail beside the rear theatre door and re-saddle the horse. Then he said: "David, be sure to give the mare a few more forks of hay. She will earn them tonight. Leave now and do not cross the lobby. Use the rear stairs in the hall to the alley and I will meet you at Herndon House at eight o'clock."

Booth, as a multitude of travelers have done before and after him, gave a quick look around, turned off the gas lights by twisting the side key, and left the room, locking the door behind him.

The night clerk exchanged pleasantries with Booth as he dropped off his key. The actor smiled as he said: "Ah, Bunker, are you going to Ford's tonight?"

"No Mr. Booth, I am the only night clerk on duty."

"Too bad George, you will miss some fine acting tonight."

As he moved out of the hotel and walked toward Tenth, the cool audacity of the man was remarkable. Arriving at Ford's, Booth checked first on his horse, or was he checking on Herold's reliability? Either way he found every thing in order, the saddlebags tightly cinched and the scattered signs of hay, nourishment for the bay mare.

Walking up the alley to the front of the Theatre, he moved through one of the arches near the box-office and again bumped into William Withers, the orchestra leader. The outer lobby clock read 7:21. Off went the two of them, through the hall and into the Saloon. Booth's cash supply appeared inexhaustible. He was picking up the tab all day. The establishment was almost empty at this hour, the bartender polishing glasses for tonight's performance. Booth excused himself to have a brief discussion with the bartender at the other end of the polished mahogany bar. I made sure to eavesdrop.

"Murdoch, When the President's two guards, Charlie Forbes and John Parker, come in tonight as they usually do; tell them that John Wilkes Booth, in tribute to their loyalty and heavy responsibility, is paying for everything they order tonight. Be sure it is your best. No need to discuss this with Mr. Tartavull."

"That is very generous of you, Mr. Booth but what you are giving me is far too much for whatever they consume, even Parker."

"What is left over is for you, Murdoch. Just fill the glasses and keep them happy."

The implications of what Booth told the bartender rang in my head like a clapper on a bell. Bound by fear, the bartender, Parker and Forbes, carried that bombshell of information in silence to their graves. Neither of the two was ever called to appear before the military trial that condemned the conspirators.

When he returned to Withers they had a bar stool conversation about whom in the cast was an easy conquest. Glasses were then refilled as Booth expressed the hope that Withers newly written opus, "Hail To The Soldiers", would be favorably received. The conversation turned to greatness in the theatre and Withers, a little tipsy, went so far as to tell Booth his father was the greatest Hamlet of all the Booths. With a sly grin, Wilkes said something that Withers thought about regretfully for years: "When I leave the stage, William, I shall be the most talked about actor in America."

Chapter 7
The Final Arrangements

Booth made his goodbyes and moved through the hall into the theatre entrance. Checking the large lobby clock, it was 7:52 in the evening. With a firm and steady gait, he walked around the corner to Herndon House on Ninth Street.

Walking up the three flights to Paine's small room, he knocked before entering.

Paine, with a half smile, was on the bed checking his weapons. The large curved Bowie knife I remembered with a shudder, and a repeating pistol with an octagonal barrel. Herold was going over the escape route maps and Atzerdrodt was sitting on a corner chair, grasping his knees tightly and moaning. He was clearly quite drunk.

"Shut up George!" Booth snapped as he shook Atzerdrot roughly: "Your meaningless life now has a glorious purpose. You would have died an unknown drunkard in an alley if not for me. Carry out your mission and your fame will last for a millennium!"

George reacted by coughing and spitting on the carpet.

Booth, in disgust, turned his attention to the evening's plans and gave precise orders: "Paine you, David and Atzerdrot will stay in this room until nine o'clock. Herold, here is my father's watch. I have set it correctly. At that time you will all go to Nailor's stable to pick up the horses and gear. Take Paine to the Seward house and dismount a half block away. At exactly 10:00 Paine must knock on the door to Seward's House. Lewis, do you have a small parcel prepared for the medicine excuse?" Paine showed him the stringed parcel. "Good, Lewis, have you rehearsed your part with Herold today?" Again nods of affirmation from both men. "It must be simple, quick and firm in tone. I know Lewis, you will not fail. Ha! You should make a fine actor. Make sure Seward is dead and make your escape. If more than ten minutes, Herold will leave your horse at a hitching post. He must meet me on time. If you can, get to the Old Navy Bridge at the bottom of Thirteenth and go to Surrattsville to meet us at the Tavern. We will wait for you there for a half hour. I will kill America's King at a moment in the second act that is covered by loud laughter. The time should be between 10:10 and 10:25. Only Harry Hawk will be on stage to stop me and he will foul his pants in fright."

Paine spoke in his gruff drawl: "Capt'n, why are you using a one shot pea shooter? If you stay with the Army pistol, you'll have a friend on the way out."

"Lewis, now that Grant will not be there one shot is enough. The size of the Deringer means hardly a bulge in my pocket. That pea shooter with cap and ball is more reliable than the pistol and just as deadly at close range. A misfire would be a disaster. I have one chance and will be inches away. My knife will then be my friend on the way out."

Booth relished the moment and then pointed at Atzerdrodt: "As for this drunken poltroon, on my way out I will send the valet up with a pot of coffee. Try to sober him up by any means you choose and give him the same information about the time and escape route. The Kirkland has a large clock behind the desk, he will not need a watch. Do not waste too much time. Get him to his horse and check his knife and pistol." He spoke as if Atzerdrot were not present, which was probably right. With Booth's eyes glaring and his voice in deep and measured tones, he said: "I have prepared myself for the possibility of this drunkard's failure to kill the Vice President. If he does fail, I hope Johnson's guard will shoot straight. Stay the course, we strike a blow for the South, for freedom and our sacred honor." I looked at Paine and Herold and wondered whose sacred honor he was talking about.

With that he grabbed both men by the shoulders in turn. There were a few more small details ironed out and by the pocket watch of Junius Booth, Sr., it was 8:51, time to go.

John Wilkes Booth left the room, walked slowly down the stairs and out the front door.

The night had become wet and gloomy. A light misty rain and wisps of fog gave the city an eerie appearance. On the opposite corner a barker stood in front of a beer barrel topped by a flickering torch, shouting: "This way to Ford's, this way to Ford's."

The actor paused on the well lit stairs of the Herndon House, then stepped to the walk and turned left on F Street. All in black, the fog swallowed him.

Wilkes arrived at Ford's as the evening audience began to stream through the doors.

There was a happy, festive feeling in the crowd. The war was over, their sons now safe and they might glimpse the most famous man in the world as the Lincoln party took their seats. The box office was still selling seats for the night performance. I noted the price as ten dollars for a box, six dollars for the dress circle and two for favored front rows of the audience. In the back of the theatre on ground level, it was seventy five cents. They were to witness the incredible events of the evening at bargain prices.

Booth stuffed his slouch hat into his coat pocket as he walked over and lit a cigar. On a high, he spotted Clay Ford behind the box office grille. Reaching his arm in, he deposited the cigar and said with a flourish: "Who e'er this cigar dare displace must meet Wilkes Booth face to face." Clay laughed and waved Booth in. Ford later testified he recognized the parody of lines from a popular burlesque farce. The real last lines of the doggerel, were: "Thus do I challenge the human race."

Booth was enjoying every moment of his carefully planned journey to infamy.

The celebrated actor's unlimited access to every part of the house was a tangible weapon in his arsenal. Without suspicion, the actor had the carte blanche necessary to carry out his plans to the last detail. After his first drink at Taltavull's, Booth did not take the inner route to the stable. The first act had already begun and he walked around the theatre and through the alley. The bay mare was restless but fully saddled, bridled and ready. A quick check of the saddle bags let Booth know they had been untouched. A young man with theatrical makeup on was standing at the rear door when Booth walked over leading his horse. He turned out to be a bit actor whose scene was just over and he was out for a smoke. Booth knew everyone and in a brusque command, spoke to him: "Debonay, get Mr. Spangler and tell him to hold my horse." The young man obediently scooted down the short stairs, under the stage and through a passageway to stage left, to deliver the message. Spangler finally appeared but by that time Booth was back to his barstool. I tarried to find out about the horse. The nervous carpenter, who probably figured that holding the horse was another nail in his coffin, then called out to Peanuts whose job it was to sit at the stage door around the corner. After Peanuts protested that his job was to guard the stage door, Spangler insisted, pulling out a half dollar to ease the boy's pain. Peanuts must have also counted on his usual generous tip from Wilkes Booth.

I went back to the bar and Wilkes was moving back and forth between drinks to check the lobby clock, getting a little tense each time. The Presidential party was late and he might have thought the plans had changed again. Booth's obsession had created some puzzlement on the face of Buckingham, the doorkeeper. Drinking alone and drinking one glass after another, the actor made one more trip out to the doorkeeper just as the Presidential carriage pulled up to the door. The rousing cheers of bystanders echoed off the red brick walls of the theatre. President Lincoln, who got out first, acknowledged the cheers with a small wave, appearing lost in thought and grim faced. Next, A smiling Mary Todd and her guests, Major Rathbone and Clara Harris came next. The group moved through the entryway into the Theatre. Booth watched all this as stealthily as possible by standing in back and to the side of one of the brick arches in front of Ford's. He slipped in behind the Presidential party and followed them. The entourage moved to the left to a stairway leading to the dress circle to the thunder of applause and cheers generated by Lincoln's appearance. Watching from a different angle from the day I spent with Lincoln, I was struck by how very sad the President looked. He brightened when Joseph Hazelton, the youthful program boy, became frozen handing out the programs. Lincoln smiled broadly after putting the boy at ease and with his wife and guests, climbed the carpeted stairs.

Booth watched intently but not from the dress circle. He moved among the cheering audience on the floor level when all eyes were on the Presidential Box. Withers had struck up the band in "Hail to the Chief" adding to the din as the Presidential party moved to their seats. On stage the actors were applauding vigorously as were many of the stagehands. I spotted Spangler stomping his feet and clapping his hands to let everyone know around him he was pro-Lincoln. It did not do him much good at his trial.

The play resumed in the middle of the second act. One of the actor's lines was about a cold draft from a castle window. Hawk's ad-libbed answer was: ". No more 'draft' by order of the President", pointing to the Box. The audience exploded with laughter as did the President whom I could see clearly from the seats below. Lincoln, a shy and private man, then adjusted his rocker and the drapes to almost hide him from view. Mary, Clara and the Major were quite visible. The play went on, the actors settling down to their roles and the audience becoming absorbed. The time was about 9:15 PM.

The restless Booth went back to the Saloon but instead of checking time, busied himself in moving back and forth from the bar to time the play, waiting for the proper moment. From this moment on, his glass was untouched. He seemed as calm as I had seen him all day and hummed a tune as he studied two of the men at the other end of the bar. It was John Parker and Charles Forbes with Murdoch filling the glasses every time they were empty. Both, as Booth had hoped, had deserted their posts. He watched calmly as Forbes pulled Parker by the arm. John Parker shook him off. Parker's post was a chair placed inside the box vestibule door leading directly to Box Seven. Tonight, that chair would remain empty.

The actor's eyes followed the unsteady Forbes, as the guard took a seat in the dress circle near the closed vestibule door. Wilkes stood in the dark shadows in the back of the dress circle, now bareheaded, watching Act Three as the comedy moved quickly along with bursts of laughter from the audience. Every time someone came in at the top of the stairs to the dress circle, Booth's head jerked left. Parker would have been another problem to solve if he returned but time and drink were on Wilkes' side. He carefully fingered the Bowie knife inside his belt under a closed jacket and patted the little bulge in the right hand pocket of his coat. The audience in front of him watched the stage intently. The actor's cue would soon be spoken on stage.

He moved down the side aisle and in front of the people in the first row, some of whom looked up in annoyance at the intrusion. When he got to Charles Forbes, he bent down to speak to him but Forbes spoke first: "Mr. Booth that was damned nice of you to treat John and I that way. Nobody else gives a damn."

Bending to Forbes' ear Booth said quietly: "Forbes you certainly deserve it. The President has invited me to join him at any performance. You can take in my card if you like." With that he handed Forbes his card.

"No, no Mr. Booth. You don't need no card. The door is not locked so go right in."

I listened to this in helpless frustration and followed Booth into a vestibule where the only light came from the open door to Box Eight. Major Rathbone was looking front and down, absorbed in the play. From this angle, only Clara's dress was in sight as she sat on the far right. Booth did not make a sound as he put the wooden bar firmly in place. Spangler had even added two nail heads to the end of the bar for more purchase against the door. It was a perfect fit. Booth then unloosened his coat and took out the Deringer and the Bowie knife. The small pistol in his right hand and the glinting knife in the left. As he waited patiently for the right dialogue on stage he glanced though the peephole in the door. His only outward movement was to swallow, quickly.

The President's stovepipe hat was off and his hair was long and unruly. He was bent to his left, peeking through the draperies at someone in the audience.

On the stage Mrs. Mountchessington, a haughty English Matron, was scolding the American cousin, Asa Trenchard, a bumbling country oaf. Asa was played by Harry Hawk, a veteran comedian who knew Booth well.

"I am aware, Mr. Trenchard, that you are not used to the manners of good society, and that alone will excuse the impertinence of which you have been guilty."

The exit line allowed her to haughtily sweep into the wings, leaving the stage empty except for the country bumpkin. Asa, with gestures, had his sharp edged reply:

"Don't know the manners of good society, eh? Well I guess I knows enough to turn you inside out, old gal... you sockdologizing old man trap!" The audience roared.

Booth stepped through the unlocked door. He silently moved forward, arm straight out and came within two feet of Lincoln's skull. The President was still looking at the audience, down and left as the pistol was aimed just right of his left ear. The Major and Clara were uproarious, as were the rest of the audience, and time stood still.

Booth's finger tightened on the trigger. The report of the small pistol was very loud and the orange flash glinted from the glass chandelier as white smoke wafted over the stage. The President did not utter a sound as he slumped forward against the wall, his right arm jerking reflexively upward. For a split second no one moved, not even Booth, staring at the mortally wounded President. The actor moved first, toward the railing. Rathbone, stunned as all were, jumped upward and forward to stop the assassin. Booth snarled like an animal and turned to Rathbone with the reflexes of a tiger, dropping the pistol and flipping the Bowie knife to his right hand, he slashed at the Major's chest. Rathbone used his left arm to parry the thrust and was cut to the bone, falling back. As the actor started his carefully planned leap to the stage, the brave and bleeding Rathbone grabbed him once more, throwing Booth's timing off as he went clumsily over the balustrade. The screams of Mary Todd and Clara Harris followed him as his left foot struck the heavy portrait of Washington, banging it fully around. His spur then caught the blue Navy banner and he landed heavily on the stage below, his left leg crumpling beneath him.

Booth was not about to blow his lines. Frenzied with pain with what turned out to be a broken leg, he struggled to his feet before an audience just starting to comprehend the enormity of what had happened. Holding the bloody knife above his head he shouted: "Sic Sempre Tyrannis!" In a grotesque hopping run, eyes wild and waving the bloody knife, he moved straight at Harry Hawk who promptly bolted into the scenery, bug-eyed with fear. Men were climbing up on the stage, a screaming audience in near panic as the assassin staggered into the wings on stage left, making for the rear alley door. Booth's drinking friend, Maestro Withers, was hurrying from the rear to the stage, looking confused at this apparition coming at him. Booth cried: "Let me pass! The startled man froze and fell back as the knife missed his throat, cut his collar and inflicted a small wound. Withers was speechless as he grabbed his neck and watched his friend Booth fling the slightly ajar alley door open, and lunging through, slam it shut.

As I moved with Booth into the alley he used his good leg to vault into the saddle of the startled horse. The loyal, but frightened, Peanuts was still holding tightly to the reins of the bucking animal. His reward for loyalty was a smash on the head from the butt of the mounted actor's Bowie knife. The blow sent him sprawling, screaming in pain and frightened disbelief. At this point a tall and determined Army officer finally broke through the sticking rear door and watched helplessly as the horseman brought the wheeling horse under control. John Wilkes Booth, grimacing in pain and hunched over the pommel, dug in his spurs and cut sharply right on F Street, galloping into the judgment of history, a judgment the actor had not foreseen.

Chapter 8
Doctor Samuel Mudd

Urging more speed from the mare at every stride, Booth headed down the near empty street, whipped right on Ninth Street past the Herndon House and went flat out for four blocks over the cobblestones. Bearing right he went over a fetid canal on the small Tenth Street crossover and made for Eleventh Street. Pulling up within sight of the Navy Bridge going east over the Potomac, he calmed the steaming horse and listened intently for any sounds of pursuit. Booth was waiting for Herold, Paine and Atzerdrot to join him and unless he was pressed, was stopping to give his confederates a chance to catch up. There was danger in standing still which made him very impatient, running the horse down to Twelfth, craning his neck and repeating the procedure to Tenth. Aside from pain, his injury covered by a tight riding boot, his demeanor was intense and excited but fully under control. He had worked out some support on the horse to ease his left leg and was fully stretched out to the stirrups only on the right.

Turning right on F Street and around the block to Ninth at the onset of his escape, was probably to fool anyone in pursuit that he was heading North instead of Southeast. Booth, a wily planner, would not waste a second. As it turned out, he was inexplicably given a four to five hour head start. There was no pursuit.

After a quarter hour Booth made his decision to move on. While waiting, he assured himself that there were no Union pickets, also inexplicable, anywhere in the vicinity of the bridge and moved at a calm trot to the bridge keeper's booth between the east and west lanes of the wooden structure.

The Navy bridge had been reinforced early in the war for the Army caissons that rolled over it hauling cannon and supplies. Wooden or not, It looked solid and dependable in the late night moonlight. The skies had cleared and the stars astonished this 21st Century observer. A horse driven transport system might have smelled a little but it was great for a clear, smog free atmosphere. It was now nearing eleven o'clock.

The bridge keeper was an old Army Sergeant, Silas T. Cobb, at your service. The following conversation I cannot quote but a cool and personable Booth started to talk his way out of the city on a bridge that was supposed to be closed at nine o'clock. The first question from the Sergeant was for identification. Why Wilkes chose to give his name is difficult to comprehend, but he said: "My name is Booth."

My only explanation was the man's mania for attention. Why do all this and remain anonymous? At the same time he might be thumbing his nose at his pursuers. Not to jump ahead, but the rest of this escape he used an alias repeatedly. I know from his conversations with his cohorts that he considered the Union state of Maryland enemy territory. He was sure that once in Virginia a worshiping citizenry would nurture him.

Pumped up and excited about his successful mission and bold escape, using his name could also have been an ego induced oversight.

After identification a conversation ensued on the reason he was there. Booth then passed himself off as a resident of Charles County who had stayed late in the city and wanted to get home. He feigned ignorance of the nine o'clock curfew and without wheedling pleaded his case. Cobb's waving him on through might have saved the Sergeant's life. Throughout the conversation Booth had one hand in his saddlebag, gripping the butt of his pistol. Cool and convincing, reflecting no pain from his broken leg, the smooth talker triumphed again. Clattering over the wooden rails, he looked back with a smile of smug satisfaction.

As the lone horseman started to climb Good Hope Hill on the Lower Maryland side of the bridge he stopped again to look for anyone of his men. He could see the Capitol lights and the nearby bridge but saw no one. Prodding the horse up to the crest of the hill he stopped again to look back down for anyone else. The moonlit night was still and the snorting of his horse the only sounds in this beautiful view of the sleeping city.

Booth rarely showed weakness but his audible sigh as he pulled the mare around was surely an expression of deep regret that no one else had made it out of the Capitol.

The horse started slowly on the down slope and Booth spotted a rider coming up toward him. Drawing even with the horseman he stopped and said, without a trace of anxiety: "Good evening sir. Can you tell me if another horseman has recently come through?" The rider said that in the last hour he had passed no one. Wilkes then asked him if the road to Marlboro turned right. Assured by the stranger that he should go straight and make no turns, the two men continued in opposite directions.

When present at the evening meeting at Herndon House, I had heard Booth and Herold go over the route to Surrattsville and got a good look at the crude map they were using. Marlboro was due East, not South. Wilkes was taking no chances that any testimony by a passerby, as to spotting a horseman, might be given to his pursuers. Throwing the Army or police off the track could give him many more hours of safety.

It was only after a few minutes of steady trot that Booth heard hoof beats behind him. There was no panic in the man as he coolly moved into some trees just off the dirt road and took out his pistol. As the follower rode by at a good clip, the actor let out a shout: "Davey, you made it!" David Herold reigned the roan in sharply, turned and had the adoring look of a man who just found God:

"You did it, you did it! I didn't let you down, Wilkes, and nobody is a' following me. For a while, I thought the bridge keeper would never let me pass. Maybe I joked with him too much but he looked me over and finally let me by."

Booth was happy to see his young companion and slapped him on the back. He was desperate for any information and anxious to share the news of his supreme moment of heroism, shooting an unarmed man in the back of his head.

"Davey, I am sure the tyrant is dead. The barrel of the Deringer was no more than six inches from his head! My spur caught in a flag decoration and I think I broke my leg in the jump to the stage." Davey reacted in concerned surprise about the injury but Booth did not pause: "I used my knife to strike at anyone in my path and was out the back door and on my horse before an Army Major broke through behind me. The mare ran like a startled deer. I had no trouble getting through the bridge gate keeper and that was about twenty minutes ago."

All this poured out of an excited Booth to his adoring sycophant as they moved toward Surrattsville. The actor, on a euphoric high, assured Davey that pain or not he could follow the plan to head for Surrattsville about ten miles Southwest. He felt that a fast trot, rather than gallop, would be best for his leg in spite of the need for haste. The two men started down the old TB road toward Surrattsville, riding side by side on the deserted dirt road, the moonlight darkened by the leafy canopy of trees. His jaw clenched in pain, Booth then asked of Paine and Atzerdrodt. Herold started to blubber and Booth pulled him together sharply:

"Davey, Stop that sniveling! I have no time or inclination to wet nurse you through this journey. Be a man or by God you shall go your way and I mine! Now, what of Paine?"

"Wilkes, Lewis and I rode to the Seward house and tarried a wee bit about a stone's throw from the Secretary's house. We went over what he should say. At 10:00 on your father's watch, Lewis dismounted and was real calm as he walked to the door and knocked. I seen him arguing with a house nigger servant about bringing in the medicine and the boy finally let him pass. I wait's for almost twelve minutes and the boy busts through the door and out to the Street yelling 'murder, murder'. A few people ran over and Lewis still was in the house and I, .. I, made sure his horse was tethered and got out quick. Wilkes, I swear it was after ten minutes, I swear."

"Davey, I told you to stop sniveling. Is that all? Did you hear anything about Atzerdrodt? About the Vice-President?

"Wilkes, Nary a thing! I was too busy trying to get over the bridge. I didn't get more than a few streets when I saw a man on a horse shouting my name. I think it was Fletcher the stable manager looking for me to return the roan. I had the horse out after I was s'posed to. I dug 'em in and skedaddled to the Navy Bridge in kinda round about way."

Well, what of the mis-adventures of Lewis Paine and George Atzerdrot? My information comes from the eye witness testimony at the military trial I had previously researched.

Atzerdrot left Paine's room after the meeting at the Herndon House still overcome by fear. Picked to murder the Vice President at Kirkland House, he got as far as the Saloon in the Hotel and after two whiskies, staggered out the door. He threw away his Bowie knife and wandered about for a place to swallow him up. Returning his horse to the stable, where he was questioned by Fletcher about Herold not bringing back his horse, he finally headed for a small, run down boarding house that provided drunks and the homeless with a cot for a few coins a night. He slept on a sofa until a cot was available and slept the night away. The only man in Washington that could have given the Police the time and place of the assassination had no trouble falling asleep. The next day, after pawning his pistol for ten dollars, he walked to another flophouse he knew, easily traced by Police, and was captured without a struggle.

Paine had a different kind of odyssey. When he left Seward's home off Lafayette Park, he ran like a wild bull through a small crowd in front of the mansion, waving a bloody knife and screaming he was a lunatic. Escaping on his one eyed bay horse, he vanished. Paine was an experienced soldier and member of Mosby's raiders who foraged off the land. He was often involved in hiding from Union troops, invisible for days. One of his aliases in the recent past was that of a Baptist preacher and he carried it off well. He could read and write, in spite of what he told his interrogators, and was not the "half wit" depicted by Carl Sandburg in his life of Lincoln. It took three days to capture Lewis and that was by sheer coincidence. When he showed up in the wee hours of April 17th at the Surratt house, his appearance was not that of a starved wanderer who had slept in trees and open fields as his testimony avers. He used what he had to disguise his well made clothes, pulling one trouser leg up and making his undershirt into a cap in an attempt to look like a laborer. The attempted disguise was complete to an old pick axe he found, propped over his shoulder.

I believe his overriding priority was the safety of Mary Surratt. By the night of April 17th, the Police and the Army had information provided by Louis Weichmann, the H Street boarder. He helped to place Booth, Atzerdrot, Herold and a man named Paine, at the Mary Surratt House to plot the conspiracy. Lloyd, the rummy who owned Surrattsville tavern, also implicated

Mary Surratt. Lloyd told the interrogator about Mary's active role in the supply drop for Booth.

At three in the morning of the 17th, Army officers and Metropolitan Police swooped into the Surratt house and arrested everyone in sight. They had made a similar raid the night of the assassination but after searching and questioning, took no prisoners. Lewis Paine, unseen for three days, knocked on the door of Mary's house just as this second raid was taking place, a rather unfortunate coincidence. He attempted to disguise himself as a laborer, complete to a makeshift stocking cap and pickaxe. His first words were: "I guess I am mistaken." He surely was.

When asked what was his business in this house he told the Police that Mary had hired him to dig a gutter. He said that when he saw lights on in the parlor he came in to ask Mary what time he should start work. Posing as indigent, the idea was to sleep on the porch. Asked to identify this intruder, Mrs. Surratt knew quite well that a mention of his name would mean the immediate arrest of her lover. Her reply: "Before God, sir, I do not know this poor man, nor have I asked him to dig a gutter."

Lewis had not disguised his face and was standing no more than a few feet away. Poor eyesight was Mary's defense at the trial when pressed on this apparent lie. Paine's story and his bizarre appearance was enough to have him booked on suspicion.

The Metropolitan Police and Army Intelligence in 1865 had a relationship that was not unlike the FBI and the local Police in our own time. It took many hours before enough information was shared by them to realize they had captured a key conspirator, a man identified as the predator who attempted to murder the Secretary of State.

Each bumbling department fell over themselves in an attempt to get the most credit for their brilliant capture of Paine. Finally the order came from Stanton to turn Paine over to a Military Prison to await trial. The War Secretary had suspended the legal niceties.

Every one in that house, including the teen age Anna Surratt and a friend, were packed off to prison. There was not even a reprieve for Wiechmann, the self serving informer, who had answered the door in his nightgown. His summary arrest was in spite of the information he had provided the authorities. Anna, her girlfriend and Weichmann were all eventually released but Mary, Lewis and Atzerdrot remained in an Army prison.

The night and wee hours of April 14th had turned clear and had the cold bite of mid spring. The ride to Surrattsvile by these unlikely companions, Booth and Herold, continued at a controlled canter. Their destination was about two hours away. Booth's leg was causing him pain that he could no longer stoically hide. Herold fussed over him when they paused to rest and attempted to stuff his blanket under the leg to buffer the jolting. Booth, pale and anguished, struck at him in anger. Any small movement was difficult to bear for Wilkes but when

Herold whined like a chastised puppy, Booth relented enough to apologize.

The village was dark and deserted, the Tavern locked tight when the two horsemen moved down the silent, unpaved street. Herold banged on the door with the butt of his Bowie knife until a lantern was lit and older man in a nightgown, after getting a shouted identification from Herold, opened the door. Word had not yet reached Lloyd, the owner, of the death of Lincoln. The staggering man was falling down drunk and Herold looked at Booth with dismay as he moved inside. The actor wanted brandy and David came out instead with a bottle of whiskey. The Tavern's liquor list was not too extensive. Ashen and in obvious pain, Booth drank deeply from the whiskey, coughed and said to Herold: "Get inside and get the goods stashed by John Surratt and yourself. Mary told me Lloyd is not to be trusted. Just get the goods and tell him as little as possible. He knows my name but we have never met."

I moved into the Tavern with David Herold and watched as he moved up the stairs with a stumbling Lloyd to a small unfinished room that was part of the attic. Herold pulled down two carbines and two more pistols from a space in the rafters along with a small wooden box that was probably ammunition. He asked if Mrs. Surratt had left another parcel for them that afternoon. Lloyd mumbled that he had gone fishing but his sister in law, Mrs. Offutt, had seen Mrs. Surratt, received the parcel and left it in the living room.

David scooped up everything and underpaid an annoyed Lloyd for the first bottle and one more for the road. Booth looked at all the goods and made a quick decision to give back one carbine as he could not, handicapped by the leg, handle the added firearm. He told Herold to tell Lloyd that John Surratt would pick up the carbine at a later date. At this point, as Herold turned to walk in to the tavern, I went with him to check on the closing conversation. Lloyd testified at the conspirator's military trial that Booth had told the tavern keeper that he had shot Lincoln and Herold had murdered Seward. In the ten minutes or so that the two men stopped at the tavern, Booth never spoke to Lloyd. The testimony was a lie. I had also followed Herold and Lloyd as the two men retrieved the weapons and field glass parcel. Davey obeyed Booth's order to discuss nothing of importance with Lloyd and got out quickly.

The horsemen sat quietly and Booth took the Army field glasses from the parcel along with a map of the surrounding roads. In the light from the open tavern door, framed by a besotted Lloyd, they looked over the map and trotted out of hearing distance. Herold had spent some weeks, sometimes with Atzerdrodt, going over the route south to Port Tobacco from Surrattsville. They had emptied many a glass at the tavern and Lloyd knew them both but had never met Booth. On a freight scow commandeered by Atzerdrodt, the plan was a night crossing to a friendly Virginia welcome. If Atzerdrodt did not make it, they would buy their way across.

The broken leg had added a new dimension to the escape plans and Booth was determined to seek out medical help. A detour to a Doctor he knew would take them many miles to the southeast but if he was to make Port Royal the leg would have to be set. His word was law and Davey, not yet the age to shave, readily agreed. It was about one o'clock when they started out and still, no signs of a pursuit. Stanton did not organize a pursuit for Booth until sunrise of the next day. For tonight, they were safe.

The trip was a painful grind for Booth. Aside from the broken leg, his back was beginning to hurt. Any pace faster than a slow trot would make him grimace with pain and the two men stopped often to rest. I felt that the ten foot drop to the stage of Ford's Theatre and landing heavily enough to break his leg, might have hurt his spine. At any rate his general condition showed steady deterioration.

My feelings at this time were not mixed. I had spent a day with Lincoln, a man I had revered ever since I could read. A man who deserved every tribute and accolade that his countrymen could give him. This man, this posturing actor, had taken his life without remorse. Booth had personal courage and an iron will but he deserved a fame only achieved by the men most reviled in the history of our country. I felt no sympathy for his wretched plight.

At the last stop, checking a signpost that read "Bryantown", the two horsemen went off the road into a small clearing. Herold helped Booth off the mare and they spread a blanket. It was not to rest. The actor took out his makeup kit and proceeded to disguise himself with a black beard sprinkled with gray. He powdered his own hair to match over the ears and fixed his slouch hat back on his head. The man applied the tricks of his craft with practiced expertise. Adding some age lines with wax crayons, the young actor could have played "King Lear". In the trials and testimony that followed, Dr. Samuel Mudd was treated with incredulity when he testified that he did not know the man who came to his door. To my knowledge, no historian has pointed out that the expert knowledge of an actor's stock in trade was used in this disguise. When he finished applying the makeup, the old man that climbed laboriously back into the saddle with the help of Herold was not, even to my eye, John Wilkes Booth.

Booth then explained to his young companion that he had met with Mudd many times.

He had been introduced to the Doctor by John Surratt, who portrayed Mudd as a rebel sympathizer. Wilkes had carefully tried to bring Mudd into the plot to kidnap Lincoln by bogus plans to have the Doctor profit from real estate and oil speculation. When he approached the possibility of Mudd's aid in sheltering his band of men, having with them "a captive that would turn the South's defeat into a victory..", Mudd backed off: "as if I had scalded his hands with boiling water." Booth continued: "I was calm and did not let him see my inner feelings but from that moment on I did not trust this man and will not now let him know my identity." Herold, ever anxious to flatter Booth, exclaimed that his disguise would fool anyone.

"Not completely, Davey, Mudd is not a fool and I cannot disguise my eyes. My effort to keep them narrow and heavy lidded might suffice, it will have to. I shall approach it as any important role I have played. God, if only I had my strength back again."

Upset for showing a weakness to Herold, he ordered an immediate departure. It was about four in the morning when a neatly lettered sign on a white picket fence was visible in the bright moonlight. The sign identified the house and farm of Dr. Samuel Mudd. The two men had traveled the eighteen miles from Surrattsvile in about three hours and were both exhausted. Booth, in obvious pain, spoke to his trusting admirer:

"David, I expect you to carry this off without a hitch. Mudd will be questioned about this interlude. When the news reaches him of the death of Lincoln, and he knows his patient was Wilkes Booth, he will betray us. If we can carry this deception off and get away at dawn, we can get to the Virginia shore unimpeded."

I was not sure if Herold knew what "unimpeded" meant, but he vigorously asserted his readiness. My own feelings were that Booth's egomania was taking over his thinking process. He was playing a role of deception that, given the nature of a medical examination, would eventually be discovered. Booth gave a few more instructions: "Tell him we are two strangers riding to Washington. When he wants to know why we stopped, tell him my horse reared and I fell hard. We think the leg is broken. When we are inside, try not to show how clever you are and don't talk too much. In case he will recognize my voice, I will say little or nothing. If asked, I shall be a 'Mr. Tyler' and your name will be 'Henston'. Remember, damn it, and be careful in what you say."

After nodding in vigorous assent to everything Booth said, Herold went to the Doctor's front door and knocked sharply, accompanied by the frenzied barking of a large dog trying to leap Mudd's stable fence to protect his turf. It took a lot more banging before a flickering candle showed through the front windows and a red headed man with a beard answered the door in a nightgown and slippers. Davey was true to the script and after explaining why they stopped, Doctor Mudd moved across the yard with Herold to the man on the bay horse.

In Mudd's testimony about this incident, he refers to Booth as the silent one. He most certainly was. Mudd helped the actor off his horse and gave him support as Booth stifling a cry of pain, hip-hopped into the house. The Doctor motioned him to sit and Booth sank into a large sofa. Mudd brought over a large lantern and manipulated the leg with the boot still on. Booth's reaction was a jerk and moan of pain as the Doctor reached a spot a few inches above the ankle. Mrs. Mudd had come the head of the stairs and asked what the trouble was. The Doctor told her about a traveler with a broken leg and kneeled again to examine his patient, saying: "I don't think it is wise for you to continue. We shall have to go upstairs and treat your leg."

Booth had wrapped a shawl around his neck and chin in a house that was warm. I was looking at Mudd's reactions and I felt a certain wariness in his body language. He looked back and forth to Herold who had not left Booth's side and the two of them helped the injured man up the stairs. The three men moved to a small bedroom with two beds. The boy helped Booth, flinching from pain, to lie down one of the beds. Ever aware of his disguise, the actor made sure his muffler did not slip. Herold, with his usual blank expression, stood nearby. Mudd tried to pull the boot off and the pain was such that Booth finally spoke, asking the Doctor to hurry, saying that he wanted to continue on to consult his own Doctor in Washington. Complaining about pain was not supposed to be the image of a southern gentleman, even to an audience of two.

I watched Mudd's reactions during the examination and he was all business, focused on his patient. The treating of a patient with a broken leg required some movement from the prone and muffled Booth. At one point the sleeve and cuff of Booth's shirt slipped upward on his left arm as he steadied himself while sitting up. Revealed were the scrawled initials of J.W.B. that he had written in indelible india ink as a youthful prank to impress his sister. If Mudd had made a mental note of that possible clue to his patient's true identity, he did not have an outward reaction. When the Doctor left the room for a moment to get a needed instrument, neither Herold nor Booth noticed the oversight. The actor was in pain, trying to hide his discomfort, while Herold was in his usual unobservant mode.

Mudd returned with a pair of steel surgical scissors and proceeded to snip the instep of the actor's left boot and cut directly up, peeling the sides of the boot down. Observing and marveling at the expert medical attention given to Seward and Lincoln, considering the limitations of diagnostic tools and modern drugs, I admired the same efficient professionalism in Mudd's treatment of Booth.

The Doctor was able to remove boot and sock without causing undue pain to his patient, disclosing an ugly purple swelling above the ankle. After determining the extent of Booth's injury he told his patient that it was a simple fracture of the bone that did not involve any other bones and had not shifted apart. Mudd's prognosis was that with the aid of a splint the bone should heal without incident and that Booth should see his own Doctor for a plaster cast as soon as it was possible. The Doctor then fashioned a serviceable splint from heavy pasteboard he cut to size. Booth did not cry out as the bone was set and Mudd firmly bound the splint with bandages.

Wilkes spoke again about severe back pain and the Doctor, after briefly examining the painful area, said it was not serious and probably caused by the fall from the horse. He suggested treatment with hot baths. After advising bed rest Mudd did not hesitate to tell Booth he could stay where he was and rest the night. Booth thanked the Doctor and lay back exhausted. Mudd had previously assured 'Mr. Tyson' that his horses would be taken care of and went downstairs to get a servant to attend to it.

Herold, Sancho Panza to Booth's Don Quixote, stayed faithfully at his master's side. The boy seemed a bit surprised Booth had decided to stay and rest, increasing the risk of capture. Booth's explanation was that a day of rest would give him the strength to make a difficult journey. His last comment to Herold before falling asleep was for Davey to borrow a razor in the morning. The idea was to cut off his mustache in case wanted posters with his likeness were being circulated in Maryland.

When Mudd returned he asked Herold to join him at breakfast as he and his wife were early risers and not much was left of the night. I felt that the Doctor's hospitality was really an attempt to pump some information out of Davey about his strange patient. Doctor Mudd got more than he bargained for in an endless stream of nonsense from Herold. Davey used the names of "Tyson" for Booth and "Henson" for himself. Close but not exactly the names Booth had wanted. Doctor Mudd, by the end of the meal served by his wife, was impatient to go to the fields with his farm workers and lay out the day's work. As Mudd excused himself, Herold asked Mudd if he could borrow a razor. The Doctor then answered:

"Young man, I see little signs of a beard on your cheeks, why do you need a razor?"

"Well sir, Mr. Tyson needs the razor to shave off his mustache. It will make him feel better. "

"Really, Hmm..I shall bring a razor to your room before I leave. Perhaps I can find an old slipper to replace the sliced left boot."

Herold, blithely unaware of Mudd's suspicions, thanked him for his kindness and moved upstairs to the small bedroom where Booth was deep in sleep.

Doctor Mudd, at the military trial, testified that this request seemed to him to be suspicious. He felt that a man, in a stranger's house, would not normally cut off a well nourished mustache or beard and that from this point on he felt that his patient was not the man he represented himself to be. I was there and certainly the Doctor reacted as a suspicious man would react. I was convinced that he was not aware, at this point, that he was harboring John Wilkes Booth. The accomplished actor had played a convincing charade. I followed Mudd as he moved to his own bedroom where his wife was fixing the rumpled bed:

"My dear, I want you to keep a sharp eye on our guests and report anything out of the ordinary when I come back in for lunch. I am beginning to have doubts about them."

"Samuel, do you think I am safe while you are gone?"

"Oh, yes, the boy is superficial and quite harmless. Mr. Tyson, whoever he is, seems like a gentleman and in any rate has been rendered equally harmless by his injury. Please tell Best (the white English carpenter) to make him a pair of serviceable crutches, he will need them. They have not slept all night and will probably not awake till the afternoon."

Mudd took a boxed straight razor out of a dresser drawer and left it with Herold as he moved downstairs. Davey, bone tired, pulled the drapes together and stretched out on the other bed alongside the silent Booth. He fell asleep at once.

The two men, Herold first, awakened early in the afternoon. Davey helped Booth out of bed and brought him hot water from the kitchen stove for shaving. The actor had taken off his false beard but did not look very well. Always pale, he now looked pasty. His eyes reflected his pain and moving about was still difficult. Best had dropped off the rough hewn crutches that Mrs. Mudd had left in the room when they were both asleep. Booth was able to use them for support and was pleased with the result. While Booth was shaving, he directed Herold to take the chamber pots out behind the stable, empty them and wash them clean at the well.

The Southern countryside, in the Civil War era, had not changed very much in the way of household amenities. The rich and the middle class of the South all had house slaves as well as farm hands. Unpleasantries did not push plumbing advances as long as someone else could do the dirty work.

Booth, mindful of his disguise, did not want a servant in the room. Removing the mustache did make a difference in his appearance. His face looked thin and a good deal younger. Even a close friend might do a double-take. Since the full mustache was his trade mark in the theatre, Booth knew it would be pictured on every wanted poster.

When Herold returned from his chores he said that Mrs. Mudd had prepared a cold lunch and they were welcome. Wilkes put back the false beard flecked with gray and aged his face. Having a proper mirror made the disguise quite effective. He said very little at the table but Herold made up for it with silly stories that did not impress Mrs. Mudd or an uninterested Booth, who seemed deep in thought and said little.

They sat on the porch after lunch and quietly discussed the necessity to move quickly.

News of the assassination would certainly be widespread this close to the Capitol. Staying any longer would be dangerous. It was agreed that Herold would ask Mudd about the possibility of purchasing a carriage. Booth could use his horse in this manner and could rest his leg. This man was running for his life, hampered by a broken leg and counting only on the village fool for logistical support. His unflagging bravado was beginning to be chipped away by the circumstances but the enormity of his crime was not a factor. He was far more interested in his "hero's welcome" from a southern citizenry who, from my observation, were happy that the war was finally over and did not wish to be drawn back into the conflict.

During the time the two men were on the porch, Mrs. Mudd used the interim to clean the room Booth and Herold had slept in. She found the sliced boot that Dr. Mudd had removed from Booth's left leg. It had been tossed in the room closet by the Doctor the night before. She examined the boot and found an inscription etched into the inside leather of the top. "J. Wilkes" stood out clearly and the woman became immediately distraught. Hoof beats sounded in the driveway and she went quickly down the stairs to her husband. Doctor Mudd greeted the two men on the porch, Booth still wrapped in his shawl, and made an inquiry as to his rest during a cursory examination of the splint.

Booth still spoke to Mudd in monosyllables while Mudd, with the "hmm's" and "ah's" that are still part of a Doctor's vocabulary, pronounced him fit to travel at an easy gait to Washington to see his own physician. Herold then piped up in a prearranged script to thank the Doctor for his kindness and settle their accounts. When payment was made of twenty five dollars, Davey asked about the possibility of purchasing a carriage for the convenience of "Mr. Tyson". Mudd said he would inquire and left at the calling of his name by his wife, inside the house. Booth and Herold were unperturbed.

The couple went upstairs together. I hurried along with them to hear what was said:

"Samuel, I must show you what I have discovered." Her husband blanched and followed her into their bedroom, shutting the door behind them. After she showed him the name etched in the boot, the Doctor sat heavily on the bed and sealed his fate with the decisions he made that afternoon:

"When I was in the south acreage with the field hands, our neighbor stopped in his carriage from a trip to Bryantown. He asked if I had heard the news of the assassination of Lincoln in Ford's Theatre. I was stunned, as speechless as you are this moment, but you will be further stunned to know that army patrols as well as metropolitan police are looking for the suspected killer. Along with the name of John Surratt, was the name of John Wilkes Booth. Both men have been guests under this roof in the past and I will now be suspected of aiding the murderer in his escape from justice or being part of the plot. How can I not be implicated? Would anybody believe I did not penetrate his disguise? I did not worry you with the suspicions I had when I spotted a J.W.B written on his wrist. I knew of his former scheme to kidnap the President but did not know what shocking crime he was running from. I felt if he would only leave us I could wash my hands of him."

Mrs. Mudd, shocked and distraught as she was, demonstrated a more level head than her husband: "Samuel, your duty is clear. Whatever your sympathies with the Confederacy this act of barbarism will and must be paid for. You must get on your horse and notify the army post in Bryantown of your suspicions. If you do that you will be held blameless."

Mudd looked grim and unyielding as he replied: "There is more to this story, my dear, than the betrayal of Booth. Secretary Seward might be dead from an attack by a member of Booth's unholy group, a member who is still at large. They say that Andrew Johnson narrowly escaped death at the hands of another conspirator who has not been captured. If I betray Booth our lives are not worth a tinker's dam. He has desperate followers that will take vengeance. Let them be gone and when questioned we shall claim a Doctor's duty to treat a stranger who came to the door, a stranger not recognized because of a disguise. How can we be faulted? How can we be part of a plot with a man who never would have come to my door if he had not been injured?"

"It is wrong, Samuel, regardless of our safety. It is wrong! If we do not turn him in we shall be damned as well!"

"You will do as I say. My first responsibility is the safety of my family and I shall take care of my responsibility."

At her continued protestations he slammed his fist on the dresser and shouted: "Enough!" Mudd never wavered and stayed with his weak and confused story right through the military trial, two months later. The trial judge would save the Doctor from the gallows but would sentence him instead with life at hard labor.

The Doctor and Herold mounted up to make a halfhearted search for a carriage or wagon that could be bought in the neighborhood. Mudd, afraid to get anyone else involved that could testify to his actions in helping the fugitives, returned with Herold to his farm within the hour, empty-handed. Booth, nervous and impatient with the light starting to fade in the late afternoon, was on the porch rocking chair with his saddle bags packed beside him. He was still using his riding scarf to cover the lower part of his face. Not trusting Mudd, Booth asked for directions in the opposite of his intended destination and in spite of his infirmity, insisted on moving out quickly on horseback.

The two fugitives really planned to go southwest and ferry to the Virginia countryside by way of Port Royal or Port Tobacco to get out of Maryland. Carrying out his own charade, the Doctor mounted his horse and offered to lead the two men to a short cut north and west. The boy strapped the crutches to the bay mare and gingerly helped Booth astride. The two men followed Mudd at a slow trot into the woods of the Zekiah swamp. It was dusk on Saturday, the 15th of April, 1865.

The Doctor led the two men to a clearing beside a pond wreathed by tall weeds. The path was beaten down on both sides of the pond. Mudd pointed out the route north and made his goodbyes. Booth, always the gentleman, spoke in the firm, deep theatrical voice that he allowed Mudd to hear for the first time. Having met Doctor Mudd several times in the recent past, it was clear that Booth wanted the humorless man to know exactly who he was. An act of bravado or a way to implicate Mudd? Perhaps it was a bit of both as he quieted the mare and said:

"Doctor Mudd, we may never see each other again and I am grateful for this opportunity to thank you for your help at a time of great distress for David and myself. Adieu!"

This was said with his old panache, doffing his slouch hat with a wave like D'Artangnan in the "Three Musketeers". Mudd never blinked an eye or said a word as he wheeled the horse and took the path back. He never reported this short conversation to anyone and was never questioned in detail about it but I am sure that if he had any doubts about who his patient was, those doubts were fully resolved.

Chapter 9
Useless, Useless

The two horsemen sat quietly without moving as Booth removed his false beard and instructed Herold to take out the maps of the country in order to get to the next stop on his odyssey. During the months prior to the assassination, Herold and Atzerdrot were Booth's advance scouts in this area. Aside from making crude maps, they also picked up a good deal of information about those citizens in the area most loyal to the Confederacy. One of these citizens was Samuel Cox, a wealthy slave owner who owned a large tract of farming land about twelve miles through the woods and swampland southwest of Bryantown. The information, gleaned from many fleeing Confederate soldiers who refused to surrender, was that Cox was an unreconstructed zealot who never turned a compatriot from his door.

Booth and Herold turned the horses in the opposite direction that Mudd had indicated and in a leisurely trot followed the path into the woods. In spite of Wilkes' pocket compass, it did not turn out as planned. Nightfall was almost upon them and the path would suddenly fork in odd directions and then disappear into a swamp. Within an hour they were hopelessly lost. Just as David began to blubber in fear a shadowy figure leading a donkey with a rope was moving down the path in their direction. An old black man dressed in tatters, had two full bags of what looked like potatoes draped across the donkeys back. He put his head down as he moved by the two mounted men.

Booth did not let the chance meeting slip by: "Hello there, boy, we want to talk to you."

This particular boy, a frightened old man, stopped but was still silent.

"We mean you no harm and are in need of your services as a guide."

The man protested that he had to return to his old woman with the potatoes and had no time for such business. He spoke in a thick southern drawl almost undecipherable to me but not to Booth, who grew up as a boy with the children of his father's slaves.

Booth persisted: "We are dead lost in these woods and wish to go to the farm of Samuel Cox. I shall pay you well for helping us."

With the absence of threats or show of firearms by the two men, the old man seemed a little more at ease: "How much is you gwine to pay me?" When Booth said that he would give him five dollars, the deal was quickly consummated. Wilkes brightened up and Herold stopped whining as the actor gave his guide the money up front. The old farm hand gave his name as "Ozzie Swann" and said he knew the Cox farm well. Ozzie, startled and pleased by the good fortune that had fallen his way, asked no questions as to who his companions were but I could see his eyes flitting to Booth's bad leg and the carbine sticking out of Herold's gun sling. The two horsemen did not volunteer any information, making the procession a silent one.

It was necessary to backtrack a half mile to a fork in the path the fugitives had misjudged and the party, with Ozzie walking in the lead hanging on to his donkey, finally but slowly moved through the maze of now deeply darkened trails with assurance. Night in the forest was not silent. The rustling of small animals, the hoot of owls and sounds of nocturnal birds were mixed with an occasional glimpse of doe and fawn. It took until the skies began to lighten in the foggy, eerie confines of the forest, before the party arrived at the Cox residence. The house was much larger than the home of Samuel Mudd, but not quite a Tara like plantation. After sincere and grateful thanks by an exhausted Booth, Ozzie turned around and in a moment was swallowed by the thick foliage.

Rather than bang on the front door and awaken the household, Booth and Herold sat quietly upon their horses until the house began to stir with the early activities of a farm on a spring morning. Herold again dismounted and did the knocking, greeted by a young man, already fully dressed. On the trails, Booth had prepped Herold as to the integrity of Cox and the need to finally confide in the people that would help in his escape. It was a risky decision but he was running out of options.

The young man at the door, I learned later on, was the son of Samuel Cox and he led Herold to his father, just sitting down to breakfast. Davey told Cox that he and his companion were fleeing from Union Army patrols and needed shelter. He would leave the details of their flight up to the man on the horse with a broken leg. Cox, who must have known of the assassination of the President did not hesitate to tell Herold to bring his friend inside for some breakfast and see if he could help them. Cox was a fiery secessionist and was consistent with his vow to help anyone in the same cause who came to his door. When Booth showed Cox his initials on his wrist and told his story there was, however, a backing away from hiding the men in his home. The risk was too great for his family but he would do all he could to help the fugitives across the river into Virginia. Wilkes, after the trials of the last two days, was relived he was being helped and did not display any rancor.

After breakfast the two men were provisioned, the horses were tended to and led by the Cox foreman, they moved a mile to camp out as best they could in a secluded grove of trees off the main path. Cox had told Booth he would notify his foster brother, Thomas Jones, a man he fully trusted, to take care of them with daily provisions, blankets and what transportation they would need to get them across to Port Royal.

On this obscure cove near the main river, Booth and Herold existed as best they could through six days of mixed weather that left the ground damp and cold. Jones brought food every day and kept saying it was too dangerous to cross. The condition of both men steadily deteriorated. Booth was feverish and disheveled, his leg painful. Herold could move a lot more freely and was in better physical condition. I might say that his devotion to Booth was stronger than his fears.

In the chill nights, he huddled close to his idol to give him warmth. During the day he encouraged the actor to eat and supported him when a toilet trip to the bushes was necessary. On Jones' strong advice they did not make a fire for warmth or cooking.

Fire or smoke could have been spotted by the Army patrols that were combing the countryside for the two men.

Booth sank deeper into melancholy each day, reading the newspapers that Jones brought and reacting with increasing despair. He read with particular anguish that Robert E. Lee, the unquestioned hero of the South, had told a reporter that Lincoln's death would be a great loss to a defeated Confederacy. Lee expressed the belief that the men now in the principal seats of power in the federal government would be far more unforgiving. How right he turned out to be. Booth's first reaction was disbelief but when he saw this view supported by many Confederate leaders, he became silent and morose. Nothing Davey could do would cheer him up as the days dragged on.

After a particularly close call when an Army troop decided to stop and rest only a few hundred feet from their hiding place, Booth speculated that the horses might give away their position by a whinny at the wrong moment. A few hours later, when all was quiet, Davey took the two unsuspecting animals several hundred yards down the river side. The tears streaming down his face, the boy shot them both. He had a difficult time with the second horse, tethered to a tree. The shining mare, who could run like the wind, reared and kicked at the sound of the first shot that killed the roan. He took a few minutes to calm the bay before he shot again. Davey walked back to the clearing, angry and morose.

Thomas Jones was true to the vow he had made to Samuel Cox. As he told the story to Booth, he was having a drink at the Brawner House in Port Tobacco, trying to learn what he could of the patrols sweeping the area and when it would be safe for the two fugitives to cross the Rappahannock to Port Royal. Sitting on the next stool was Captain William Williams of the Union Army. Looking directly at Jones, he said he would give 100,000 dollars to anyone who knew where Booth was hiding. Jones laconically replied: "such a tidy sum really ought to do the job if anyone knew the answer." Instead of commenting on his protector's integrity, Booth's remark was right in tune with the actor's ego:

"I should think a crime of this magnitude would bring far more of a reward from the federal government."

The next day, 21st, Jones overheard a conversation by a Union Calvary officer that chilled him. The officer had information that Booth had been seen in an area that was very close to his hiding place. Jones knew that the time for Booth to get to Virginia was at hand. For several days Jones had Cox's servant fish in the river near the hiding place. Each night the man secured his skiff in a patch of foliage that made good camouflage. It would be ready to take Booth and Herold that very night.

Booth mounted their guide's horse with Davey's help and the three men made their way to Jones' house. After stopping for more food it was a few hundred yards more to the river. Tom Jones and Davey pulled the boat from its hiding place and the two fugitives boarded the tiny vessel. Booth, always gracious, thanked Jones for the help he and Cox had provided in spite of the danger to themselves. Jones then outlined the escape route and listed people that could be trusted to provide a meal or temporary shelter. Booth, Herold and my ghostly presence moved away from the shore as Davey wielded the oars. The small figure of the loyal Jones receded in the twilight.

A strong tide on the river forced them to the shore for another cold, damp night. The crossing was at dusk of the following day. Scenes of rejection as well as compassion by southern loyalists were common the next few days. At war's end, they were feeling the heat of a outraged government who had mounted an intensive manhunt in the area for Herold and Booth. Ladies came out of their homes to provide a meal but did not provide shelter. A Doctor Stewart, on Jones' select list, refused to let him in the house. Booth's last night before finally crossing to Virginia was spent in the broken down shack of another black man who took him in. A free slave who worked for Stewart.

My memory of this dignified man, Bill Lucas, is sharp and clear. I wonder if Booth felt the irony of being helped by a second black man. People whom he had designated as farm animals during his lifetime gave him guidance and shelter without betrayal. The white southern loyalists, other than Cox and Jones, had turned him away.

Sitting on the floor, after giving Booth his only chair, the old man spoke in a measured and dignified manner:

"I don't knows who you is but I does know you is a'runnin'. Ize bin on dat skared run for my freedom. I git caught twice and dey brung me back for a whupping both times. You all can stay put and in de mornin' I'll hitch up the wagon and takes you to dat ferry at Port Conway. Dey will take you to Po't Royal on the Virginny side. I hopes you all will stop de runnin' some day."

I watched Booth closely and there might have been a welling of the eyes. With only a single candle for light, I was not sure. Booth and Herold shared their meager provisions with the old man who provided them with some home made cornmash booze that immediately lightened the gloomy mood. Or so I thought. The powerful "white lightning" also revealed the steady mental deterioration of the assassin. Booth ripped some blank pages from the notebook he wrote in every day and scribbled a short and very sarcastic note to Dr. Stewart regarding the man's lack of hospitality. I remember one sentence that says it all: "...I would not have turned a dog from my door in such a condition.." The actor, proud to the end, enclosed two dollars and fifty cents for the food the Stewart family had given them and rubbed in a quote from Macbeth about the manner in which a kindness is extended: "...the sauce in meat is ceremony, meeting were bare without it." He folded the letter carefully and asked Lucas to deliver it the next day.

The ex-slave was able to bring their maps up to date in a forty mile parameter before exhaustion and booze overtook them all. Sleeping on an old saddle blanket placed on the clapboard, uneven floor of the shack, Herold slept soundly but Booth restlessly moaned and twisted throughout the night. In the gray cool light of the morning Bill Lucas, who had slept in his chair, his white topped head on folded arms, was as good as his word. There were no troops or guards at the Port Conway ferry crossing and soon the small wooden scow took Booth and Herold on the way to the promised land. Lucas, who protested that he did not want it, was paid and thanked effusively. The bent old man stood on the shore as we moved slowly across the river.

The ferry took them to a scrubby spit of land that jutted out into the river and the two fugitives disembarked. Herold was like a frightened puppy and did little but whine. Booth remained calm but he was in bad shape after nine days without real shelter, the pain and stress taking a fearful toll. Unable to focus, he lay back against a tree trying to collect his thoughts. As he talked to Herold in a gloomy discourse about possible plans, he admitted that shooting the horses might have been a mistake weighing the risk at that time against the need for transportation now. Since Herold was mobile, and Booth still had funds, buying two horses in the countryside would have to be the first priority. Davey spread out the maps on which Bill Lucas had marked the location of the various homes in the Port Royal area that corresponded to the names on the loyalty list given to them by Jones. While studying the maps, they heard the sound of hoof beats and a trio of horsemen appeared, slowly approaching the docked wooden scow that served as a ferry. They turned out to be Confederate officers on the way home to nearby Caroline county ready to turn themselves in to a federal provost or parole officer. In disbanding the defeated troops, the federal government required a loyalty oath to the Union that had to be signed and notarized. Thousands of men were meandering home to take up the life they had left and most seemed to be fulfilling this requirement without rancor. This chance meeting, like the inexorable flow of a coastal tide, was to be another fateful step toward Booth's final destiny.

Herold, prompted by Booth, introduced himself as David Boyd and Booth as James W. Boyd. The latter name was an attempt to explain away the J.W.B. on his left wrist.

Herold explained that Booth had been wounded at Petersburg and because of an altercation with a Union patrol in which an officer was wounded, they needed a place to hide. Two horsemen introduced themselves as Lieutenants Bainbridge and Ruggles. The third as Captain Jett. What struck me at the time was that not one of them looked scarcely out of their teens. The rapid depletion of a decimated Confederate Army must have moved many such fine young men quickly into positions of responsibility.

The trio were quite friendly but not too forthcoming with help. Booth, fraught with anxiety and feeling the Union net closing in on him, had evidently made up his mind to stop being cautious. Within a few moments, the actor blurted out his real identity along with Herold's. The three men, who were fully aware of the manhunt the Union Army had mounted for the killers of Abraham Lincoln, were too stunned to speak. Jett, the Captain, agreed to do what he could to help them and urged Bainbridge and Ruggles to do the same. Booth told them he could no longer walk and had difficulty mounting a horse. He wanted shelter in a secluded house where he could recover his strength and find patriots in Virginia to help them escape. Booth told the officers that once in Canada he would have the means and aid from "certain sources" to take flight to England. The two other Confederates agreed that it was their duty to help this man. With that settled, Booth was lifted on Ruggles horse and the five men, with Ruggles and Herold on foot, boarded the ferry on the second leg to Port Royal.

The first stop after landing was the home of the Peyton sisters a few miles from the ferry landing. This was a time of formal manners and two unescorted ladies, though hospitable and friendly, would not have men in the house unchaperoned. Booth then sank into a silent lethargy, muttering to no one in particular that he would never be taken alive. Ruggles, on foot, led the procession to the next stop on the journey about three miles south and west on the road between Port Royal and Bowling Green. He was leading them to the farm of Richard Garrett who was high on Jones' loyalty list.

They all agreed that the secret of Booth and Herold's identities should be kept from the Garrett family. Richard Garrett had harbored many a passing soldier during the war and both of his own sons were Confederate veterans but the notoriety of Booth's deed and the punishment that would be meted out to a benefactor, made a request for concealment too much to ask and possibly too much for any man to give.

Ruggles, carrying the two crutches, was still leading his horse with Booth slouched on top as he and Jett moved to the front door of Garrett's family home. It was about three in the afternoon of Monday, April 24th,

1865. Herold and Bainbridge stayed at the fence gate. Jett knew Garrett as a friend of his father but had not seen him since childhood. The man who came to the door was of medium height and in his fifties. His black hair was graying and his features were lean with high cheekbones.

"Mr. Garrett, I suppose you hardly remember me".

"No sir, I surely do not."

"I am the son of your old friend from Westmoreland County."

"My gosh, how is your Dad, Is he still well?"

Jett, anxious to get to Bowling Green to see his girlfriend, a Miss Goldman no less, made short of the amenities and cut right to the chase:

"This is my friend, Mr. James W. Boyd, a Confederate soldier wounded at Petersburg.

He is trying to get to his home in Maryland. Can you take care of him for a day or two until his wound will permit him to travel?"

Mr. Garrett, with his pre-teen namesake Richard peeking around his legs, not only agreed but invited Jett and his other companions to join them for a rest and dinner. Jett was adamant but very polite as he declined the offer. His buddy Ruggles, with no romantic attachment to cause haste, seemed disappointed but said nothing.

Booth was helped from the horse by Jett and Ruggles and handed his crutches. Herold, who was to go with Bainbridge to a house of a friend nearby, looked on the verge of tears. As the actor hobbled up to the veranda, he turned for a moment and waved to his young, loyal companion, who biting his lip, waved back. The shallow boy had never left his mentor's side in the most trying of circumstances. In spite of my strong negative feelings for the fugitives, I felt a wave of pity for both.

The party broke up and went their separate ways as Booth sat down gingerly on a porch rocker and leaned back in relief. Garrett invited him in, but Booth, using his best Virginia manners, said he would rather rest for awhile and admire the magnificent grove of locust trees that surrounded the yard. The tired fugitive almost dozed off immediately but Garrett asked his curious young son to bring "Mr. Boyd" a cool glass of water and some pillows but not to disturb him further.

That night at a family dinner Booth had another audience that invigorated him. Garrett's two older sons had just returned from the Appomattox surrender and were in faded and torn uniforms, telling tales of raw combat that were stirring in detail. Booth was a central figure at the table, the pain in his leg forgotten, as he charmed the family with talk of all the cities he had traveled to. Afraid of his lack of military knowledge, he avoided talk of his fictional soldiering. At one point, in another sad indication of his increasing lack of caution, he asked one of the sons to exchange his uniform for the suit he was wearing:

"I am not going back to my home until all chance of the South's recovery is gone. I shall make my way to North Carolina and join Johnston's Army. I intend to stay a soldier and your battles are over. I shall have need for a uniform and you shall need a suit."

In spite of "Mr. Boyd's" logic the offer was declined. Garrett noted later that his suspicions were aroused by these remarks as I certainly thought they would be.

Booth, his black hair washed and bright in contrast to his fashionably pale features, had made one conquest, as he did with all women. The brown eyes of the boy's sister Annie, just in her teens, had never left his face. The oldest son, with Booth's arm slung across his shoulders, helped the actor up the stairs and to a small bedroom. It was nine o'clock and a working farm family retired early. The next morning Booth awakened to a nudge by the eleven year old Richard:

"Mr. Boyd, we are going have breakfast in a little while and my father asks you to join us." While speaking, the child's eyes grew wide at the gun belt hanging on the bedpost. It held two large revolvers and a Bowie knife. Booth did not seem to notice as he smiled at the boy and accepted the invitation. When the boy Richard Garrett became an old man, he still remembered his feeling that something was not right. All the soldiers he had seen were deeply tanned and weather-beaten, in contrast to this man's features. In an era when little boys were seen and not heard, he did not tell his father of his observations.

All morning the house guest lounged in the grass under the shade trees and played with the two young children. He showed them how the needle on his pocket compass would always point North as he moved it around. In the balmy, sun splashed orchard, Booth sitting with his back against a locust tree, it was easy for him to forget for a little while the dire peril he was in. His pale face took on a degree of color and his body regained some of the strength that had seeped away in the past week. He was able to use the crutches to get up and down unaided.

During lunch that afternoon, the two older Garrett brothers talked of the assassination of the President. They had both been to Bowling Green in the morning. The senior Garrett was not at all convinced the murder had happened at all. "Mr. Boyd" inquired about the man who did the deed and was told by Jack Garrett that he had not seen a poster but it was rumored to be the actor John Wilkes Booth or a man named John Surratt. I watched Booth carefully and the trained actor simply buttered his roll and asked how much of a reward was being offered. When told it was a hundred thousand dollars, the actor remarked that the reward, considering the "so called" crime, was not as much as he would have expected. Jack, with a laugh, said the man better not come this way for he would be sorely tempted to take the money. This time, in spite of his effort to remain impassive, "Mr. Boyd" remarked with some heat: "Would you betray him for that?"

"Mr. Boyd, I fought for my country honorably for three bloody years and haven't got a nickel to my name. I sure would give it a passing thought." When every one laughed around the table, the actor slipped back into his role and laughed along with them.

Booth was in his favorite chair on the veranda when Ruggles, Jett and Bainbridge pulled up on horseback to the front gate. Herold, who was snugly mounted behind Bainbridge, jumped off and hurried to see his mentor seated on the long porch. The news that Booth eagerly awaited was not good. Yankee mounted troops had landed at Port Royal and were moving toward Bowling Green, stopping to question each homeowner. Herold ran to Booth's room to bring down the gunbelt and saddlebags. The three horsemen galloped off toward Bowling Green as the two well armed fugitives moved into the woods behind the farmhouse, Booth hip-hopping on his crutches. Mr. Garrett and his older sons, who were working in the fields, and Mrs. Garrett, in the house, had missed this action but not the children. They excitedly told their father and brothers all about it when they came in at five o'clock. Annie said the man with Mr. Boyd was introduced to her as Mr. Harris. A few minutes later a troop of Yankee Calvary moved by at a gallop, raising a cloud of dust on the road to Bowling Green. I assumed they had been given information that pointed out Bowling Green as the destination for a passing party of four men. Herold, who was scouting the road from the woods, saw the troops rush by. The two men, Booth now fairly agile on crutches, made their way back to the house.

No matter what explanations they made for this behavior, I could see by the body language and faces of the Garrett family that the actor and his cohort had worn out their welcome. Such strange behavior was indicative of men being hunted. I do not believe that the possibility of either man being involved in the President's murder crossed their host's minds. I moved invisibly about and was in the yard during a conversation between the Garrett's. Jack and Mr. Garrett were afraid that their guests must be guerrillas, deserted from Mosby's raiders, that had committed a serious crime. It was decided that the men must leave the house tonight to protect the family. They should be quartered in the tobacco barn and must leave early in the morning. After dinner this evening they would discuss this frankly with Mr. Boyd and Mr. Harris. The senior Garrett was angry with Jett for using his father's reputation to bring in fugitives that were not merely soldiers but something quite more nefarious. He then told Jack and his brother to sleep in the corncrib and keep a sharp lookout on the tobacco barn.

Jack Garrett did the speaking that night at dinner and did not mince words. He was upset that the two men had not been truthful with the family and had endangered all of them including the children. No effort was made to question Booth and Herold about their situation.

Indeed, for the sake of their future safety, Jack made the comment that they did not want to know. Booth, to his credit, made the following reply:

"Mr. and Mrs. Garrett and family, some day you will know all the facts in this matter and my hope is that you will think more kindly of us. Without doubt, Mr. Harris and I will move tonight to the barn. We will take our belongings with us and be gone in the morning with the warm memories of a loyal Confederate family that took me in at my darkest hour."

That was said like the old Booth, like a soliloquy at the end of a play. His audience, however, was not greatly moved, with the possible exception of thirteen year old Annie. Booth then tried to buy two of the family's farm horses but was firmly turned down. Jack, probably more anxious to see "Boyd" leave than for any other reason, said he would arrange in the morning for a former slave who owned a horse and wagon, to carry them for hire to their next destination.

The tobacco barn, the first such structure I had seen, was a solidly built two story barn with large double doors on each side. The walls were not solid clapboard. Tobacco drying probably needed good air circulation and the side boards were separated by two inches on either side of each board. One side of the barn was being used for storage of furniture. Mr. Garrett, a spare, practical man, must have rented space to his neighbors. Dressers, wardrobes and side pieces were all covered loosely by hay.

Leaves of curing tobacco were hanging on tight ropes strung from side to side. A not unpleasant smell of hay and tobacco permeated the structure. Booth and Herold were armed with three pistols and the carbine picked up at Lloyd's Tavern. Wilkes was calm and determined. Herold, on the other hand was jumpy and obviously frightened.

They made makeshift beds out of piled hay and each used a saddle bag for a pillow.

Both ready to rest, Herold blew out the lantern Jack had given them. Darkness descended, with some moonlight filtering through the slatted walls.

The two men talked for a little while of their plans for the morning and beyond. Booth and Davey were going to take the hired wagon they were to use in the morning to Guinea railroad station and go North by rail to Boston. There he would make a contact with a Confederate agent that would take them into Canada for eventual escape to Europe, possibly to England or France. Herold brightened considerably as Booth outlined the scheme and with his fears soothed, dropped off to sleep. Booth too, after some restless moving around to ease the pain in his leg, slept as well.

Hearts racing, the two men sat bolt upright in the wee hours of the morning as the neighing of horses, shouts of men and the jangling of weaponry filled the night. I moved effortlessly through the walls of the barn and found the yard jammed with Union calvarymen. A burly

Colonel and young Lieutenant dismounted and moved to the front door. The Lieutenant pulled his pistol and used the butt as a hammer on the thick door, whacking it so hard it made gouge marks on the hardwood. It was enough to waken a hotel full of guests. Garret, his wife and younger children behind him, came to the door with lantern and nightshirt, trembling in the crisp cool night.

"My God, what is the commotion. what do you want?"

The Colonel, called Conger, wasted no time in pleasantries:

"You Rebel bastard, where are the two men that you have been hiding here today!?"

"I have been hiding no one Sir"

At this time Garrett's two older boys had rushed to the door from the corn crib, awakened by the din. Conger's face darkened as he turned to the Lieutenant:

"Let's waste no more time Baker, hang the old bastard to the top of one of those locust trees. Then we'll talk to the boys."

Mrs. Garrett and the children screamed with fear as Baker pulled a rope from the bridle of his horse.

"Well Garrett?" Garrett, shaking and stammering, made a frightened reply:

"They have run off to the woods. I don't know who they are or what they have done...they were sheltered here in an act of kindness to a wounded soldier!"

"Damn it you fool, we have Captain Jett with us right now! We know they are here! Baker, waste no more of our time with this bullshit, string him up!"

Baker yelled for one of the men to make a hangman's knot and began to tie up the elder Garrett to a chorus of screams by his family. Jack Garret broke the impasse:

"Hold it, for God's sake. I will show you where they are. They are locked in our tobacco shed."

Jack and his brother were convinced that "Boyd" and his companion might steal the horses during the night and locked the doors an hour after making sure the fugitives were asleep.

Garrett was not untied but taken to the yard still in his undershirt, shivering with cold and fear. The troop, on orders of Baker, surrounded the barn and Jack Garrett was instructed to go inside and disarm the two men.

Jack had been a brave soldier, but not a stupid one, replied: "Why would they listen to me, Lieutenant? I have no arms, why would they not shoot me?

"They are your buddies, Garrett, if you don't go in I'll shoot you where you stand and then send your brother in."

Jack did not answer and pulled out the axe handle that barred the way across the door pulls. Baker shouted to the men inside: "We are going to send in Jack Garrett, on whose premises you are, to get your arms and deliver yourselves to my command!"

Jack took a deep breath and stepped inside. I went with him.

Booth stood defiantly in the hay strewn center of the barn, a Bowie knife in his hand, leaning on one crutch. Herold stood to one side, unarmed and eyes welled with tears. The actor spoke before Jack could say a word:

"You cowardly bastard, you have betrayed me. Get out of here!"

"Boyd, the barn is surrounded by troops. There is no escape. For God's sake come out with your arms turned down. My father will be hung as a hostage!"

Herold blubbered at Booth: "Do it Wilkes, for God's sake do it.."

Wilkes reply was to reach for a pistol in the gun belt lying in the hay. Garrett ran to the door and begged to get out or he was a dead man. Baker, rather foolishly holding a lighted candle which made him a perfect target, allowed Jack to bolt through.

"He is desperate and determined to die. If I go in there again he will shoot me!"

The Colonel and Baker decided quickly to give Booth the option to come out with arms down or the barn would be burned to the ground. Baker shouted those terms to the men inside. Booth was enjoying his only moment on history's center stage. Determined to die, eyes bright in flickering candlelight, he made up the script as he went along:

"Well Captain" (Booth would never parley with a mere Lieutenant) "That is damned hard, to burn an innocent man's barn. I am lame. Are you afraid to fight? Draw up your men before the door and I will come out and fight the whole command."

The latter was said in deep theatrical tones and projected right to the rear seats.

Baker answered: "We did not come here to fight but to take you prisoners."

In the barn, Davey, almost speechless with fear, tugged on Booth's arm and begged him to surrender. On center stage he spoke to his audience again:

"Captain, there is a man here who wants very much to surrender. Go, you damned coward, I don't want you with me."

I then witnessed a poignant scene that will stay with me forever. Booth lifted Davey, now on his knees, and gave him a strong embrace before pushing him to the door.

Davey looked back at Booth with streaming tears and shouted to Baker to let him out.

Baker insisted he bring his arms and Davey insisted that Booth had them all. The actor then spoke his next line:

"Captain, the arms are mine and you will have to kill me for them. This man is not guilty of any crime."

The exasperated Colonel Conger then said with some heat:

"Let the damned prisoner out, Baker, and get ready to burn the barn."

Baker opened the door enough to let the shaking boy through and he was immediately tied to a tree for safekeeping.

Baker and many of his command were carrying lighted candles. Inside the barn, Booth shouted again:

"You are a brave man Captain and a perfect target in candlelight. I could have picked you off like a strutting pigeon but spared your life. Tell your family and they will pray for me."

With that remark, the abashed Lieutenant placed the candle on the ground a few feet away. Booth, wild eyed, may have had the illusion that he was really on a stage. He struck a theatrical pose with his free arm extended above his head and emoted:

"Well, my brave boys, you can prepare a stretcher for me!"

The Colonel then directed several men of the now dismounted troops, to fire the barn. They reached through the slats for hay and lighted the makeshift torches. Booth could see clearly as the inside of the barn lit up in the flickering yellow light. The men thrust the burning hay through the slat openings and the fire spread rapidly. The licks of flame spread upon the hay piled up on the stored furniture of Garret's neighbors and climbed the stairs quickly to the upper storage areas.

Booth was still not frightened and his voice was firm as he shouted:

"One more stain on the old banner!"

Baker then opened half the door and the resulting draft intensified the flames. Booth hip-hopped toward the door where Baker, backed by Colonel Conger and several armed soldiers, watched his every move. He had dropped the crutch and was carrying the carbine in one hand and a large pistol in the other. Neither weapon was raised to shoot but he had his fingers on the triggers. I was so focused on this ghastly scene that even though I knew it was coming, the blast of a pistol through the open slatted walls of the barn was terrifying. Booth went down like a cut down punching bag, rolling over on his side, a pool of blood from his neck staining the hay floor. I could swear there was a trace of that wry smile on his face. The heat of the fire was searing, the flames shooting into the second story and engulfing the barn. Baker and two men dragged Booth out to the yard as Davey Herold, tied to a tree, watched with horror as all his dreams came to an end.

I looked over Baker's shoulder as he emptied a canteen of water on Booth's face.

The Colonel and the Lieutenant began arguing about who fired the shot. Conger's first impression was that Booth had shot himself. Baker was adamant that the shot had come from one of his men. As the fire became an inferno, Booth was dragged again by his heels. Doherty, in technical charge of the men, said he would question the troops about the shooter. Strict orders had been given to take Booth alive. Within a few moments the Lieutenant brought Sergeant Corbett to the Colonel. Conger asked him in stern tones why he shot Booth and disobeyed orders. Corbett replied at stiff attention:

"Sir, the man was carrying a carbine and a-moving t'wards the open door. He coulda kilt you and the Lieutenant. I did my duty and God guided my hand".

The Colonel said nothing more as Corbett was led away. The sharpshooter was later absolved of all guilt by the Secretary of War, Edwin Stanton.

Booth had been shot as Lincoln was shot, from the left rear. Struck in left side of the neckline, the bullet must have severed his spine as he was paralyzed from the waist down. The exit wound was on the opposite side. The wound was as mortal as the President's and nearly in the same area. The actor's lips stirred and he forced out the words, melodramatic to the end:

"Tell mother...I died for my country."

The heat of the collapsing barn was so intense that Booth was moved to the house veranda. A Doctor Urquhart was summoned from Port Royal and speaking in the same somber tones that Lincoln's Doctors' had used, said there was no hope and little time left.

John Wilkes Booth revived once more and asked for his arms to be lifted. His last utterance as he looked at his flaccid hands was said with tears of despair:

"Useless. useless.."

Chapter 10
Treason

My presence, unseen and invisible, lingered on that front porch. A wagon was brought for the body of Booth, driven by a former slave that had stayed with the Garrett's as a field hand. The old man was shaking with fear, afraid to be near the body of a murderer. Patrick Garrett was hogtied and arrested, still in his nightshirt. His older sons were also taken along as prisoners as was a babbling David Herold, protesting his innocence. The Garretts, as I knew in hindsight they would be, were let go in a few days. Davey, the callow youth who worshiped his mentor Booth, was imprisoned to stand trial for conspiracy in the assassination of President Lincoln.

I did not follow. Shutting my eyes and ears to the bedlam, I focused on my next objective and when the sounds of the Calvary troop died away, I opened my eyes to a walk down the staircase of the White House just after the morning cabinet meeting had adjourned. It was the early afternoon of April 14th, 1865. I was following the stocky figure of the Secretary of War as he walked with his aides across the colonnaded front portico and down the steps to the walk below. Stanton paused for a moment and told one of his aides that he wished to refresh himself with a walk in Lafayette Park.

"Shall I send your driver to pick you up, Mr. Secretary?"

"No, no Dana, the day is bracing and the walk to the War Department is only a five minute one. I may also stop in to visit Secretary Seward to discuss the Cabinet proposals so don't tell anyone of the Generals I deserted my post for an hour."

Charles Dana, the Assistant Secretary of War, chuckled and walked with the group toward the drab old building on the right of the White House gardens. I followed Stanton as he crossed the wide avenue and moved into the park. He walked slowly along the cobblestone path, shaded by tall trees and graced by beautiful flowered shrubbery. In a short frock coat in dark brown, with matching vest and trousers, a white shirt and light tan silk cravat, the bewhiskered Stanton looked every inch the wise authority figure. The way he walked, hitting the rubber tip of his cane firmly on the pavement, with shoulders back and chest out, he reminded me of a bantam rooster spoiling for action.

The record showed a somewhat different picture of a man who could inexplicably do and say things that bordered on instability. One of his deep seated phobia was a pathological fear of death. In 1833 he was served

Daniel J. Weingrad

a meal in a boarding house by a pretty young girl who suddenly died of cholera that same evening. It was the practice to bury plague victims shortly after death. He went to the graveyard with a hired laborer later on that night to dig her up to convince himself she was dead. In 1841 his daughter died. She was a small child, carried away by sickness as were so many children. After her burial in a family plot, the child was then exhumed at Stanton's orders. The coffin was to remain in his bedroom for over two years. The same behavior took place after the death of his wife in 1844. He dressed her in her wedding gown and refused to have her buried for days. Aides and family finally forced the internment. As a witness to Stanton's power to command in a Cabinet meeting among his peers and the extraordinary performance in the Petersen house after the assassination, I was aware of the administrative ability of this man but his psychological pitfalls were clearly an area of apprehension.

I stayed with the Secretary as he bounced along to a secluded and shaded area in the right rear of the small park. An enclosed one horse shay with the shades drawn was a black presence in an otherwise bright afternoon. The quiet horse was jet black as well. There was no driver, the reins tethered tightly to a wrought iron hitching post, one of many about fifty yards apart. As Stanton neared the carriage, the door on curbside swung open and the Secretary moved inside. My presence moved in as well.

My first look at Thaddeus Stevens made me chuckle inwardly. Looking back, that was the last time I thought anything amusing about the man. He seemed to me the image of the mean Mr. Potter in the role that Lionel Barrymore made immortal in the classic movie "It's a Wonderful Life". Thaddeus had that same chilling countenance. Stevens had on the same black bowler hat, the high starched collar, black tie and black vested suit that Potter had worn. Sitting opposite Stanton, he was in his sixties, old for that era, with a face carved out of white marble. His black eyes were bright and piercing but it was his mouth that betrayed his character. It was a thin lipped slash across his face that seemed tight even when speaking. A photograph of Stevens by Matthew Brady, featured in American Heritage, has this heading: "The South, looking at this granite visage, stared into the face of its most implacable foe."

James Truslow Adams, the dean of American historians, said of Stevens: "...perhaps the most despicable, malevolent and morally deformed character who has ever risen to high power in America."

Stevens was the leader of the Republican Radicals in Congress, Lincoln's primary political opposition. His grasp on their leadership was absolute. Abruptly, he opened the conversation with Stanton without wasting time for polite amenities:

"Well Stanton, do you have news for me"?

In spite of my suspicions, to actually hear the facts, was shattering. The most powerful man in the Cabinet, the Secretary of War, calmly talking and listening to the most powerful man in Congress in a discussion of mind bending treason. Stanton started by giving a complete review of the historic Cabinet Meeting that morning. With every description of Lincoln's strong views on benevolence toward the defeated Confederacy, Steven's face darkened and his jaw muscles tightened. He never interrupted.

When Stanton was finished, there was a moment of silence in the dark confines of the buggy. Thaddeus Stevens, who couched his language in the flowery phrases of an orator, spoke as Satan must have spoken to Eve in the Garden of Eden:

"It is time Edwin, time to strike down the man who could destroy all we have sacrificed for in the last four bloody years. Lincoln was the right man, the only man to have led this country to a successful victory in this grisly conflict but is now poised to destroy the very things those men died for. That man must be gone! Only you and I, Edwin, stand at the breech to stop Lincoln from this monstrous crime. You, Stanton, are the right man and the only man to head our government and lead the nation on the path of righteousness. I may not live long enough to see the fruits of our labor but long enough, by the blessing of the Almighty, to see you President.

Johnson, the inebriate tailor who is Vice President, will be easy to handle and if not, easy to remove when the time comes. I do not mean by the bullet. I have enough votes in my pocket to impeach him. You will still be the

War Secretary and we can insure your Presidency over the weakling Seward, if alive, at the next nominating convention. If we hesitate, if we do not seize the moment, our battle will be lost."

Stanton did not reply but his tears dripped steadily on his beard.

Stevens, aroused, gave the Secretary a vicious tongue-lashing: "For God's sake Edwin, why are you blubbering? You give an impression of a man with nerves of steel. Did I pick the wrong man to lead our country!"

The Secretary's face reddened in anger at this allusion to perceived weakness:

"You know full well I have done my part. This morning I had to confront the President about taking Major Eckert to the theatre. The Major would have been the best of all bodyguards. Thaddeus, I cry as Abraham must have cried when he lifted the sacrificial knife to strike at his only son Isaac. He did not waver in his duty and I will not waver in mine! It is a hard choice to kill a man you have grown to respect despite his political views. Lincoln is such a man. America will not see his like again. Father Abraham must die so his children will live in peace for generations to come. I have not a single doubt as to the justness of our cause and I am not ashamed of my tears."

Stevens spoke with a trace of apology:

"Well Edwin, I am relieved and heartened by your words. We must now go over the details as my driver will be here in a half hour and you must be gone before that. Not a single crony of mine, no matter how close, knows of our financial support of Booth and our plans. The egotistical actor and the idiots he has surrounded himself with will make perfect sacrificial lambs. He thinks his money came from the Confederates through our own operatives posing as go betweens. Even our operatives think they are double agents working for the Union Army. You must see to it that the military conducts any trial that follows. You can then ensure the verdict. Booth must never live to stand trial. That should be relatively simple, you need no strategy from me. Grant will not attend Ford's Theatre tonight. Julia Grant took care of that, she hates Mary Lincoln. Grant also has the fearless bravery to stop Booth and the General's absence shows the hand of providence. The carpenter at the theatre has given our contact the details of preparation by Booth at Lincoln's box. He also believes his information is for the Confederates as a way to keep track of Booth's nerve. The actor may be playing a role within his fevered brain but by God, I am positive he has the stomach for it. Anything can happen but the odds are for success. One of Booth's men, the brute Paine, will go to the Seward House to kill Seward. The weak link, Atzerdrot, is assigned to Johnson. He is a drunken coward and will not succeed. It will be a perfect non-attempt. Johnson must stay alive if Seward lives as the Secretary of State will be next in line for President. Stanton, are you listening to me!?"

The Secretary had become distraught once again at the mention of an attempt to murder Seward. He could hardly get the words out:

"Not Seward, not the man I have nursed through a horrid accident. Not Seward."

Stevens again went on the offensive: "Edwin, Seward is a rubber-stamp of the President's policies and is a threat to be your opponent at the nominating convention as he was the chief threat at the Wigwam in Chicago to Lincoln's nomination. If he should be the nominee all our plans are for naught. We have nothing to do with Booth's choice of victims. He is a loose cannon that goes his own way. No more romantic kidnapping adventures! We must let Booth take the reins. Stanton, this is your acid test. You have not flinched in sending troops into blood baths that destroyed the flower of our nation's youth. A sick and wounded old man is but another casualty of that war." Stanton, no longer in tears and staring at his polished boots, pushed his glasses higher on his nose and sat back with a sigh.

"Edwin, our time is up. If my driver should see you with me, I must eliminate him and good coachmen are hard to get." Thaddeus cackled in morbid amusement looking carefully at Stanton and clapping him on the shoulder: "Go now and keep the faith."

Stanton did not say another word as he opened the door, stepped on the hanging iron step and descended to the cobblestone walk. His shoulder's bent and eyes down, the rubber tip of his cane did not rebound from the walk as it did when he started out. Nearing the War Department he paused for a moment at the start of the entrance path. As he squared his shoulders and composed himself, I knew he had finalized his position. Thaddeus Stevens and his own lust for power had clearly made up his mind.

D'Isreali said: "Patriotism is the last refuge of scoundrels" He was right on.

I had witnessed a bombshell. I could hardly believe what I heard and saw. My role was to observe, not to change history. I was the only witness to this astounding revelation of murder and treason. A witness That could not stop a shocking deed that would put the nation in mourning and effect events in our nation for a hundred years of civil strife. Taking a gesture from the perfidious man I followed. I mentally squared my shoulders and moved on.

The pace of work activity in the War Department picked up as the Secretary walked down the hall to his office. There was no doubt of who was in charge. Following in his wake I was struck by the difference in today's work climate. There was a total absence of females. In 1865, the Government was a man's world. All work staff right down to the file clerks, were male.

The end of the war left the country in a quagmire of logistical problems that had to be planned for and solved. To dismantle the formidable war machine the Union had created was not to be an easy task. How the defeated South would be brought back into the Union was a political issue but also a humanitarian one. Food, shelter and medical care was an immediate need for thousands from Richmond to New Orleans.

Stanton was a dynamo of concentrated activity. Aides scurried in all directions with one order after another. Telegrams were sent and received and orders to the Generals still in the field all bore the scribbled signature of Edwin McMasters Stanton.

On the late afternoon of April 14th, 1865, as shadows darkened the windows, the President again visited the Telegraph office to check the dispatches from Union Armies still facing Confederate troops. General Sherman was haggling over the surrender of Confederate armies far south of Appomattox. Surrender was inevitable, considering Lee's surrender of the Army of Virginia, but negotiations were difficult. Confederate General Johnston, not whipped in the field, was an irritating stumble block.

Lincoln, making his daily trip to the telegraph office, was impatient at the stalling but understood the difficulties of "tying all the ends together" as he put it to Stanton, standing tall and bare headed in the Secretary's Spartan office. The Secretary was a bit edgy as he assured his Commander in Chief that negotiations were difficult but were moving forward.

The President smiled and said:

"I am not pointing the finger of blame, Mr. Secretary. I am aware of the herculean efforts you are putting in every day. I guess I'm becoming a crotchety old man."

"Stanton, are you well? Is there anything the matter?"

The Secretary's eyes had welled up in tears and he pulled out a large handkerchief, blowing his nose loudly:

"Oh no, Mr. President, each Spring the blooming flowers give me a runny nose."

Stanton turned quickly away from Lincoln and blew his nose again, trying to cope with his emotions. As he wished Lincoln a pleasant evening at the theatre and as the President left, he closed the door, giving orders to his aides not to be disturbed. I did not waste time in sympathy for this man who was crying uncontrollably.

Around ten that evening a tiny pistol that could be concealed in the palm of a man's hand would be detonated in a theatre box and the history of the United States would be changed forever. It would take more than one hundred years before the South would begin to loosen the grip on discrimination and the results are still far from resolved.

Was Col. Lafayette Baker (not to be confused with the young Lieutenant Baker of the Garrett barn raid) to make any positive use of the information he had about an attempted assassination?

Standing outside the War Department watching the departing President and his aides, the late afternoon sky began to cloud up and the scene took on a gloomy mood. Baker was my next objective and I focused on the President and Mary Todd's trip to the Navy Yard that afternoon. In a heart beat, I was transported back to the Montauk tryst.

I came back below decks as the President was laughing about the old turkey who always escaped the axe. Col. Baker did not seem quite as taken by the story as Lincoln was. The President, bending his neck to avoid hitting the oak rafters, took his leave. The Colonel stiffly held his salute until the door closed but then moved very quickly. He threw a long Navy cape over his uniform and clapped a naval officer's cap on his head. Gathering up all his documents in a large brief case, large enough to accommodate his army officer's slouch hat, he opened the door and moved up the gangway to the deck above, jammed with officers and men paying loud homage to the President. He merged with the crowd and made his way across the gangplank to the boardwalk. Walking briskly, he climbed into a waiting carriage that moved at a fast trot away from the Navy anchorage.

Regardless of all you might have seen in those costumed English movies, each carriage I have been in on these time trips seemed more uncomfortable to the occupants than the next. This jolting, bouncing ride was the norm in this era and Colonel Baker hardly noticed, a determined scowl speaking of his inner turmoil. His destination was the Herndon House, just a few blocks from Ford's Theatre and the same hotel in which Lewis Paine's room was Booth's meeting place.

In this era before elevators, the favorable rooms were on the first floor up from the lobby and they became cheaper and less desirable as you climbed the stairs.

As Colonel Baker, registered as a Mr. Llewellyn, sat at his desk with the contents of his briefcase spread about, I tried to get inside his brain to tell him that the man who was to kill the President would preside at a meeting of his cohorts that evening just two flights above his room. He never stopped focusing on his work as I strained with every ounce of my mind's power to contact him telepathically. The effort was a failure.

Glancing at the small pendulum clock on the mantle, I had about four hours left to alert the Colonel. There was no certainty that Baker would have the slightest interest in any stray thought I could implant. There was even a fear of having history changed if I could make contact and Baker acted on the information. I had began to believe that these were questions to which no one had answers except the writers of science fiction. Could I depend on a screen play of "Back To The Future" to guide my actions?

Einstein had postulated that time would slow down for any one moving at the speed of light. Experiments in space travel and astronomy had proved the theory. We were centuries away from having any scientific proofs about the time travel paradox of never changing the past and having our own time take a different course. If I messed around in an attempt to stop the assassination, would I come back to the same world I had left? I also had to stop Annie Surratt from being in the prison courtyard when Mary Surratt was hanged. Was that also a change of the past that would wipe out my familiar world?

The hours spent with Baker moved at a glacial pace. Many men moved in and out of Baker's room with the latest intelligence reports on the possibility of plots against the President. Several reports caught my attention. One such report involved Louis Weichmann's interview about the kidnapping attempt on the President in March. It named names, Paine, John Surratt and Booth among them. Weichmann gave the address of the house on H Street but not a good deal of credence was given to facts that certainly were alarming.

I did not blame these earnest men in dismissing facts that to them must have been seen as flights of fancy. A crew of misfits led by a matinee idol? Intelligence was too wrapped up in the theory that agents of the rebel army paid by the Confederate government must be the culprits. I had the benefit of hindsight. It was too easy to be smug about how dumb they were and how smart I was. In my limbo existence in this era of slow communications and the lack of technical tools, it was so frustrating not to be able to lead them to the right conclusions in order to save the President.

The evidence of a political conspiracy that Col. Baker shared with Lincoln never surfaced that afternoon. I presumed that the Colonel would move only after he laid all the facts he knew before Lincoln and await his orders on how to proceed. One large leather dispatch case was never opened and locked with a heavy padlock. It was the same case Baker had carried to his meeting with Lincoln on the warship Montauk.

When the Colonel left for the theatre later that evening he was to lock that dispatch case in the hotel safe.

Baker gave orders for twelve of his best Union Army operatives and two experienced civilian Pinkerton detectives, to dress in plain clothes and mix among the audience at Ford's Theatre that evening. They were to spread out in the ground floor seating area. He and his chief aide would be seated in the dress circle on the same level as the box seats. All the men, including the Colonel, would be carrying firearms.

The modern Secret Service send agents in advance to check every shooting angle that could be used to shoot a President attending a public event. A theatre box occupied by the President would be minutely examined. Remember that in 1865 no American Head of State had ever been assassinated. Baker, thorough as he was, did not have any reference on which to draw. To murder the President was almost inconceivable and Baker, along with many others close to the President, were considered alarmists.

McKinley was gunned down and Theodore Roosevelt, Franklin Roosevelt and Harry Truman were missed by assassination attempts. John Kennedy was murdered and Reagan was hit and luckily survived. The learning process was not a rapid one and even in our own era of wireless phones and hovering helicopters, it is not foolproof.

When the Colonel and several of his aides went to dinner in the Hotel restaurant about six o'clock, uncharacteristically, I did not follow. I needed an undistracted hour to reflect on my plans which rested squarely on my ability, even slightly, to change events in the past. In the case of a world famous leader, changing events might have long reaching consequences but I could not buy the theory that my modern world would be suddenly replaced by a wholly different universe. In the election that gave Lincoln a second term, the Radicals were also swept into greater power in Congress. Could a live Lincoln have changed civil rights history? Not a sure thing. As to my own problem in the exorcism of Mary Surratt, in the life and death cycles of billions of people over the centuries, I was sure that a small change of Mary's daughter's destiny would not cause a ripple in the fabric of time. On such a thin thread, I was betting my future, my family and my life.

I followed a thought pattern used in decision making to break down whatever assets I might possess and make the most of them. I was an experienced hypnotist. How could I use that experience being cut off completely from contact in the world about me? A long shot, just a chance, evolved in my thoughts. If words or thoughts could not be transmitted it might be possible to transfer visual images. It was grasping at straws but I had no other options.

John Wilkes Booth would start to walk the few blocks from the theatre bar to Herndon House at about ten minutes to eight. That would put him climbing the stairs to Paine's room at about eight o'clock. The head of the stairs, from the lobby to the first level, was two rooms down the hall from Baker's room. The common floor men's room was on the other side of the stair well. This proposition may seem far out, but if I could get Baker to go to the bathroom at that precise moment, the sight of Wilkes Booth moving up the stairs might alert the Colonel whose reports implicated Booth in the aborted kidnap attempt on the President. Baker had read the report and because he believed that Weichmann was an unreliable witness he gave the information little credence.

Helping him to form a mind set about Booth was his macho military man's conviction that the celebrated actor, who cultivated the image of a dissolute dandy, would not have the courage to commit himself to such daring adventures. The ex-corporal Napoleon made the same mistake about the elegant Lord Wellington.

Colonel (Lieut. Colonel to be precise) Baker came up from the dining room with a handful of trusted aides at 7:16 pm, according to the loudly ticking clock on the fireplace mantle. He sat at the room's mahogany desk with the seating plans for Ford's Theatre spread out before him.

"Neeson, I want you to distribute the tickets you picked up this afternoon from the box office, for all our plain clothed operatives and myself to be seated without raising suspicion. They should not come not as a group and must attract as little attention as possible. Side arms should be well hidden. Major, you did a fine job in purchasing all the box seats on both sides of theatre. The Presidential party will be in the combined boxes seven and eight, here on the right side facing the stage. Lieutenant Alston here tells me that Clay Ford needed some convincing. Well done."

In the back and forth discussion of procedure at the theatre, I was concentrating on the clock and fighting a rush of adrenaline. Writing that seems odd, considering my ghostly state, but my mouth was dry and my pulse was rapid nevertheless. I have witnessed the same reactions with a patient in deep trance state and my body back in my office chair must have been breathing heavily. Real heart stopping fear can also be felt in dreams. What I felt seemed to intensify my focus on the visual image I was trying to transmit telepathically to the mind of Colonel

Baker. Looking back, it was dead serious but humorous as well. It was all my mind could come up with.

It was a simple picture based on the many times I have had to give an unwilling urinary sample for a lab test. It was a hand holding a glass of water and pouring it in a high, thin stream into a dry metal basin. The sound, of course, an integral part of the image.

The visualization I was able to produce, with my ghostly eyes closed and in intense concentration on Baker's mind, was as sharp and clear as a color television picture.

If I pissed my pants in that office chair, so be it. The minute hand was moving toward eight o'clock when Baker pushed back his chair and excused himself for a few moments. In the euphoria of making contact at last was a rush of anxiety. Anxious because in 1865 or even in 1999, all time pieces did not exactly line up with each other. Booth could be still not through the hotel door or even upstairs in Paine's room.

Baker moved down the hallway and as he neared the stair, Booth, fashionably dressed for the performance of his life, hit the top of the first flight and without looking to his left moved past the bathroom and climbed the second flight of stairs a few steps to the right. I am positive the Colonel recognized the famous actor by his expression on his face. It was not the reaction I was hoping for. Instead of a worried frown, it was a hint of a nod, knowing half smile and barely audible "..hmm.." I did not immediately understand. I waited in the hall for Baker and followed him back into his hotel room, my mind stunned in disbelief.

Angry with frustration, I would have whacked him on the head if I could. How could he be so stupid as not to react? In reflection, it was a example of stupidity on my part as I listened to him reciting a juicy bit of gossip to his aides:

"I just spotted that actor Booth in the hall heading upstairs. I bet he has been in more hotel rooms in this city than most carpet layers. I could smell the Bay Rum and whiskey from six feet away." The comments were awarded with the guffaws of locker room humor. The Colonel continued: "I wonder what assignation he has tonight? They say his latest mistress is Lucy Hale, the Senator's daughter. No matter, we have more important fish to fry."

It was stupid on my part because of hubris. My detailed knowledge of every moment of this dreadful Good Friday night in 1865 could not possibly matter at all. His mistake, a common one, was for Baker to underestimate his unknown adversary. Booth was not really under suspicion in spite of undercover reports on the house on H Street. To the Colonel, the thought must have been preposterous.

A series of men moved in and out informing the Colonel of the whereabouts of the Presidential party. Lincoln, despite the curtain going up at Ford's, had not yet left the White House. The men around Baker left to take care of their special duties which included mingling in the crowd in front of the theatre that were waiting to get a glimpse of the Presidential party. The message finally came that the Lincoln's were finally on the way to pick up Major Rathbone and Clara Harris.

The Colonel, a dashing figure in evening clothes and high hat, managed to hide the formidable Army pistol he carried by pushing back the holster to the rear right of his hip, under his three quarter length evening jacket. He sat up and down a few times to make adjustments for comfort. Glancing at the clock for the last time, showing 8:42, he left the room and walked down one flight to the lobby. By my calculations he was not to see Booth do the same thing ten minutes later. Doing without the sophisticated fax equipment of our own era and records that included photographs, he would not have recognized the three other men, Paine, Herold and Atzerdrodt even if he did see them. Giving his room key to the clerk he walked out of the hotel into the cool, misty night and walked the city block to Ford's Theatre.

His plan was to present his ticket and walk the half flight up to the dress circle as unobtrusively as possible. There was no nod of recognition to one of his men heading for the ground floor orchestra and the man also feigned indifference. Baker stopped to get a program and took his aisle seat. With the lights turned down in the middle of the second act and not having to step over people, no one noticed his entrance. Baker, all business, hardly noticed the action on the stage and kept his eyes moving.

Baker was in direct line of sight to Major Neeson, also in plain clothes, who was surveying every entrance and exit as well from a seat further back and across the circle. They were to be in eye contact and had worked out a series of signals if either found something or someone suspicious.

The arrival of the Presidential party in the dress circle was greeted by tumultuous shouting and applause. A very critical time for Baker and Neeson who both were standing with a hand on pistols under jackets, looking over the crowd with glowering intensity. This chaos was a perfect opportunity for a killer to strike. The President and his party entered the boxes reserved and decorated for them. Charles Forbes, on the White House guard detail, took the end row seat just outside the door. If the President noticed the empty chair without the other guard Parker, whose post was just inside the box vestibule door, we will never know. The robust martial strains of "Hail to the Chief" drew to a close and the audience finally took their seats, the excited buzz of conversation dropping off to a murmur as the light comedy resumed.

From the Colonel's seat on the aisle in the middle of the dress circle, he could not see much of the Presidential party. Major Rathbone was visible on the right side in what was usually a separate box in regular performances. Rathbone sat forward enjoying the play, turning from time to time to share the pleasure with Miss Harris, partially blocked from Baker's view. The President and his wife were further back and hidden by the long curtains that afforded the couple a degree of privacy. Lincoln, his unruly hair more carefully brushed tonight, could be glimpsed as he occasionally leaned forward to get a better view.

Baker did not spend his time looking at the box. He was trying to scan the house without raising any suspicion from the people around him. It was not an easy task.

The best time for observation was during some of the sustained bursts of laughter that broke out at intervals. When every eye was on the stage, Baker and his adjutant Neeson, who was more to the back of the circle, managed to scan and re-scan the audience. Only a rough third of the audience below was visible but the Colonel was counting on his carefully spaced operatives on the ground floor to do a thorough job of surveillance.

It was about ten o'clock and the curtain had gone up on Act III when Baker first noticed John Wilkes Booth in the "standing room only" section at the back of the dress circle.

The same adrenaline reactions I experienced at Herndon House made my heart pound. There was no signal from Baker to Neeson. Booth at the theatre to see the President seemed perfectly natural to Baker. The house was full of important people and the famed actor did not cause any alarm. When Booth started down the aisle he walked right past Baker who glanced at him without interest. The Colonel then observed that the left side curtain of the box was pulled slightly open, Lincoln looking down to his left, doing a little audience scanning of his own, probably for political cronies who might have attended.

A visual image was easier to project the second time around. My mental focus, again spurred by a pounding heart, was sharper. I concentrated on Baker's mind and visualized a famous lithograph published in "Harper's Illustrated" a few days after the assassination. It showed Wilkes Booth standing in the Presidential box with his arm extended, holding a small pistol and firing a bullet into the head of a slumped and dying Lincoln, both men wreathed in smoke. As Wilkes was conning Forbes to let him into the President's box, the Colonel reacted to the image in horror. He leaped to his feet and shouted: "Major, Major!" Neeson reacted instantly but had to take a less direct route. The Colonel reached the box almost as the door closed, furiously brushing a standing Forbes aside. The sturdy door moved a half inch as Baker pushed the knob but then the door was as immobile as a tree. The Major, arriving at that moment, was the first to slam against the jammed door and bounced off just as Booth's pistol shot shocked the house. Baker, almost insane with fury, lowered his shoulder and charged the door. In one of those inexplicable twists of fate his head was thrust outward a little further than his shoulder and there was a sickening crack that could be heard above the shouts and screams of an hysterical audience. He dropped in a crumpled heap as the Major, with pistol drawn, could not get an unobstructed shot over the balustrade at the scuttling figure of Booth, hip-hopping his way across a stage already filling with other people. He turned immediately to help the fallen Baker who had not regained consciousness. Checking his Colonel's breathing and pulse, satisfied with the man's vital signs, he half carried and dragged Baker through the chaos of a stampeding audience and down the stairs to street level. Hailing one of the carriages for hire that awaited the theatre crowds, he bundled the Colonel in and waved the driver to Herndon House. Feigning drunkenness and supporting his supposedly inebriated friend, the Major secured the room key from the clerk and struggled upstairs with his burden.

This behavior was consistent with the undercover roles the men had assumed. There was just a small circle of trusted men who knew that Baker was not in New York where he was sent by Stanton. Major Neeson's responsibility was to get the Colonel well enough to travel to a small lodging house south of Baltimore and near a railroad water and coal stop. Baker was then to board a New York to Washington morning train when it made the supply stop and arrive in uniform at the Capitol. His aide in New York would receive Stanton's telegram at five in the morning of April 15th, telling Baker he was in charge of the manhunt for Booth, the suspected assassin of President Lincoln. The same aide would be on the train, meet Baker and accompany him to the Capitol.

The Major was not a Doctor but during the Civil War an officer was well schooled in the bloody engagements he had been through to care for his men. Neeson, a highly decorated officer, was no exception. He tended Baker with the skill of a male nurse with cold compresses and warm blankets. Baker awoke sitting up, coughing from a swallow of strong brandy from a pocket flask held by the Major. Several of his men were in attendance. His first tortured question was of the President:

"Does the President live?"

The answer came from one of his operatives that had moved into the Petersen house with the men carrying the fatally wounded President. He brought the news that the President was fighting to live but the bullet in his brain was a mortal wound. He could not live much longer. Within a half hour of a question and answer session Baker knew all that was known of those heart-stopping moments at Ford's theatre. He was told that none of his men had been able to get off a shot at Booth in a theatre crowded with screaming men, women and children. Only the Major and the Colonel, seated in the dress circle, could give a positive identification of Booth. In the pandemonium that followed the shot, the armed men planted in the orchestra seating area were not sure of the killer's identity. There was no mounted Calvary that could give chase.

Awaiting orders seemed the most prudent course of action.

At the end, it was agreed that the Colonel, sporting an egg-sized lump at his hairline, was well enough to carry out the original plan to come to the Capitol. As head of Army intelligence, Baker knew he would be called upon to lead the man hunt for the assassin after his arrival in Washington. He was also told that Stanton was now the seat of power in a confused city, his headquarters in the Petersen house, a few steps from the dying President.

The Colonel requested privacy and a few hours of rest before he started the trip north.

Then and only then, in the darkened room, did the tears of anguish burst forth.

There was little rest before an aide knocked on his door to inform the Colonel that it was time for his journey. Baker again dressed as a civilian, entrusted his locked briefcase to the care of Major Neeson. The party jounced and bumped on another long carriage trip and made the connections on time to board the southbound morning train. It was just after sunrise on April 15th, about the same time that Lincoln drew his last breath at the Petersen house and Wilkes Booth slept soundly in the upper bedroom of Doctor Mudd's home in northern Maryland.

Chapter 11
The Confrontation

Trains in 1865 were gritty and smelled of the belching fumes of a coal-burning engine. Shirt collars became dark with soot, especially in late spring and summer with open windows providing the only ventilation. There was no rest for Lafayette Baker in his small train compartment. Exhausted, he had dozed off several times in the two hour trip to the nation's capitol. Nearing his destination he had read the telegram Stanton had unwittingly sent to his supposed Hotel in New York. His brows had furrowed and his eyes were narrowed in a steely look of anger and purpose:

"Major, when we get to Washington I want you to take a fast horse from the men who will meet the train and go directly to the War Department. It will be late in the morning and Secretary Stanton will be at his desk. Tell him that Lt. Colonel Baker requests a private meeting as soon as I arrive by carriage at his office."

"Yes Sir, Colonel"

"Now pull down the brief case from the upper bunk and give me some privacy. No one is to enter this room except at my command. Post a sentry at the door. If you wish to speak to me it must be of utmost importance. Knock once, twice then once to identify yourself."

"Is anything wrong that I can be of your service?"

"Wrong, Major? We have witnessed the most despicable act in our country's history, an act we were powerless to stop. There is still more wrong than you might imagine but for the present I must carry this burden alone. You will be apprised in due time. Until then I need only your absolute loyalty."

"You shall have that, Colonel, to my last breath."

Baker locked the compartment door from the inside, set the briefcase beside him on the bench seat and began to read every note, dispatch or memorandum pertaining to the treason of Edwin McMasters Stanton, Secretary of War and Thaddeus Stevens, Pennsylvania's longtime Representative in Congress and majority party leader. When he was finished and the papers safely tucked away, he moved back in his seat and looked through the streaked and dirty train window at the lush farmlands of northern Virginia. His beloved country was about to get another crippling jolt and the immense weight of his responsibility affected him deeply.

The Colonel shaved and dressed carefully, attaching to his dress uniform all his medals for valor in the field. Opening the compartment door, he told the sentry to have Neeson meet him in the dining room car for breakfast. From my vantage point of a fly on the wall, whatever trepidation he might have had for the meeting with Stanton seemed to have been resolved. He appeared eager for the battle to be joined.

Later that morning, the Colonel sat stiffly in a chair just outside the Secretary's office, his right hand on the briefcase beside him. A civilian aide to Stanton had gone in to tell the Secretary of Baker's arrival. The aide beckoned him in and we both went through the open door. Stanton was seated behind his desk in his shirtsleeves, thanks to the warm day, glasses well down on his nose and dictating to his private secretary seated nearby. Looking at the Colonel he spoke in a rapid staccato:

"A terrible business, Colonel, a terrible business but with you at the helm we shall track down this wretched assassin and bring him to justice. Let me first go over the testimony I took from eye witnesses and from detectives that have been swarming over northern Maryland and Virginia since the early hours. I have been in touch by telegraph and post riders all night through. As soon as you are apprised of the situation, I will then seek to rest, knowing there are no better hands than yours to lead the hunt." Baker was standing at attention, stony faced and stock still. When he spoke it was with grim seriousness:

"Mr. Secretary, please ask your clerk to leave us. What I have to say is for your ears only. I would also appreciate it if your outer door sentry would be given a brief rest until we finish our business."

Stanton, who was unaccustomed to orders from subordinates or superiors, even when politely phrased, looked up sharply at the Colonel's tone. What he saw in Baker's face was enough to evoke a gruff cough and instructions to his aide to give them the privacy Baker requested.

Stanton did not explode at the first damning memorandum, seemingly determined to read them all. His hands trembled and droplets of sweat began to appear on his balding forehead as he moved slowly from one page to another. Throughout this twenty minutes of agony for the Secretary, Baker had not moved or spoken. As Stanton put the last piece of paper face down on the small stack in front of him he looked up ashen-faced and in a whisper asked the Colonel to be at ease and be seated.

"I prefer to stand, Mr. Secretary."

Haltingly and searching for words, Stanton, began to justify his role in the conspiracy to murder the President and Commander in Chief:

"What you do when you leave this room is the most important decision you will ever make in service to your country. You must not make that decision rashly, driven only by raw anger and emotion. You, like so many of your countrymen loved Lincoln. I am included in that group, even more because of my proximity to this great man every waking hour."

With those words spoken, Baker erupted in anger:

"Mr. Secretary, do not compare yourself to Brutus who loved Rome more than Caesar. You would do anything to be President, including murder. Do not dare to justify your foul deed. If you have anything else to say, say it. Any further chicanery, I will have a troop of men loyal only to me come to this room and arrest you on the spot!"

"All right Baker, It is your love of country that I wish to address. No more talk of my motives. The deed is done. Lincoln is dead and the country is prostrate in grief. Can this nation survive another blow at this critical time? There are men out there with the power to bring down this democracy and ride in on horseback as saviors. Grant or Sherman with the loyal backing of the Union armies could dissolve the Congress and declare a dictatorship. It is a move that a disillusioned country might welcome. Damn the politicians will be a battle cry. Washington has gone to hell! Think deeply on your next moves as a patriot. Would my head in a noose along with Thaddeus Stevens serve our country? The old guard is passing and in a few years death will take us to be judged by the Almighty. The United States will and must survive. Will it survive the exposure of its leaders at a time when the people of this nation already feel that the ship of state no longer has a stalwart Captain at the helm? An inebriate tailor has been sworn in as President. He must have strong men in his cabinet that will move this country out of these troubled times. Do you trust that stewardship to Andrew Johnson? Think well Colonel, of your next decisions."

For a length of time that seemed to be measured in hours instead of minutes, the two men stared at one another. It was difficult to tell what emotions and thoughts ran through the mind of Baker. He did not betray any emotion and remained stoic. Stanton on the other hand, began to slowly break down. He finally bowed his head and stared at the desk, waiting for Baker to speak:

"Mr. Secretary, I am aware that the threat to our democracy is real. Especially when I have seen it trampled on by men such as you. The only civil rights you recognize are those that will perpetuate your own selfish power. Make no mistake regarding my intentions. If I should decide to keep this terrible secret for the good of my beloved country you will go to your grave and will never lead this nation. I will hold this sword over your head to strike you down if you reach for the Presidency."

Stanton looked stunned, his eyes bulging in anxiety.

"You have read the copies of these documents that damn you. If you ignore my warning and allow the Party to put forth your name as a nominee for the Presidency, the original documents will appear on the editor's desk of a great newspaper in opposition to Radical policies. You and Stevens will die in prison or be hanged first. That promise also protects my own person as I leave you to stew in your agony. I know full well that murder is a tool that men of your ilk will use without a moment's reflection. When I leave this room I will be at the top of your assassin's list. You would never trust me to be silent. Only a bullet with my name on it will give you peace. If that is your choice and I too am murdered, a trusted confederate will carry out my mission to bring the facts before the nation as quickly as possible. You and your evil partner in this despicable deed of murder and betrayal will pay for your treachery. I will bring back the assassin, John Wilkes Booth, to stand trial for the President's murder but from this very moment we will confer only through aides. I will not suffer your presence again."

Colonel Baker did not make any by-your-leave amenities. He collected his papers from an uncharacteristically docile Stanton, turned his back and strode from the room.

The Secretary slowly heaved to his feet and walked to a cabinet in the corner. He then pulled out a bottle of what looked like sherry wine and poured himself a stiff drink. Walking to his window overlooking the gardens, he looked at this lovely scene without really seeing anything. His face bore the stunned expression of a cocksure defendant in a murder trial that has just heard a verdict of guilty. I stayed with Stanton, curious to see how this powerful man dealt with such a crushing blow. He did not break down but the level of sherry fell slowly in the bottle. Stanton began to scribble memo after torn up memo. I put myself in a position over his shoulder to read the precise script that became a scrawl as more and more wine was consumed. He was testing a plan of action he would take in disclosing the shattering news to a man that held the key to his political future. Thaddeus Stevens, whose hands were also steeped in blood, would have erupted in a fury that would consume them both. I could follow his thinking as the memos progressed. "Stevens need not know anything at all. Business as usual."

"Johnson is the President and the next election is four years ahead." "Anything can happen." "My operatives are as smart as his and I hold the power."

One memo was chilling: "Get Sgt. Corbett (the Army's noted marksman) into the troops that will hunt for Booth. Booth must die! Trial of Booth dangerous. Promise Corbett generous pension for life and scare him into secrecy or kill him. Don't get involved personally.. use the General." No name was given.

Any knock on the door and Stanton would keep it simple: "Go Away".

After coming to the end of this exercise, Stanton burned all his notes in the cold fireplace. He then moved to a small dressing closet that held a dry sink, porcelain pitcher of water and matching washbasin. The Secretary freshened his appearance and by the time he summoned his door sentry to get his secretarial aide, there was a semblance of normalcy about the man. A little more subdued, a little less bluster, but finally in command of himself.

The night before, Stanton held executive power in his own hands. He ruled by decree and pulled the administration of the government together. It turned out to be his high water mark as power is defined. As War Secretary under Andrew Johnson he attempted to put in motion a hard line reconstruction policy toward the South. The firm hand of Lincoln was gone but Andrew Johnson, a southerner by birth, wanted to carry out the outlines of Lincoln's more temperate policy. Stanton, pushed hard by Stevens and the Radicals, became a thorn in Johnson's side that led to the Presidential call for the War Secretary's resignation. That led an infuriated Thaddeus Stevens to lead an impeachment drive against the President. He used the call for Stanton to resign as proof of the President's treason against the United States. Steven's Radicals took the lead in the bitter Congressional debate and incredibly, considering the charges, delivered the votes to impeach the President. When the impeachment trial in the Senate failed by one vote, a bitter and vengeful Stevens vented his spleen in the well of the House.

The Congressional Record, July 7th, 1868:

"I have come to a fixed conclusion. that never will the Chief Executive of the nation be removed by peaceful means. If tyranny becomes intolerable, the only recourse will be found in the dagger of Brutus."

To soften this polemic, the sanctimonious bastard then said: "I pray it will never come to that.." Majority Leader Stevens died of cancer within two years. Stanton, relegated to the dustbins of history, died some six years later. Thaddeus Stevens and the Radicals of the Right left a wound in the body politic that festered for another hundred years. The South hardened into suppression of black rights that lasted right into the civil rights wars of the 1960's.

As a last but interesting footnote to the post-assassination record, the nemesis of Stanton, Col. Baker, sued the former War Secretary in Federal Court for Stanton to return what Baker felt to be the property of the Government; the missing pages from the diary that Booth kept active during his escape that were given to Stanton by Colonel Conger. Stanton lost the suit and the pages were returned to the War Department. To this day, the contents have not been made public.

My schedule was tight but our family calculations regarding the elapsed time in our own space continuum, my office in my home, were right on the money. I moved out of Stanton's office and to a shaded park bench under a huge bush of blooming lilacs.

It was the perfect place to rest for a few moments as I thought about my next immediate goal. That goal was to stop the daughter of Mary Surratt from attending the execution of her mother. To stop the unholy possession of body and soul that would end, God willing, in my office 143 years in the future.

My fourteen day time trip was drawing to a close. Using the formula that my son Donnie had worked out (he is a math whiz) to transpose the exact hours and minutes that have elapsed in the escape and death of Booth and the time spent with Stanton, my wrist watch gave me enough time to complete the mission.

Chapter 12
The Family Plan

The only way I could make a side trip to the day of Mary's execution was to make enough of a distraction for the waiting couple from hell in my office that would make my objective go unnoticed. Jennifer at this very moment would be opening the side door to the garage. Donnie and I had worked on the hinges and lock with squirted oil. It would not betray us with noise. Jane had always parked her car in my driveway and entered my office through a small hallway. To a patient, the garage was not visible but the sides of the hallway did not go up to the ceiling of the garage. There was a foot and a half opening on top.

My son and I had taken off the garage office door and with a rotary saw I took a full inch off the bottom for more ventilation. Donnie had made absolutely sure that the garage was spick and span. Jennifer's job was to walk to the whitewashed oil drum, strike a lighted match and drop it into the oil soaked rags that Naomi had prepared from some old stuffed coverlets. We had tested the results over and over to make sure that there would be no flare up to put my daughter in danger. Done just right, with a moderate amount of lighter fluid for a quick start, It would be the best damned safe smoky fire you ever saw. Donnie experimented again and again for the exact formula and amount of rags to keep things safe and still produce the required amount of smoke. Naomi, of course, played Fire Chief.

Jen was then to display all out hysteria as soon as the hallway filled with smoke and had started to stream under the door. I had purchased a self contained gas mask from one of those weird Internet web sites. It really worked. Jen had practiced with it and was to put the mask on after pounding on my locked door. Mary's old instructions about leaving the door unlocked would not be a factor. Jen was to scream: "Daddy, Daddy, the garage is on fire", over and over. The other door to the office was left unlocked and led to a paneled den and the stairway to the upper hall and front door. In the den waiting for Jane/Mary to bolt out of the only unlocked door were Donnie and Naomi. They were to be out of sight, the den was big enough for that, and as soon as Jane/Mary would hit the top step to the upper hall, Naomi would release me from the trance state using the process I had taught her and I in turn would awaken Alfred.

Donnie would run to help his sister. Jen, who looked like an alien in a gas mask, would put out the oil drum fire with a foam extinguisher and then open the garage door. So as not to alert the neighborhood fire department,

Donnie and I had disconnected all the house alarms. Was this all too simple? Perhaps. I believed that plans that did work were usually uncomplicated. Was the plan foolproof? To that I would have to answer no. Was it the only plan we could think of? Yes.

I was counting on Surratt's fear of fire that must have been magnified over the five generations she had lived with her hosts. As the ultimate survivor, a fatal fire would have been her destruction as well. That intense fear of fire was our salvation. Mary would hang and the only person to deal with would be a frightened Jane Gotting.

The reporters of the Civil War period might have been a little overblown in the choice of words they used to describe an event but as to exact time and dates they did the job.

Perhaps better than our own news sources. Research told me that the traps that were sprung to execute Mary Surratt, Lewis Paine, poor David Herold and George Atzerdrodt, were tripped at eleven minutes after one on the blazingly hot afternoon of July 7th, 1865.

All of our calculations rested on that precise moment. It was time to take a trip about two months in the future from that park bench under a sweet smelling lilac tree. If we were wrong and my power could not get me back to my own time, I would be trapped in an eternity whose boundaries were endless, my wife and children forever gone. I closed my mind's eye and visualized an 1865 calendar with the date of July 7th encircled in brilliant red. Alongside the date hung a pocket watch similar to the one used by Booth's father Junius. It was set at 8:00. Alongside the watch, also in red, were the letters AM. I then visualized the majestic columned portico of the White House and exerted all of my concentration on the move.

Chapter 13
The Anguish of Anna Surratt

I was there, the portico bathed in sunlight. A teen age black youth dressed in the formal livery of a White House servant was sweeping the steps. From the way his collar was soaked in sweat and the quick moving fan of a lady walking into the great entrance hall, I knew the historical description of today's weather was accurate. Men as well as women walking on Pennsylvania Avenue used umbrellas. If it was this hot in the morning, I could imagine the scene in the prison courtyard that afternoon. I was smugly happy that my disembodied state had the wonderful property of not feeling heat or cold.

Why the White House this morning? It was where President Andrew Johnson now lived. Johnson, some two months before, had been escorted from the Kirkwood Hotel to the Petersen house when Lincoln fought for life and escorted back rather quickly when Mary Lincoln objected to his presence. Chief Justice Chase swore him in as President in his hotel suite the early morning of April 15th after Lincoln was pronounced dead. He had given Mary Lincoln a period of time to move from the White House and was now sitting down for breakfast in the family dining room upstairs. This was the same dining room that had rang with the laughter of President Lincoln teasing Tad about his lemonade business in the White House garden.

This morning a brave but distraught young woman was to make a final plea of clemency regarding the death penalty for her mother, Mary Surratt. Exhausted by a night of agony in her mother's cell, the two visitors, Anna and her Aunt, were assailed by the sound of heavy carpentry before sunrise just outside in the prison courtyard. A gallows was being erected with traps for the four doomed prisoners. Another detail of soldiers had the macabre duty of digging the graves just alongside the rough hewn structure. The reporters gathering early could hear the piteous wails of Mary, her sister and daughter Anna from the cell windows in the prison walls. Surratt's priest, Father Wiget, had been at her side the night through, offering whatever comfort he could during the long, humid night.

My time schedule was very tight and the impressions above were not my eyewitness observations but rather my research into the newspaper accounts of the coming execution.

I waited for at least an hour until Anna arrived. Bareheaded and disheveled, she moved slowly up the stone steps to the White House entrance and inside the entrance. She was accompanied by Mr. T. Aiken, one of her mother's capable defense attorneys during the preceding trial. They were there to ask for clemency in regard to the death sentence. There was more than just a groundswell of support across the nation for the President to commute her sentence to life imprisonment. Many of the country's great newspapers, joined by clergymen of all faiths were calling the execution of a woman to be a barbarous assault on the religious and moral concepts that underlined the American experiment in democracy. Many felt there was a fine line between committing a murder and aiding and abetting one. The Radical Right and even many from the moderate center called out for blood.

While this storm raged the business of the court moved inexorably to its conclusion.

The President of the United States was the only man that could change that conclusion with a stay of execution. Abraham Lincoln had put his signature on hundreds, possibly thousands of such stays and pardons that robbed the military gibbets of victims.

Andrew Johnson, new to the Presidency and sniffing the political winds like a basset hound, was a different kettle of fish.

In 1865 the White House was the people's house and no hand reached out to stop the progress of this seventeen year old girl and Mr. Aiken. Up the great stairs they went, the bewhiskered lawyer steadying Anna by the arm and at one point stopping for her to gather her strength. I had few positive emotions for her mother but this display of emotional grit by Anna struck right to the heart. Not that much older than my own daughter who, at this moment, was displaying a little grit of her own to save her father.

When they reached the benches outside the Presidential office, Mr. Aiken formally introduced himself to the young aide to the President outside his office and asked for a meeting with the president for himself and his young charge, Anna Surratt. There were many people at this early hour already seated or standing about with the same request. When they heard Anna Surratt's name a hush fell in the hallway and more than one person came up to tell Aiken that they would defer their own requests if she could be admitted first. Anna gravely thanked them each in turn. No one in the hall demurred. The aide did not immediately appear and as the minutes dragged on the poor girl became more and more distraught. Mr. Aiken was grateful for several of the women who helped to comfort the young lady. I then saw a few visitors in the hall, who had recently arrived, take out the familiar reporters notebook to describe the scene.

The young man who had carried the request into the Presidential office finally opened the door, closed it behind him and said he had a general announcement to make:

"The President is indisposed this morning and has canceled all his appointments. He will see no one"

The wail of anguish from Anna reverberated through the great hall. She threw herself at the young man's feet and begged him to go back and ask the President again.

The aide simply repeated the same words over and over: "He will see no one".

Within a half hour of this outpouring of grief the petitioners were escorted from the hall by White House staff. Anna, hysterically refused to go and Mr. Aiken firmly supported her position. The Press was not asked to leave when their credentials were displayed.

When an usher warned that he would have to get members of the White House guard to remove Anna, Mr. Aiken reminded the man that the reporters were present and that he better get someone in charge to come out of that office or he would do a great disservice to the President. Unlike the press of our own era, these men made no move to even come close to Anna and her counsel. We all waited together and in a while Anna's sobbing ceased. A large bearded man came out of the office and Anna's face momentarily brightened. His face was grave as he introduced himself:

"Miss Surratt and Mr. Aiken, I am General Muzzy, the President's first Secretary and responsible for the Presidential Staff. I have heard your entreaties and my heart breaks for what I must say. The President will not change his mind and will not see you this morning."

The anguished wail from Anna was difficult for anyone to bear let alone a battle hardened General. The tears welled in his eyes as he pulled the girl upright from her knees and tried to soothe her. I had heard enough and wanted to see this man Johnson who would not even speak to the girl. Moving through the closed door into the business office of the President, I knew I would find him where I first saw Lincoln. In the small study just off the office overlooking the Potomac. He was seated at the same polished desk but not on the rocker. A larger overstuffed chair had taken its place. The wails of poor Anna could be heard clearly. Johnson was a short man, stocky and powerful. His head was large, with a full shock of black hair and the coarse features and bulbous nose were set like stone into a stubborn pout. He was wearing a shirt with a white collar dangling loose on one side. It was about eleven o'clock but Johnson was drinking heavily. The bottle of brandy was half full and he refilled a glass as I watched. That stone expression with the rheumy eyes said it all. Nothing would move this man, nothing.

As I moved out Aiken was trying to make a case for Johnson to just listen to their pleas:

"General we are not here for a pardon. The court, even though it was a court that I believe had no jurisdiction in this case, has made a judgment of guilt we cannot overturn. We ask for a commutation of the death sentence for legal and humanitarian grounds. Legal because Mrs. Surratt was a tool in the hands of a dominant personality schooled in theatrics and the power to make people do his bidding. John Wilkes Booth shot the President and Lewis Payne attempted to murder Secretary Seward. Booth is in his grave. Lewis Paine should stand alone on that scaffold today and the whole world knows it. Vengeance is not a legal or constitutional concept and in Civil court that case could have been made. Let Mrs.Surratt pay her debt in prison so this young girl can live knowing she can see, hear and touch the woman that gave her life."

General Muzzy was touched as I was by this impassioned plea but he did his duty to his Commander in Chief and in a broken voice said:

"I am deeply moved but again I must obey the wishes of the President. He will not see you. Not now or not if you stay alone in this hallway all morning. He will not see you.

This morning, The President acting as Chief Magistrate of our nation, signed the death warrants of the conspirators issued by a duly appointed military tribunal after a trial that allowed a full defense. The warrants bore the signature of Justice Holt, the Chief Magistrate of the tribunal. Duty can be a heavy burden for those that have the responsibility to lead. The President has done his duty and his decision will stand.

My heart goes out to this innocent child but I will do my duty to the President. I have given orders that you will be made comfortable and not be disturbed but the answer to your plea is still the same. The President will not see you."

With those words spoken, the kindly man turned and closed the office door behind him.

A single soldier in blue stood guard and wept as well. Aiken, with soothing words of comfort managed to get Anna to her feet and moved her toward the great staircase that curved into the rotunda below.

I had to jerk myself back from my own deep feelings of sympathy into the reality of my predicament. I must stop Anna from being at the hanging of her mother or my life as I once knew it was over. Anna got three or four steps from the top and sank to her knees, sprawling out and hanging on to the railings. She screamed again and again:

"No, no it cannot be over, he must see me, he cannot refuse me...he must come out and when he does, he will listen to me, he will listen to me.."

I could feel for Mr. Aiken as he did everything in his power to get the girl to leave peacefully. He told her of the writ of Habeas Corpus he had submitted early in the morning designed to delay the execution. He was not hopeful but must see Holt at his office before leaving for Surratt's final moments at the prison. It was a desperate attempt to hold off the hangings that would be carried out at one o'clock.

If Anna listened or understood Aiken, I did not know. How she was able not to collapse after a pitiful night with her Mother and the hysteria of this morning was in itself a tribute to her strength. Aiken, seeing that nothing he could do would budge Anna from her determined effort, managed to get her back on one of the leather covered benches outside the Executive office. A heavy set black woman, one of the White House kitchen staff, had been sent by the Chief Usher to help after General Mussy had spoken to the Chief Usher. The ample lady entreated Anna to rest and armed with pillow and coverlet, got the exhausted girl to lie down. Anna first exacted a sworn promise from the woman that if the President was to walk through the door she would be awakened. Aiken too had to promise he would pick her up with his carriage on the trip to the Arsenal Prison.

My own prior research had given me the time of execution in 1865 and my son's formula of the minutes elapsed in his time in ratio to the days and hours of time travel that I was engaged in had to be correct. Had to be because it was all we could hang on to.

Aiken and I left Anna deep asleep upon that bench in the White House. The reader and I know full well the answer of Judge Holt to Mr. Aiken's petition. The execution went as scheduled. Aiken sat in the jolting carriage with his head bowed in sadness.

He really had no hope that his petition would be accepted and the heart rending experience this morning in the attempt to see the President must have taken its toll.

As it was, Holt did not even have the courtesy to speak to Aiken directly. His outer office secretary simply handed the lawyer the denied petition without a word.

Mr. Aiken was not surprised or shocked. He had sat in that so-called courtroom on the top floor of the prison since early June, sweltering with all the rest. It was really a small conference room with table's chairs and desks added. Two windows looked out upon the high walled courtyard where soldiers walked the watch atop the thick masonry. Beyond was the shimmering silver Potomac and floating, suspended in a deep blue sky, the majestic white dome of the Capitol.

Aiken had listened to objection after objection by the lawyers for the defense only to be denied by the senior and junior officers that served as the tribunal judges. There was no jury of their peers. These were the hand picked judge and jury of a court-martial of civilians. Stanton had done his picking well. The show of legality was carried out to the end. An impassioned plea of some forty minutes, representing the combined defense of all the conspirators, was made on constitutional grounds that this tribunal had no jurisdiction over American citizens that were not members of the Armed Forces. Reading this plea you are struck by the polished professionalism of the brief's arguments. The Officers never left the courtroom to make a ruling on the issue. A few passed notes, a buzz of whispers and within ten minutes the plea to change venue to a Civil Court was denied. No wonder the melancholy of Mr. Aiken showed so clearly.

The minutes of the closed discussions that approved the sentences of death to Surratt, Paine, Herold and Atzerdrot and life at hard labor for Dr. Mudd, have never been released by the War Department. My pressing time constraints did not allow me to attend the conferences but the written record showed that it did not take very long by our standards for the prisoners to be apprised of the results.

The lesser figures such as Spangler, Arnold and O'Gloughlin were all punished in varying degrees. The record and my own observations showed the last three men were members of Booth's conspirators. The missing John Surratt, Arnold and O'Gloughlin were part of the kidnapping plot. Spangler willingly helped in preparation for the assassination and in Booth's escape.

As for Dr. Mudd he made the self incriminating mistake of hiding any prior relationship with Booth and not going to the authorities when he knew Booth was the man he treated. That may have been aiding and abetting deserving punishment but certainly the life sentence for being part of Booth's conspiracy was a travesty of justice. A simple question, one his defense was weak on, was: "Would Booth have stopped at Dr.Mudd's house if he had not broken his leg?" I believe no civil jury would have convicted him on the grounds of being part of the conspiracy to murder the President.

Lewis Paine had called in a well known and influential clergyman that night before his last day to plead for

Mary Surratt whom he portrayed as innocent of all wrongdoing.

This plea did not sway the court but it did serve to make the storm of criticism against Mary's execution grow much louder from pulpits and newspapers across the country.

Within a few weeks after the hangings the storm was loud enough for Congress to hear it. Holt, the Chief Justice of the military court, testified that a recommendation of clemency for Mary Surratt was forwarded to President Johnson along with the sentences of death decided by the court. Johnson then claimed that no one had ever shown that recommendation to him. As long as both Holt and Johnson lived some measure of this fundamental disagreement stayed alive as well.

There is more to be said of the Stanton role behind this kangaroo court. Ignoring the constitutional prohibition against cruel and inhuman punishment, Stanton had ordered leg and hand manacles twenty four hours a day. Immune to constraint, he reached back into medieval times to order thick canvas hoods that covered the heads of each prisoner with the exception of Mrs. Surratt. He made sure of Mary not talking by isolating her cell to prevent a conversation with anyone. The news of this treatment did not get out for an effective reason. The Press was barred from coming into the main body of the prison. You can imagine the sweltering conditions of a blazing Washington summer. Humane guards were the only reason the four lived to be hanged.

When the guards leaked the news, the outcry was loud enough for even the Secretary of War to hear. The hoods were removed. Stanton ordered every Army prisoner that had been incarcerated, other than the conspirators, to be removed. The accused were separated by row after row of empty cells. Fearful of any conversation that might have implicated any government or military figures, Stanton had again found a way to insure that would not happen.

It was about a twenty minute carriage ride back to the White House and Mr. Aiken bounced along with the sad expression of a man who had to deliver the news to Anna that death for Mary Surratt was inevitable. I had only twenty minutes to achieve my goal; to keep the daughter of Mary Surratt from being taken to Arsenal Prison to witness the hanging of her mother. Anna had told her mother of her mission to the President on the last night of Mary's life. Anna and her Aunt had both made their final, wrenching goodbyes before daybreak.

It was easy for me to rationalize that it would be traumatic to the breaking point for Anna to see the cruel ending of her mother's life. To this moment I have not lived with guilt about this decision. Whatever the room for argument, my family's life hung in the balance.

If ever I focused the power of my mind it was then. I used the skills of visualization honed over fifteen years of professional practice. The man in front of me had good reason for a rational excuse to ride by the White House without picking up his charge.

It was up to me to give him that reason. A picture was drawn in his mind of Anna sound asleep on the bench where we had left her. Her face was angelic in needed rest.

Aiken wiped his hand across his brow as his face reflected his troubled thoughts.

I moved the visualization to his awakening Anna to tell her the news that his last legal appeal had been denied. The reaction of the tortured girl was full blown and poignant. The inner scenes then turned to the prison courtyard and the scaffold looming overhead. There was Anna's agonized face looking upward before the trap was sprung. Aiken sat bolt upright as we drew near our White House destination. I prayed for his decision.

"Thomas, do not stop at the Executive Mansion. Go directly to the prison. Wait for me as we will be stopping for Miss Surratt later when this awful event is over. We will then leave her in custody of her Aunt."

I know my body in the trance state at my office had just sobbed tears of thankful joy.

Chapter 14
The Execution

To draw the picture of that prison courtyard is easy for me. The scene pictured in a book in my library at home was the first thing I looked for after the initial shock of meeting Mary Surratt in my office. Being here now was a strong feeling I had traveled this road before. The prison courtyard was set off by huge oaken doors to the cellblock on my left. Studded with brass spikes, they looked impregnable. The courtyard's central feature was now the rough hewn structure of the gallows on the western side. Wide steps, I counted fifteen, led to the platform above on which two double traps had been built to hang all of the doomed prisoners at the same moment. Not counting an oaken beam the length of the platform above the traps, I estimated the trap height to be about ten feet.

To the left of the gallows were four coffins. The open pine crates were lying aside four freshly dug graves, the mounds of earth damp and brown. Men were busy on the scaffold with sand bags that were dropped through to the ground when the double traps were tested. These men were dressed in civilian clothes, some in the simple garb of workmen. A man dressed like that was checking the working of the four expertly made nooses that hung from an oaken beam above each trap. Two ropes about three feet apart for each double trap.

The audience about me, no more that twenty or thirty people, were mostly men although several women dressed in black mourning, were in attendance. Soldiers and officers in Union Blue were about, including many simply lounging on the grassy banks of the high masonry walls. Above, on those walls, were soldiers in groups of two or three looking for good vantage points. Some were at attention and on duty but several were onlookers like the audience below. The audience was dotted with black umbrellas that were being used to block the intense heat of July mid-day sun. It was the seventh of July, 1865 and time moved toward one o'clock as the wide doors creaked open.

Aside from the two guards that opened the door, the first person through was Mary Surratt. She was dressed all in black with a large bonnet and veil of black lace that obscured her face. A priest on either side supported each arm and tried to comfort her. She was unsteady and her progress up the fifteen steps was slow. At the top the guards had provided a chair for her. Still unsteady, she had to be eased into the seat.

If she spoke it must have been in a soft and muffled voice. There were no screams or hysteria. The on looking audience was silent.

There was some murmuring when the next prisoner appeared. Lewis Paine, alias Powell, alias Wood, walked tall and straight and shook off the hands that were helping him. His hands were manacled behind him and there was a gasp when he walked up the scaffold stairs with perfect balance on his own. He was dressed in the navy cotton, close fitting shirt he favored. The garment was perfect to show off his neck, shoulders and muscular arms. Refusing to sit, he stood erect, gazing at the Potomac beyond the walls and not uttering a word.

Then came Herold, the young naive boy that worshiped his master Booth. He was talking in a stream of consciousness that ran on as he ascended to his death. It was a garbled paean of disbelief that this could be happening, protesting his innocence. I had the same sympathetic rush of feelings at the moment in Garret's yard when David finally realized the playacting was over. He was staring at Booth lying on the ground in the hot light of a burning barn, soaked with the blood of a mortal wound. When the boy Herold was seated he glanced at the open graves below and burst into tears.

The pig barge owner, George Atzerdrot, was the last to move out of the prison doors. He looked dazed and uncomprehending. Jerking from side to side he needed help on both sides to climb the stairs. Once on top the jerky movements became a shaking fear as he was calmed by the Minister along side of him.

It took a few moments to prepare all the doomed conspirators. Mrs.Surratt's only outward signs were that of physical weakness. One New York newspaper reported she was suffering from menopause. She did not scream or sob. The people around her held an umbrella over her head and strips of white linen were used to bind her long skirt around ankles and thighs. A thin white linen hangman's hood was put over her head. I watched closely as the bonnet and veil were removed and the linen hood was pulled down. Only for an instant did her face became visible. There was a look of determined defiance.

Lewis, because of his large head and bull neck, was another problem. His face seemed bemused at the difficulties the hangmen were having. Breathing normally, he showed no fear and made no comment as they adjusted the noose again to accommodate his neck. The linen cap was too tight but it did not seem to matter.

Herold needed more than one person to help. Hardly able to stand and sobbing without let up he was bound and prepared. As for Atzerdrodt, he was the only one to shout something before the trap was sprung. In a thick and guttural German accent he called out loudly: "Goodpye my boys, I shall zee you all in eternity!"

His last request must have been a bottle of whiskey.

The loud clatter of the sprung traps was startling in a courtyard that had been mostly quiet. The bodies dropped with a thud somewhat like the sandbags I had heard earlier. Mary was the quickest to stop moving. Her body twisted somewhat and struck the platform with a hollow thud. She then swayed with the stillness of death.

Lewis was true to form. He fought the noose by a tremendous effort of his neck muscles. His neck never broke in the common flip to one side. The last to die, it was from suffocation some ten minutes after everyone else. The photographer was set up in the courtyard with a huge camera. The bodies were not cut down until he was finished.

I had only a few minutes left to get home. There was no time to think about my chaotic emotions about the revolting execution I had witnessed. This time trip home would be my last and I was bone chilling afraid that I would not be able to get back home after the death of Mary Surratt.

Long before this time and place I knew what focused visualizations I could trust. The strongest emotions I have are the love for my wife and two children. My focus was on their faces and my hands reached out to them.

My first impression on my return was the strong smell of smoke. My wife was leaning over me with an anxious frown and then grabbed my face with a series of smacking kisses. I moved out of my chair and over to the seated Alfred on the couch. Getting him out of trance state was smooth and quick. His first question was for the whereabouts of his wife. Naomi reassured Mr. Gotting that all was well and hurried him upstairs to Jane, giving soothing explanations as she went. I heard the overhead garage door come up and Donnie dragging the oil drum out across the concrete floor of the garage and out to the double driveway. I opened the inside door to the garage fumbling with the button lock as Jen, gas mask and all, jumped into my arms with hugs and very metallic kisses. I was as deliriously happy as both my children.

Later in the evening we were in the master upstairs bedroom, the excited kids and my equally excited wife going over every detail of my return. When Mary heard Jennifer screaming and saw the smoke moving under the door, she had bolted the room alone. Jane's husband was simply left behind. Naomi awakened me from the trance state with the technique she was taught in self-hypnosis to ease lower back pain. I, in turn, awakened Mr. Gotting who did not need much urging to run upstairs, concerned about his wife when he smelled the leftover smoke in my office. He joined his wife Jane. Jane, not Mary, sat dazed in my hallway still half in trance and needed my attention.

The couple were shown the oil rag cause of the fire, explained as a stupid but harmless accident and breach of home safety rules. They rested, calmed down and went home. We had set up another dual session for the following week.

Our family pajama party went on much longer than it should have. In bubbling energy everyone tried to talk at once about their exploits. Naomi, black eyes flashing, was as excited as the children and so was I. A little later the mood and excitement died down.

Is it really over? The question of the evening was repeated and felt by every one of us. We all comforted one another with the absolute certainty that it had to be. Mary had died on the gallows without the flesh of her flesh that was required for soul transfer.

I could have exploded with pride the way my family reacted in this unbelievable crisis that we must forever keep to ourselves. A family secret that would bind us forever.

The science fiction movies are sure that all memory would be wiped out of my time travel episode. It did not. The travels back in time were sharp and clear. I will cherish the details throughout my life.

Later on in the evening as I lay on the bed basking in the satisfaction of our success, Naomi walked to me from her shower. My wife is the shy type who manages to get dressed or undressed without revealing any goodies at all. In contrast, in the darkness of our bed, she is passionate and uninhibited in her expressions of love. Tonight she did not turn off the lights and walked toward me in a sheer dressing gown that revealed all of her body. Naomi's breasts were deep and full, a large russet aurora circling each aroused nipple. Her waist curved inward framing a belly that was smooth, silky and ripe. Swelling thighs nurtured a glistening pubic triangle, a black arrow pointing to our shared place of pleasure. My penis awakened in erect tumanescense as she got in bed and turned to me for the deep kiss that always started our lovemaking.

Her eyes were gray.

Afterword

It would be unusual if the reader who is interested in American history would not have questions about what is truth in this novel and what is fiction. The historical record was faithfully followed. The blanks in that record were filled in by fiction. I collected more than thirty photographs, of every main character and old maps of the city to spotlight every scene of the action. It helped to give my protagonist, the fictional Dr. Borin, the ability to describe the feeling that you the reader, was there as well.

During eight years of research, the most important resources were American Heritage magazine, The New York Public Library and most importantly, The Library of Congress. I could examine source material such as: "The Trial of The Lincoln Conspirators". It was the actual minutes of the military court that tried the four convicted conspirators and decided the fate of Dr. Mudd, Spangler and several others. The trial was convened by order of Secretary of War, Edward Stanton. There was not a person in the military on trial. The defense, lead by a United States Senator, wanted to have the trial moved to a civil courtroom. The effort was useless.

President Lincoln was the easiest study, partly thanks to memoirs published by his best friends and two faithful secretaries. One or the other was at his side from early morning to late evening, carefully noting everyone he spoke to that day and what was said.

Time travel started with the carriage accident to Seward, Secretary of State. The description was taken from the diary of his daughter Fanny. Her account of the attack of Lewis Paine, attempting to kill her father, was fascinating and yet horrific. The attack on Seward was investigated with the help of eyewitnesses. Included was the testimony of the young house servant who admonished Paine for making too much noise climbing the stairs. The minutes of this somber trial include a note of: (laughter)

Everyone that talked to Booth, the day the President was shot, was brought in to testify. That includes his barber, the hotel clerks, the girl in the alley and any other men or women he had spoken to. Despite eyewitness facts, hourly blanks were numerous.

The perfidy of Stanton and Thaddeus Stevens was never proved but hotly debated in the 1880's. The conversation in the black carriage was fiction. Colonel Lafayette Baker was in New York when Lincoln was shot. His meeting with Lincoln at the Navy Yard was fictional.

Lincoln and Mary Todd's trip to the Navy Yard was real as depicted.

Colonel Baker, head of Army Intelligence, suspected Stanton and years later sued him in federal court for withholding vital evidence regarding Booth. Baker won his suit without the help of his fictional locked briefcase.

When I taught history I made every attempt to make it real to my students. I hope that the readers of this novel will achieve the same result.